"My beloved," Gabriel said.

Gabriel kissed the woman deeply. She wrapped one arm around him as his face moved into the hollow of her neck, becoming lost in the tangle of dishwater-blond hair. Her entire body convulsed as if she'd touched a power line. He was in her. Her hands closed and opened, her entire body quivering in the vampire's embrace of love and death. . . .

By Michael Romkey
Published by Fawcett Books:

I, VAMPIRE
THE VAMPIRE PAPERS
THE VAMPIRE PRINCESS
THE VAMPIRE VIRUS
VAMPIRE HUNTER

VAMPIRE HUNTER

Michael Romkey

FAWCETT GOLD MEDAL • NEW YORK

A Fawcett Gold Medal Book
Published by The Ballantine Publishing Group
Copyright © 1999 by Michael Romkey

www.randomhouse.com/BB/

Library of Congress Catalog Card Number: 98-93467

ISBN 0-449-00200-4

Manufactured in the United States of America

First Edition: January 1999

10   9   8   7   6   5   4   3   2   1

For Carol, Ryan, Matt, and Drew,
once more with love

She sinks into her spell: and when full soon
Her lips move and she soars into her song,
What creatures of the midmost main shall throng
In furrowed surf-clouds to the summoning rune:
Till he, the fated mariner, hears her cry,
And up her rock, bare-breasted, comes to die?

—DANTE GABRIEL ROSSETTI

1

✧

Egypt, 1870

DANTE GABRIEL ROSSETTI awoke to the sound of an animal shriek coming from the darkness.

He sat up and looked around, blinking dumbly, his mind a jumble of feverish images and pieces of dreams, unable to remember where he was or how he'd come to be there. His shirt was soaked in sweat, his mouth too dry to swallow. His eyes burned in their sockets, and his bones throbbed with dull pain. His fingers came automatically to his neck, but they found no trace of a wound—no evidence of the twin punctures that had thrice cannulated his jugular vein, no hint of tenderness in the skin or underlying musculature.

The animal screamed again, an inhuman howl that began as a tremulous cry and ended as a whimper.

A jackal.

Recognizing the inhuman cry brought the puzzle pieces tumbling back into place in Rossetti's mind. They had left London on a hazy August day in 1870, journeying across France by coach. They rode by horseback through Italy, pausing in Rome long enough for Rossetti nearly to die. When he was well enough to travel again, they boarded a Venetian sloop and crossed the Mediterranean, making for the Nile delta and the ruins of ancient Egypt.

They sailed up the Nile from Alexandria, making camp near the ruined temple of Amon at Luxor, the ancient city of Thebes. There, surrounded by images of fallen glory, Rossetti took the final of the three sacraments. He planned to put his past behind him, exchanging his human heart for an immortal organ he prayed would prove more indifferent to disappointment and pain.

The canvas tent walls trembled in the desert wind. Rossetti listened to the soft rustling of sand and the crackle of fire. He could hear the murmur of voices huddled around the fire, whispering in Arabic. Lower still, the quiet rush of water between the Nile's banks came to him, delivering the kiss of life to a thin ribbon of vegetation in the midst of the hostile, sun-blasted wasteland.

The darkness was nearly absolute in the heavy canvas tent, but his eyes, like his hearing, were preternaturally acute. He could perceive hues in the darkness, but faintly, as if he were looking at a faded watercolor painting. The skin on the back of his hands was drawn, shrunken around tendons, veins, and bones. The fever had spent the last of his body's reserves. He'd never imagined he could be so sick. Not even in Rome, ill unto dying with typhus, had he suffered so severely.

The animal cried again.

"Bloody jackals," he muttered. The cowering animals had dogged them wherever they went, slinking along in the dust, loitering at the edge of camp, more oppressive even than the legions of beggars in Alexandria.

Rossetti swung his legs slowly out of bed. His movements felt curiously disembodied, as if his limbs belonged to someone else and he were but the puppet master. He pulled on his Wellington boots and stood up tentatively, his balance uncertain. He brushed his head against the canvas roof. He wore his chestnut hair long, but it seemed to have grown six inches or more during his fortnight of delirium. He looked around briefly for a ribbon with which to tie it back, but finding nothing, he satisfied himself by pushing the thick, curly locks behind his ears.

The brilliance of the light when he pushed back the canvas door momentarily blinded him. The porters had built a bonfire at the far end of the camp, flames licking into the air. Behind the fire, overawing them, the gargantuan stone head of a nameless pharaoh lay over on one side, staring at them blankly. The guards stood aloof from the others, cradling their antique flintlock rifles, barefoot silhouettes dressed in Egyptian cotton caftans.

None of the servants moved a muscle to help Rossetti. They were a skittish lot, superstitious about ghosts and the old gods said to be haunting the ruins. The porters stared at Rossetti—newly bearded, hair wild, cheeks sunken, and eyes that still burned as if with fever—with undisguised fear. He might have been the falcon-headed sky god Horus, materialized out of the ether to revenge himself for Osiris's murder, and not some sad and wasted Englishman, disoriented after two weeks of burning up with fires of the change.

Rossetti's eyes ranged over the scene. The frightened Egyptians stared at him through the dancing tongues of the fire. The starkly illuminated face of the ancient colossus loomed over them from behind, swathed in shadows that suggested the presence of an incomprehensibly vast and menacing mystery beyond the circle of illumination cast by the fire.

A light came into Rossetti's dark eyes, an expression of rapture. Ever since childhood he had been subject to what he thought of as "visions"—moments of ecstasy released in his soul by a particularly pleasing arrangement of light and shadow, by a rich or unexpected combination of colors and textures, by an elegant line of poetry. These visions had been virtually lost to him near the end, visiting with decreasing frequency until they ceased to come at all. The wall Rossetti had built to separate himself from his pain had also closed him off from his passion. Now, he realized with a feeling of happiness that approached bliss, that this inner barrier, along with the other infirmities, sorrows, and limitations of mortal being, had been miraculously transcended.

Ignoring the Hunger gnawing at his vitals, Rossetti ducked back into his tent to rummage for his sketchbook and pencil. The strange tableau was still there when he returned on unsteady legs. He sketched as quickly as he could, afraid the spell would be broken before its essence was distilled to paper. The artist envisioned a vast oil canvas, rich Rubinesque golds, reds, and browns at the center, emerging from a darker chiaroscuro shadow painting. Footsteps approaching him from behind did not distract him. In another few minutes he was finished, the pad and pencil hanging from the ends of his spent arms like lead weights.

"Permit me," a familiar voice said, taking the drawing from him. Byron tilted the drawing toward the firelight and smiled. *"Bravisimo!"*

"It is but a quick study," Rossetti said, though his work pleased him full well. It had been years since his art had breathed with such inner power.

"You learned much from the Dutch masters."

Rossetti bowed his head slightly by way of agreement. He had been tarrying in Amsterdam, ostensibly studying the works of Rembrandt, when Lord Byron had found him. In truth, Rossetti had been spending most of his time in his hotel on the Grand Canal, devoting most of his energy to his drug addiction.

Byron had admired Rossetti's art—more so than he did Rossetti's poetry—and had decided to seek out his acquaintance because of an old connection he had with a member of Rossetti's family. Through one of those strange coincidences, Rossetti's uncle, Dr. John Polidori, had once been Byron's physician and companion. Byron and Polidori had spent the summer of 1816 together on Lake Geneva, sharing Villa Diodati with Percy Bysshe Shelley and his wife, Mary. When the weather proved stormy, Byron decreed that they would each write a ghost story to pass the time. Polidori's modest effort, *The Vampyre*, was published in London in 1819 and quickly forgotten, unlike Mary Shelley's *Frankenstein*.

Rossetti owed his life to Byron. He would have died in Amsterdam if the vampire hadn't come to his aid.

"How perfectly you capture the flames prancing in the darkness, illuminating the toppled statuary," Byron said. "And the fear in the porters' faces. How greatly it contrasts with the serenity in the statue's stony eyes. The men of our company seem small and pathetic before the evidence of ancient glory. What will remain of them two thousand years from tonight?"

"It puts me in mind of—"

"I know," Byron interrupted. He could read Rossetti's thoughts, when he wished, though Rossetti found this unpleasant intrusion of his innermost ruminations unworthy behavior for a British gentleman. Byron ignored his irritation, as he was wont to do, and recited:

> "I met a traveler from an antique land
> Who said: Two vast and trunkless legs of stone
> Stand in the desert . . . Near them, on the sand,
> Half sunk, a shattered visage lies, whose frown,
> And wrinkled lip, and sneer of cold command,
> Tell that its sculptor well those passions read
> Which yet survive, stamped on these lifeless things,
> The hand that mocked them, and the heart that fed:
> And on the pedestal these words appear:

'My name is Ozymandias, king of kings:
Look on my works, ye Mighty, and despair!'
Nothing beside remains. Round the decay
Of that colossal wreck, boundless and bare
The lone and level sands stretch far away."

The porters gaped at Byron as though he were chanting an incantation to bring the dead back to life rather than quoting Shelley.

"Percy had it all wrong, poor lamb. These ruins leave me mute with wonderment. What must it have been like, to breathe the rarefied air that sustained such culture? And so strange a culture, dedicated with such fierce passion to art and death equally. I confess to a certain kinship."

"I did not think death much occupied your thoughts."

"My dear fellow," Byron said, taking Rossetti by the arm, "even as *Vampiri* we are never more than a step away from death. It is always there, just behind us, within the shadow."

Rossetti followed Byron's gesture. The shadows of their bodies moved slightly from side to side in the flickering light with a simulacrum of life.

"You are weak," Byron said solicitously.

Rossetti nodded, reluctant to acknowledge his mounting need.

"A little of the fever remains in you, I see. Your face has an almost tubercular glow. Come," his mentor said, taking his arm. "We must find you nourishment."

"I do not know whether I can make myself—"

"Leave everything to me," Byron interrupted, his tone brooking no disagreement.

Rossetti returned to his tent to put on his waistcoat, jacket, and cloak, for the desert was surprisingly cool at night. Except for his white shirt, he was attired entirely in black. Black was the British gentleman's color of fashion, and had been ever since the Queen went into mourning after Prince Albert's premature death in 1861. Byron did not share his friend's somber High Victorian tastes. Exuding always a romantic air of decayed nobility, Lord Byron favored the same sort of bottle-green velvet trousers the scandalous Disraeli wore. He owned a vast collection of silk waistcoats, none of them black, to Rossetti's knowledge. The waistcoat Byron wore that night beneath his blue jacket was afire with brilliant color.

The guide they had retained in Alexandria materialized out of the night with a pair of Arabians. Rossetti was too weak to lift himself by the stirrup. Mohammed helped him into the saddle. The Egyptian stared up at him, his face as stony as the statue of the pharaoh in their camp. Rossetti kicked the horse in the flanks and galloped after his companion.

A half hour's ride brought them in sight of a village Byron said had occupied the same place beside the Nile for thousands of years.

"Time has not changed this place at all. The mud-brick buildings, the date palms, the graceful *dableahs* tied up along the riverbanks, the stars in the sky, all are the same as they were in Mark Anthony's time two thousand years ago, or in the time of Amenhotep, two thousand years before Anthony."

The landscape's unreal timelessness was oddly comforting. Riding across a stark wasteland littered with ancient ruins, Rossetti felt he was but one of many apparitions that comfortably shared a country too bewitched to notice the passing millennia. At home in London, he would have felt like an alien, a stranger in his own land.

A boy took the reins to their horses as they dismounted outside a coffeehouse. Rossetti followed his friend inside. A dozen fez-clad men were scattered about the room, lounging on pillows. The air was dense with the smell of powerful Egyptian tobacco welling from a hookah in the main room. In a side room, a group of men sat smoking *kif*, the aroma of hashish adding its peculiar spice to the dense atmosphere. A musician sat on a carpet on a low platform against the wall. He played a mandolinlike instrument and wailed one of those plaintive Arabic love songs that Rossetti could not bring himself to associate with music, though Byron, who had lived among the Turks, seemed to take pleasure in it.

One of two men playing backgammon at a low table stood to greet them. Byron conversed with him in Arabic. The man nodded several times and put out his hand, into which Byron dropped several coins. The man wanted more, but Byron shook his head. After a few more fruitless attempts to haggle, the café's proprietor relented and motioned for them to follow. He led them into a back room and through a door opening onto a claustrophobic alley. An old woman wrapped in black robes, her face veiled in the Islamic custom, nearly collided with Rossetti as she squeezed by, her garments snapping in the dry, chill wind.

The Egyptian rapped on a door opposite the café. A female voice answered. The Egyptian looked back at Byron with a crooked leer, then returned to his establishment, shutting the door behind himself.

"I am hardly in any condition for wenching," Rossetti said in a harsh whisper. A terrible need—the Hunger—was growing in him with every beat of his heart. His upper jaw was on fire with pain, as though the bone was splitting open from the inside.

Byron said nothing but opened the door and stood to one side so that Rossetti might enter first. The tiny oil lamp was inadequate to illuminate even the cramped space, its weak yellow light serving mainly to draw the shadows from their corners and bring them to life. The room was sparsely furnished: a single chair, a washbasin, a bed. The woman sat on the bed, wrapped in a cotton sheet.

"The Hunger is screaming so loudly within you that *I* hear it, my friend."

A cold trickle of sweat ran down Rossetti's spine. He was afraid to look at the woman, afraid he would lose all control and throw himself on her, tearing out her throat to satisfy his maddening desire.

"You must satisfy the Hunger before it takes possession of you," Byron counseled. "Your real lessons as a vampire begin tonight, my friend. Learn them well."

Rossetti felt his eyes dragged toward the woman, as if controlled by mesmeric powers. She was young, not much more than a girl. She had a waif's big eyes. She was naked beneath the sheet. Rossetti could see the outline of her tiny, pear-shaped breasts. He shivered with self-loathing to feel the desire flare hotter within. He had lived freely enough as a Bohemian artist in London, taking his pleasure as he wished, yet he still possessed a Victorian's sensibilities. Though Rossetti had been an appallingly wicked man at times, he had never stooped to avail himself of the Haymarket dolly-mops, who could be had up against an alley wall or pressed back over a barrel for a few pence.

The girl smiled slowly at Rossetti, parting her lips with the tip of her tongue. She was willing enough for whatever adventures the infidels had paid to enjoy.

"This is a vile country," Rossetti said, scowling as if he'd just drunk bitter wormwood oil. "I propose that the greater the height a society reaches, the farther it plunges in decline."

"An interesting observation," Byron said dryly, his tone reminding Rossetti that resistance to the task at hand was impossible.

"What do I do?" Rossetti asked in a hoarse whisper, trembling with need.

"Remove your cloak."

The wrap fell to the floor.

"Go to her."

Rossetti sat sideways on the bed. Byron perched on the edge of the chair. The girl looked past Rossetti to his companion, a wanton smile playing across her unpainted lips. She thought Byron intended to take his pleasure in watching.

"Touch her," Byron said.

Rossetti didn't dare.

"Go ahead. This Cleopatra will not bite."

Rossetti put his shaking hand lightly on the girl's naked shoulder. Her skin was soft and moist and cool to his feverish touch. He felt dangerously near to a complete loss of self-restraint. The Hunger was screaming in him, a jackal fighting for possession of his soul, driving him toward a whirlpool of hysteria where eroticism and violence swirled together to become a single, irresistible, protean force.

"Steady on," Byron said, sounding very far away.

The universe compressed itself into a sphere where only Rossetti and the girl existed. Her pulse pounded in his ears more loudly than the sound of his own racing heart. He smelled her sex and blood commingled as one, a narcotic perfume that anesthetized his inhibition. She put her small hand on his thigh—a provocative gesture that shocked some fast-receding part of the artist's sensibility. Rossetti looked down, drinking in the gentle curve of her breast and the memories of her life in the squalid village in one continuous, intoxicating draught.

He drew her to him. As she lifted her arms to embrace him, the sheet fell away, revealing her figure, as tiny and golden as the flame illuminating it. She threw one leg over him, winding herself sinuously about his body.

The pain was excruciating in Rossetti's jaw. It was as if two red-hot pokers were being driven down toward his teeth from above and behind. The girl didn't seem to hear the crunching of bone and marrow inside his head, or the sharp hiss of pressure releasing inside his face, the front of his skull about to explode. A sudden gush of warmth flooded his mouth—blood, his own blood. The blossoming agony forced open his jaw. Then Rossetti's mouth was full of the saltiness of the skin in the hollow of the girl's neck. With the dull click of bone and cartilage, the twin blood teeth came down out of their recesses and snapped into place.

Suddenly, desperately, Rossetti wanted to stop. But it was too late. The die had been cast when he accepted Byron's invitation. The Hunger took him over completely. Instinct—a vampire's instinct—warped him. Rossetti was the servant, Hunger was the master.

Rossetti buried his teeth deep into the girl's neck.

She gasped in his ear as the first splash of steaming hot blood exploded against the back of his throat. The Hunger was gone in that instant, replaced with bliss infinitely beyond anything he had known as a mortal. A nova of pleasure burst within, illuminating every atom of his being with celestial light as his teeth clamped more deeply into the living mortal flesh. It was as if he no longer had corporeal reality; his physical body was transformed into the luminescence of pure rapture. Flesh was made spirit. Rossetti the man, Rossetti the vampire, had transcended to a higher sphere of being, transformed by a heavenly light that vibrated with a quickening pulse with every swallow of blood he drank.

"Easy now, old boy!"

The warning voice belonged to Byron. His companion and teacher was at his shoulder now, bent over him and the girl as they lay together on the bed, locked in a mortal embrace.

"You do not wish to kill her," Byron said.

It was true. Rossetti did not wish to kill the girl; he did not have to, to get what he needed to satisfy the Hunger. But the joy—oh, Jesu, the heavenly joy!

"Enough!" Byron cried.

Rossetti felt the hand tighten on his arm. It required an act of superhuman will, but he somehow managed to make himself release her.

Rossetti sat up in bed, the sense of bliss diminishing by degrees, replaced by a sensation of well-being and tremendous power. If only he had his oils and brushes, the work he could do! But then he noticed the girl, crumpled and small, lying against the wall, her skin a deathly shade of white.

"What have I done?"

"She will be all right by morning, though a little weak for a day or two," Byron said, leaning over him to cover her. "She will remember nothing. Here." He offered Rossetti a silk handkerchief. "Your mouth."

As Rossetti wiped his mouth, the handkerchief stained with a vivid crimson smear.

"Do not upset yourself unduly. You have everything now: beauty, charm, genius, immortality. And the love of at least one friend. Oh, and money. An artist always needs money," Byron said with a laugh. "You shall have all that you need. You will find such things are easily managed."

Rossetti did not answer. He was no longer looking at the girl but into the shadows.

"You are thinking of Elizabeth."

The artist did not deny it. He absently twisted the ruby ring he wore on his little finger. It had belonged to his beloved.

"We have many powers, my friend, yet we cannot bring the dead back to life," Byron said gently.

"I know," Rossetti said with a deep sigh.

"You must turn away from your grief. It was consuming you when I found you in Amsterdam. It can consume you still, if you let it. Only now the stakes are higher."

Rossetti looked up at Byron.

"You were not the first to turn yourself into a beast to escape the pain of being a man."

"I behaved despicably," Rossetti confessed.

"Put it behind you, my friend. You have not yet begun to know your new powers. You may employ them as an artist and benefactor. Or, if you take the wrong path, you may squander them doing monstrous evil, drowning yourself in blood to escape the past the way you once did with drugs."

"I would never do that."

"I should hope not," Byron said. "Your heart is good and true. Otherwise, I would have never considered helping you make the change. You must learn to treat the Hunger with respect. You need not fear it, only maintain its need. Above all else, my friend, do not try to deny the Hunger its due. That will only lead to disaster."

"I see that plainly enough."

"Cherish your memories, my friend. Only a fool would allow remembrances to poison his heart. Love will come to you again. You must believe that. Otherwise, there is no reason for any of us to go on living."

Rossetti was suddenly too overcome to reply. Beloved Lizzie, his precious rose, plucked too soon from the garden of life, a victim not of the Reaper but the sadness of life—a sadness he could have done much to alleviate but for his own selfish desires.

"Look to the future. Think of the great paintings you will produce. You may even make great poetry! Your father tempted the Fates to name you after Dante, the incomparable master. In a Grecian tragedy, that sort of hubris would have guaranteed your doom."

"Will I still dream?"

"Whatever do you mean?"

"Now that I have . . . *changed*," Rossetti managed after an uncomfortable pause. "Now that I have become a vampire, will I still dream when I sleep?"

"But of course!" Byron replied with an incredulous laugh. "Whatever could make you ask such a strange question? You know there is nothing to the ridiculous Carpathian myths about our race. We do not hang upside down from the ceilings or sleep in coffins. And you know I adore garlic."

"I dreamt of her every night before this last fever," Rossetti said. "I dreamed of Elizabeth," he added unnecessarily.

"You are the last of the Romantics, dear boy," Byron said with a dismissive wave. He put a handful of coins under the girl's pillow—far more than he had given the procurer. "We will leave her enough money to allow her to go to Alexandria or Cairo and make a new start, if she so desires," he said. "Life is so cheap throughout most of the world. I would save them all, if I could."

"What would you have done if I had been unable to stop myself?"

"That is what I meant when I told you to learn your lessons well," Byron said. "And you did admirably, as I was certain you would."

"Would you have stopped me if I had let the Hunger carry me off?"

"A vampire without the necessary self-control is subject to the most grotesque excesses. I would have had no choice."

Rossetti did not need to ask Byron what that would have meant. There was only one way Byron could have separated him from reveling in the glorious wine of life. Byron would have had to kill him.

"I would have wanted you to stop me," Rossetti said, opening the door to the night.

Byron looked into his eyes a moment, then nodded. "I know."

2

The Present

THE SUMMER SUN tamed the North Atlantic's chronic distemper, gradually warming the water, altering the currents, bringing a few short weeks of mildness to the cold, often violent reach of ocean. The sea ran in low, lazy swells, the water deep blue with hints of jade. The weather was perfect throughout the last week of July, the cloudless azure sky shimmering with the crystalline purity seen only in the mountains, in polar regions, and far away at sea.

The *Bentham Explorer* had its bow turned into the wind, riding its sea anchor, holding its position south of Newfoundland. The air on deck smelled of salt, sunblock, and coffee, mixed with the occasional stink of diesel. The ship's engines idled low in the background, an almost inaudible hum, driving the generators.

The crew had a healthy, windblown look, their skin tanned and hair streaked with highlights after weeks at sea. The *Bentham Explorer*'s permanent crew members were easily identifiable in short-sleeved khaki jumpsuits. Half of the others aboard worked for Meyer Naval Salvage, most of them Portuguese-Americans who'd once had jobs with New England's fishing fleet, presently fallen on hard times. Movie people made up the final third of the ship's contingent.

16

The real sailors dressed for work, but Nick Drake's people seemed to think they were on a Windjammer cruise, wearing shorts, polo shirts, and jewelry that glittered in the sharp Atlantic sunlight. Several of the men had even dared to appear on deck in sandals, which would have made the sailors hoot with laughter if they hadn't been intimidated. Almost to a man the sailors treated even the lowliest gofer on the film crew as a superior, as if working in Hollywood made you a member of an elevated caste.

Two outboard motors sputtered to life and a pair of inflatable Zodiacs sped away from the ship, splashing over the swells, off to collect the morning dive team. The men had been down for an hour, hooking up the air hoses running to the *Bentham Explorer*'s big Cummings-powered compressor. Air pumped through the lines would inflate an array of flotation cells that would—if everything worked the way the engineers planned—gently lift from the ocean floor what everybody on the ship simply called "the prize."

The chief diver scrambled out of the water into the nearest Zodiac. He pulled off his mask and wet-suit hood and gave the thumbs-up sign.

The camera, mounted on a lemon-yellow dolly crane bolted to the deck amidships, panned from the diver to a man in a battered captain's cap leaning over the railing. Nick Drake flashed a grin and returned the diver's thumbs-up sign. He then turned to the camera, making a slashing motion across his throat with his hand.

"Cut!" he ordered.

Sam Meyer came up as Drake turned away from the rail.

"We'll be ready to pump up the cells in a half hour," the retired Navy chief reported. Meyer had charge of the technical part of the operation. He was built like a bear, with enormous arms, a beer belly, and a hearing aid in each ear. He had first worked for Drake the previous summer, when Drake was filming a PBS documentary on a sunken German submarine.

"Super!" Drake cried, slapping Meyer on the shoulder. "Mark, we'll need to set up that shot," he said, talking to someone over his shoulder. "We need to get Patricia throwing the switch that brings the prize to us."

"Right," the cinematographer said, already on his way, a gang of camera, light, and sound engineers trailing after him.

Drake dropped into a director's chair—labeled DIRECTOR— and removed his captain's hat so Melanie Wilson could freshen his makeup. His personal assistant brought him the script and a mug of cappuccino. Drake had brought his own espresso machine on the expedition, a restaurant-quality Krups he'd bought in a shop on Rodeo Drive before flying east to join the rest of the crew.

He leaned back as Melanie patted powder on his nose, which tended to be shiny.

"Ready for your big scene, Patricia?" he asked the woman in the chair next to his. She turned toward him, fixing him for a long moment with an impassive stare. Her eyes were hidden be- hind Ray•Ban sunglasses.

"Certainly," she answered.

Patricia Solberg Mobius was not an actress, though she had the looks. She described herself as a "professional adventurer." The heiress was financing Drake's expedition, and the film he was making about it, because he had promised her high adven- ture. The reality had been mostly high tedium, but that would change the moment the front third of the sunken ocean liner began to rise slowly toward the surface.

Patricia was very beautiful and very rich—the ideal combina- tion of characteristics in a woman, Drake thought. Her blond hair was bleached almost white by the sun, which had also tanned the firm, athletic body she had shaped to aching perfection by a steady regimen of running, skiing, and climbing. Patricia's only flaw, so far as Drake could determine, was a husband somewhere in the distant background.

"We're almost there, Patricia. Can you believe it?"

Patricia gave Drake another long look, her face revealing nothing, no hint of emotion, no betrayal of what was going on behind the dark glasses. Money made you regal, Drake thought. The rich had taken the place of the royals as patrons of the arts.

And then she smiled at him!

Patricia had a beautiful smile. Her teeth were perfect, and when she parted them a little, he could see the tip of her tongue. Drake was completely smitten. The executive producer for his previous documentary had been a Lebanese millionaire whose head had been permanently enveloped in a cloud of blue cigar smoke.

He reached over and squeezed Patricia's hand. He continued to hold it in his, tenderly, appreciatively, for as long as he dared. Drake burned to get Patricia Solberg Mobius into bed.

"We're making history, darling." Drake called everybody darling. "This is something people are going to talk about for a long time. The preparation, the planning, the danger. Nobody will ever forget that your faith in this project made it happen."

"We're not there yet, Drake."

"I know that, darling. All we need is a little more luck."

Patricia's free hand came up to touch the quartz crystal she wore around her neck, her good-luck necklace, the one she'd worn since her last adventure, which had ended in disaster.

After they shot Patricia's scene, they went up to the bridge to watch the historic moment slowly and deliciously unfold. Drake had Patricia stand with her hands on the ship's wheel, even though nobody actually needed to have the helm while they were riding at anchor. Drake stood in the foreground, in front of the camera, holding a rolled-up chart. The cinematographer had the camera angled so the frame would include the *Explorer*'s deep-sea sub, *Andy,* chained to the deck below the bridge.

"This ship, stout as she is, is only a fragile outpost in the midst of a vast and merciless sea," Drake intoned to the camera. "The sea is the mother of life, but she is an indifferent parent who can take away mortal life as easily as she grants it. The North Atlantic can be especially unforgiving. The weather is unpredictable. Winter gales whip the frigid water into towering waves. And then there are . . ."

Drake paused a beat for effect.

". . . icebergs," he said with heavy emphasis. "North of here, along the coast of Greenland, the glaciers calve gargantuan mountains of ice into the water. The icebergs float slowly south toward the shipping lanes, hidden in mist and darkness. It is impossible to be at sea as we are now, even on a day as bright and sunny as this, and not remember that we are, as mortals, fragile creatures afloat in a world that is essentially hostile to our existence."

"Drake. Sorry to interrupt."

Sam Meyer came onto the bridge, Francois Guiles close on his heels. Despite the captain's hat Drake wore, Guiles was the *Bentham Explorer*'s real skipper. The Frenchman worked for the Bentham Corporation, the company that had leased Drake the ship until September, when it had a contract to spend the winter sounding for oil formations off the coast of Brazil.

"Cut!" Drake ordered.

"It's Tony and that other crazy kid," Meyer said, pointing at the window. "They're out there in a Zodiac over the rise area."

"They must not be there, Monsieur Drake," Guiles said in heavily accented English. "It is not to be allowed."

"God damn it!" Drake swore. "Give me a radio."

One of the crew handed him a walkie-talkie, but before he could use it there was shouting from the deck. "She's coming up!" a sailor yelled, pointing toward what everybody was already looking at as they ran toward the starboard railing. The ocean was boiling with air bubbles. The men in the Zodiac were caught in the midst of the roiling water, the rubber inflatable boat spinning in drunken circles. Even from a distance it was obvious from the men's body language that they were close to panic.

"Roll film, Mark!"

Sam Meyer shot Drake a disbelieving look.

"Damn it, Sam, it was supposed to take another hour to get her to the surface," Drake complained, but even as the words left his mouth he realized his luck had run out. Meyer snatched the radio away from him.

"You two, get the hell out of there, now!"

But the Zodiac was already rising into the air on what appeared to be a gigantic hot air balloon launching itself from the ocean. The flotation cell, freed from the deep when its cable snapped, continued to swell as the gas within expanded to equalize itself with the surface air pressure. The men and their tiny boat were nearly one hundred feet in the air when the cell exploded like a bomb going off.

"My God!" Patricia gasped.

Drake was too busy to worry about his executive producer. Calm in the midst of the chaos on deck, he ordered the camera to follow Meyer and Guiles as they scrambled down the side of the ship to try to rescue the cameramen. His voice was steady, with only a hint of the excitement that it would have been tasteless for him to display too openly, as he directed a second crew to set up on the bow and begin filming. These were the moments that separated the real directors from the technicians. Drake knew he was probably watching the summer's salvage effort end in failure, but capturing the death of two film men was exactly the kind of dramatic tragedy that would make the film part of his project a success.

3

NOTHINGNESS, WHEN IT came after an eternity of suffering, was as forgiving as the kiss of God.

If Paradise's gates would never open to someone so wicked, then at least he had the comforts of oblivion. There was a gradual thinning of awareness, a loss of definition too subtle at first to be noticed. A peaceful blankness enveloped him in stages, slowly nullifying everything—what had been; what was; what might be. Agony was replaced by a creeping numbness. Memories lost focus, dimmed, melted away in dying whispers. Dreams and nightmares stopped. Time lost its meaning, a seamless, looping continuum without beginning, middle, or end. All thoughts, conscious and unconscious, ceased. No sense of self remained.

Suspended in the dark, hermetic void, measurable signs of life disappeared one by one. There was no breath—for there was no air to breathe. The heart stopped, and with it came cessation of all pulmonary activity. Blood, no longer moving along veins and arteries, congealed into a thick, viscous paste. The last faint arcing of electromagnetic activity stopped within the brain cells.

It seemed death itself had come at long last. The pain was gone, replaced by an undifferentiated, unchanging void.

Years brought changes to the corpus. Adipose tissues dissolved in the icy bath, shrinking the skin tight around the bones, cleaving to sunken cheeks and hollow eye sockets, tightly molding muscles, tendons, and bones in a manner familiar to anyone who has seen a mummy stripped of its linen wrappings. The etiolated skin turned translucent. Internal organs—purplish, blue-green, or dirty yellow—became visible.

Tendons and muscles shrunk, drawing the arms and legs into the fetal position. There was something embryonic about the body, yet only in a perverse sense. It might have been an aborted specimen preserved in a jar of formaldehyde, a curiosity for medical students to study. Or perhaps it more closely resembled a child of Death, misshapen and misbegotten, a ghastly abomination.

The vampire had no awareness of these things. He had gone away, far away, beyond thinking, beyond feeling, beyond the pain. It seemed preposterous to think that he might ever return. It had not occurred even to him, as his mind burned away in Hunger's purgatory, that life in certain viral entities can diminish to the point of the merest technicality. Systems shut down when conditions become hostile. They know the trick of remaining inert for years, perhaps for centuries, waiting for conditions to change, startling them once again to life.

4

D R. RICHARD MOBIUS poured himself a tumbler of Glenfiddich and settled into his favorite chair.

He was alone in the big new house overlooking Lake Mac-Bride, a sprawling modern takeoff on the classic Frank Lloyd Wright prairie style. Soft strains of the Brandenburg Concerto emanated from eight tiny speakers cleverly hidden in the Arts and Crafts oak cabinetry. The faint music obscured the fainter whispering of the climate control system that automatically maintained the house at the optimum in temperature and humidity.

Mobius took a sip of scotch.

"Hmmmm."

His reaction was to the Glenfiddich, not Rebecca Isaac's dissertation. Glenfiddich was his working drink. He reserved his Usquaebach for pure pleasure. And this, he thought, turning past the title page, was definitely work. Rebecca's topic was "Early Feminist Stirrings in Romantic Literature." The subject was appealingly up-to-date, if a bit trendy. The best scholarship had social relevance, Mobius believed. Learned academics needed to say something to society, to address the social issues of the day: sexism, racism, homophobia, pollution, AIDS, global warming.

The prose was plain and straightforward—a little too plain and too straightforward. On the other hand, the arguments were logical, progressively offered and well-ordered, the assertions carefully buttressed in fact. This set the dissertation above the typical first-draft English Ph.D. pap that Mobius was accustomed to scanning. He'd winced through more than his share of shrill diatribes. Personal opinions were all well and good, as long as they were liberal enough to demonstrate genuine enlightenment, but they needed to support the case in chief, not replace it.

When he was finished, Mobius got up and poured himself another scotch, thinking deeply about what he'd read.

It was Mobius's duty to show his Ph.D. candidates the way, but it was not always easy. He sat down and flipped through the pages absently. Upon further deliberation—about half the second scotch—he decided his chief complaint was that the dissertation was simply too easy to understand. In a word, the paper needed to be more scholarly. An acceptable dissertation displayed a scholarly gravitas that did not seem to exist independent of a certain opacity of language.

Mobius's stomach growled. He disliked cooking and tended to eat out or skip meals when Patricia was away. She was often gone on her so-called adventures. If there was a downside to being married to his beautiful young wife, it was that she was constantly dashing off to some far corner of the world to climb mountains or canoe through cannibal-infested jungles in search of rare flora and fauna. Mobius shared his wife's love of travel, but running the university English department made it impossible to say hang-all in the middle of the semester and jet off to Nepal.

Mobius had met Patricia the year she inherited Solberg Agri-chemicals, a sickeningly profitable corporation that manufactured poisons for farmers to spray on crops. The headquarters was a two-hour drive away in Ames. Fortunately, the distasteful business intruded in their lives only once a year, when they were compelled to attend the annual stockholders' meeting and dinner. Mobius found the company executives and investors a dreary lot, but he made it a point to be charming during his yearly excursions into Babbitry. It was a small enough sacrifice to make his wife happy. Patricia had a blind spot when it came to the company, which her father had founded and built into a thriving multinational concern.

Mobius had to work at not resenting money that came from a company dedicated to destroying the environment. Fortunately, there were benefits that made it easier to bear. Solberg money built their new home. It continued to subsidize Mobius's unprofitable literary quarterly, *The Prairie Review*. The money also made it possible for Mobius to indulge in his budding passion for nineteenth-century art. A John Everett Millais watercolor hung above Mobius's desk. There was a Ford Madox Brown oil above the fireplace in the living room. These things made Mobius's life worth living.

Patricia was chairperson of the Solberg Foundation, a vast, money-burning machine designed to transfer hundreds of thousands of dollars of her inheritance to whatever cause she was interested in at the moment. *The Prairie Review* had been the first recipient of a Solberg Foundation grant. Other beneficiaries of Patricia's largess included a shelter for battered women and a recycling center in Iowa City. More recently, she had steered grants toward causes that gave her entertaining things to do with her time. She'd funded an expedition to Antarctica to hunt for fossils, and paid for an all-woman expedition up Mount Everest that had nearly gotten her killed.

Mobius was far too intelligent to object to his wife's adventures. Patricia was ten years younger than he and required a certain amount of youthful excitement. If he could manage to get her pregnant (now that they were trying), she would stay closer to home and everything would be perfect.

Mobius was unenthusiastic about Patricia's present adventure. Though he'd glanced through the engineering study—a wonderfully opaque document—he doubted it was possible to successfully raise a section of the *Titanic* from the depths of the North Atlantic. A documentary filmmaker named Nick Drake had put the project together. Drake was filming the salvage operation for a PBS program. If the project was a success, Sony had agreed to manage a general theatrical release of the best footage. That would be quite a coup, Drake said, since documentaries almost never made it to the mall movie houses.

If they managed to actually float the hulk, Drake planned to tow it to New York harbor for "study." The *Titanic*'s remains eventually would be opened to the public, the centerpiece to a billion-dollar Disneylike tourist attraction that Japanese investors would die to build around at a Manhattan pier complex.

Mere spectacle, Mobius told himself, swirling the remaining whiskey in his glass. The lowest form of entertainment, as Aristotle observed in *Poetics*. It was grave-robbing dressed up to impersonate history. A circus for the mob, thought Mobius, who despised pop culture.

He let the rest of the scotch race down his throat, not bothering to savor the smoky flavor of peat-roasted barley aged in oaken casks. He felt the alcohol immediately. Maybe he would pour an Usquaebach. It would be extravagant to get drunk on $130-a-bottle scotch, but what did he care? It was tainted money. Fish died to make that money. Deformed tadpoles were born in runoff waters downstream from fields polluted with Solberg Agrichemicals fertilizer. It made him misty to think about that—frogs born blind or with an extra set of legs. He'd seen pictures. It was dirty money. Blood money. There was almost a moral obligation to squander it, to make it fly away as fast as possible.

Money itself was a curse, Mobius thought. The wealth that

marriage had brought him had never rested easily on the former campus radical's conscience. Patricia's millions paid for his liquor and the Millais watercolor, but they also kept her away from him for months at a time.

The telephone stopped him on his way to the bar.

"Dr. Mobius? This is Rebecca Isaac."

"Rebecca."

"I hope I'm not being too pushy, but I was wondering if you've had a chance to look at my dissertation."

"As a matter of fact, yes. I just finished."

"And?"

Mobius observed how quickly tension mounted in the silence. He'd written a poem about it once.

"Have you . . . Did you . . . I'm sorry, Dr. Mobius. I really don't mean to bother you."

Mobius could almost feel her blushing through the telephone. Students were so vulnerable. Little wonder some of the professors he knew—and it wasn't only men—took advantage. Every year he had students who breezed through the course work only to freeze up when it was time to write their dissertations. Not taking your doctorate after all that work—it was like sex without orgasm. Some students had nervous breakdowns; some endured bouts of drunkenness and drug abuse; some got divorced. He'd even known candidates who committed suicide. All over a little scribbling. Astonishing.

"I thought your work was very well researched and grounded in fact."

"You did?" Rebecca almost gushed.

"Though there are, of course, one or two points I would like to discuss."

"Of course." She sounded disconsolate, as if he'd had to break the news to her that the spot on her X ray was cancer.

A face floated in front of Mobius's eyes, vaporous and unbidden: Patricia. Thinking of her filled him with the sort of longing that an evening spent watching pornographic movies in his media room couldn't satisfy. He loved his wife, but he was beginning to resent her long absences from their home. It wasn't fair that he should be alone for months at a time, without a soft body next to his in bed for company and comfort.

"I could drop by your office tomorrow when I finish teaching my undergraduate Hardy class."

"Yes," he said, and paused. "You could do that."

Mobius forced the image of his wife from his mind, conjuring Rebecca in her stead. She had waist-long black hair and a face with a mysterious, almost cabalic beauty. She wore ankle-length black skirts and long-sleeved, lacy white blouses with a cameo at the neck, looking as though she'd stepped out of a James McNeil Whistler painting. It was not an uncommon look for a female English student to affect. While the French students summered in Provence, women like Rebecca spent their days inside, meditating on the sublimated passions of the Victorian age. Rebecca was Mobius's idea of how a female graduate student in English should look. As for his other candidates, the only things that distinguished them from the wretched poor were the secondhand Volvos and Saabs they parked in the English-Philosophy Building lot. One might affect the flannel shirts and torn jeans of minimumwage laborers, but Mobius knew true members of the underclass did not drive Volvos and Saabs.

"If you're not doing anything in particular, we could discuss your dissertation tonight," he offered with sudden daring. "I don't believe you've been out to our new house."

"I was in Missouri over the holidays and missed your party."

Missouri? Good God, she was from Missouri? It would have to be St. Louis.

"Yes, I remember," Mobius lied. "I haven't had supper, Rebecca. I was thinking about making Thai chicken. You're more than welcome to join me, if you haven't eaten. We could talk about your dissertation. Or, if you prefer, you can stop by the office tomorrow."

In the ensuing pause, Mobius wondered if Rebecca had taken note of the fact that he'd failed to mention that his wife was away, that the two of them would be dining alone. It was amazing how so small an omission could suddenly loom large and significant. Everybody in town knew Patricia was spending the summer on a ship anchored over the wreck of the *Titanic*. The local rag wrote about Patricia's activities with great zeal. The newspaper's editor apparently thought of Patricia as Amelia Earhart reincarnated.

"Tonight would be great," Rebecca said softly, "if it's really not an imposition."

Mobius began to smile. "Perish the thought," he said sweetly.

He hung up the telephone and padded toward the wine cellar, the Usquaebach forgotten. Wine would be Rebecca's drink. Something red. Not a Bordeaux. A Bordeaux would be too heavy, too ostentatious; it would only make her ill at ease. He still had a case of Nouveau left. That would be perfect. A completely unpretentious little wine, light, sweet, full of Keatsian sunburnt mirth. A bottle of Nouveau was exactly what the occasion demanded.

Mobius flipped on the light over the basement stairs.

"No," he said out loud, correcting himself. "Two bottles of Nouveau."

5

✧

IT WAS NOT a gentle awakening.

A mighty tremble shook through the torn section of ship.
Cables cried out sharply as they pulled tight against the hull, a
discordant concert of metallic shrieks and doleful groans. Somewhere far above, flotation cells blossomed like silver thunder-
clouds in the inky water, straining to drag the *Titanic*'s bow
section free from the muck that had cradled its broken spine for
more than eighty-five years.

The hulk moved a ways, then abruptly stopped. The ship
seemed to be actively resisting the efforts to wake it from its long
rest. The flotation cables stretched and strained, approaching the
snapping point. The ship seemed hopelessly trapped in the mire
of the ocean floor, motionless, as solid, fixed, and unmovable as
an underwater mountain.

Then, without warning, the bottom all at once released its
death embrace.

There was the sudden sensation of movement, of a tremendous mass moving through the endless night at the bottom of the
sea. The wounded leviathan was climbing from its watery grave,
ascending from the depths with ominous Wagnerian majesty.

Deep within the ship, trapped in an inner cabin, the ancient
embryo floated in the saline darkness of its rusting artificial

womb. Its eyes opened. The irises were green and shining, like those of a cat.

Unseen things moved inside the hulk, sliding, crashing, falling as the flotation cells righted the section of ship to its old sailing trim. Doors wedged shut by debris when the *Titanic* went to the bottom banged dully open when obstructions skidded out of the way in the darkness, as if pushed by a ghost crew.

The eyes slowly blinked, regarding their surroundings without the least glimmer of understanding.

It was a birth of sorts, but without innocence or joy. It was also a resurrection—a resurrection of the Hunger. The awakening creature, twisted, larval, inhuman, was entirely without mind or identity. It was an entity that would devote its energy to one violent purpose.

The Hunger had lost none of its power during its years of inertia, sleeping within the cells of its insensate host. Its need was utterly undiminished. If anything, the Hunger was stronger than before, purified and concentrated over time, like brandy aged in a cask.

The embryo's arms began to tremble. They were turned inward against the chest, like a coma victim's. Slowly, painfully, struggling against atrophied tendons, the wrists began to twist outward. The hands were claws: elongated bony fingers, six-inch-long fingernails strong enough to tear wood—but not steel. The clenched fingers opened a little and stopped. They opened a little farther and stopped. Then a little farther still. Seized joints and muscles broke free. The hands clutched uselessly at the frigid water, a perverse imitation of a newborn babe grasping at empty air, grasping for its mother.

The entity's mother was the Hunger.

It began to move through the water, more from intention than physical ability to propel itself. Its body was mostly useless, a thirty-pound bag of bones, decalcified and rubbery, bound in sinew and semi-opaque skin. It approached the unseen space in the darkness where the door was to be found. It pressed against it. The door opened. The unthinking entity felt no relief at being freed after eighty-five years of imprisonment in the claustrophobic cabin. It was conscious only of the Hunger, the force driving it through the darkness, toward light, toward life, toward blood.

Water moved in currents through the passageways in the rising liner, beckoning. Hunger guided it through the blind labyrinth, a confusing tangle of passages and chambers, some empty, others clogged with wreckage, a three-dimensional puzzle. A snarl of twisted metal blocked the staircase leading up to the main deck. The creature's bones were flexible enough to bend at odd angles without breaking, allowing it to squeeze into impossible angles to get through.

The ship lurched drunkenly to port.

The entity stopped, turning its misshapen head slowly to one side. A weird sound moved through the water, as if a huge harp were coming unstrung. The entity drew its thin upper lip back in an angry snarl, displaying two supernumerary teeth distended from the cavities in its upper jaw. Like a rabbit that sees the shadow of a hawk moving swiftly across the meadow, the entity recognized a threat.

One of the cables connecting the ship to the flotation cells had snapped. The added strain was more than the remaining cables could withstand; they snapped, too, in quick succession, an arpeggio of disaster for the rising section of the ocean liner.

The ship was no longer moving. The sensation of stasis held a moment longer before the movement recommenced, only now the ship was going in the other direction, sliding backward toward the bottom at a far faster pace than it had been rising.

Frantic now, the entity found an open porthole and squeezed through, kicking free of the hulk. It hung motionless in the water, passively observing the ship slide by in the darkness, a mute and unthinking witness to the *Titanic*'s second death as the mountain of metal returned to the ocean floor.

It tilted its head back, looking upward. Its glowing green eyes detected the faintest hint of radiant light many fathoms above.

But there was something else there, too—a memory, or the shadow of a memory, though its brain was functioning at far too primitive a level to know it as anything but pure sensation. It was a smell, a sharp stimulation to the limbic system, the most intoxicating aroma imaginable. Thrills of pleasure pulsed through the creature hovering in the water, twitching with the sensations unleashed by the almost cloying perfume, as sweet as opium burning in a pipe.

The entity kicked its deformed feet and thrashed its birdlike arms, desperately driving itself toward the surface, toward the only sacrament that would please the wailing god of a savage world where the only law was the Hunger.

6

✧

"**F**ORGET ABOUT HOW your father feels for the time being. I want to know how you feel. Does the situation bother you, Mitch?"

"Why should it? It's an accident of birth. As long as my sister and David love one another, why would I care?"

"It's a different culture. Different traditions, different holidays . . ."

"Aren't you Jewish, Dr. Bloome?"

"That's not really relevant."

"I just don't want to offend you."

"Don't worry about offending me," she said with the merest hint of sharpness. Psychiatrists needed to establish relationships of authority and trust with their patients. The fact that Dr. Abigail Bloome was young, female, Jewish, and a new arrival in a small southern city were considerations she had to be prepared to overcome in her patients' minds.

"He's not a religious sort of person, Dr. Bloome."

"It's not always apparent."

"It is in David's case. My sister wants to get married in a Lutheran church in Naperville. That's fine with David. They gave each other Christmas presents. He's a completely regular person.

36

And, frankly, if he asked Linda to convert to Judaism and she wanted to, I'd say more power to them. It's not an issue with me."

"But it is with your father."

"Yes." Mitchell Cunningham's face turned dark with unhappiness. "I don't get it. I can count on two hands the number of times we were inside a church when we were growing up, and probably half of those were weddings and funerals. Dad doesn't go to church now. Not even on Christmas or Easter. He says churches are filled with hypocrites who think sitting in a pew for an hour on Sunday makes it okay to lie, cheat, and steal the rest of the week. He's pretty critical about religion. He's pretty critical about everything, actually."

"And you're a more tolerant person?" Dr. Abigail Bloome asked.

"I like to think that I am. We all have prejudices, though, even if we try to pretend we don't. Don't you agree?"

"Hmmm," the psychiatrist said ambiguously. "So how did the telephone conversation about your sister's engagement resolve itself?"

"It was a complete disaster," Cunningham said, falling back against the chair. "Dad was drinking. He doesn't slur his words or anything, but I could tell. The more he drinks, the more illogical and argumentative he becomes. He kept asking me over and over again what I thought he was supposed to do about Linda marrying a Jew. I tried to just listen at first. Not agreeing or disagreeing, just listening, letting him vent. I finally made an effort to outline the other side of the argument, to help him see it from Linda's point of view. He didn't like that at all." Cunningham let out a long sigh.

"I doubt he's capable of seeing another point of view, Doctor. He's from another generation. Blacks couldn't even drink from the same water fountains in Calhoun when he was growing up."

"He's as capable as he wants to be, Mitch. You don't need to make excuses for him."

"No, I don't," Cunningham said with a flash of anger. "In the end, everything has to boil down to how it affects him. He's the center of everything. Nothing matters but in its relation to him. You know what I mean?"

"I'm familiar with the type."

"Then, absolutely without warning, he went off on a tangent. Every time he calls the house at night and I'm not there, he said, my wife is—and this is a quote—'washing one of the kids' god-damned feet.' He said he'd had it with her."

"Does your wife avoid his calls?"

"*I* avoid his calls, Dr. Bloome. To start with, he almost never calls before nine-thirty at night. My theory is that's how long it takes him to get loaded enough to feel like picking up the telephone to start a fight. When the telephone rings at nine-thirty and nine-forty-five, I know exactly who it is. Besides, he knows what nights I'm home and what nights I work late. If he calls at nine-thirty and my wife is home alone, chances are she is giving one of the kids a bath or putting the baby to bed."

"How did you respond to what he had to say about your wife?"

"I didn't get to respond. He said—it's too embarrassing." Cunningham stopped talking and broke eye contact, looking down at his hands, which were clenched into fists.

"Go on, Mitch. I want to hear it. What did he say?"

"He said my wife could take the telephone and fuck herself up the ass with it," Cunningham said, his voice rising. His face turned a mottled red from his spiking blood pressure. He was still deeply shocked and offended by his father's comment.

"How did you respond?"

"I said, 'You can't talk like that.' He said, 'I just did, and I'll do it again. Fuck her up the ass with the telephone!' " Cunningham's eyes were furious. His chin was trembling.

"And?"

"I hung up on him."

"Good for you."

Abby turned sideways in her chair and looked out the window, giving Mitchell Cunningham an opportunity to get his emotions under control. It was astonishing the way some people treated their children—even their grown children.

The ceiling fan turned silently overhead, moving just enough air to make the fresh-cut flowers on her desk tremble slightly. There were more flowers on the credenza. She had a passion for flowers. Though it was a sweltering summer day, the office was always chilly—over-air-conditioned, Abby thought. The sun came slanting through the blinds. Her office commanded a view of the Calhoun Hospital's grounds. Two gardeners in gray uniforms were trimming bushes. One man had an electric trimmer plugged into an orange extension cord, its shiny metallic teeth flashing in the sunlight as they ripped through the lush green foliage. The other man's job seemed to be standing there motionless and observing his colleague. South Carolina had blessed the city with a perfect climate for gardening.

"Where are we going with all this, Doctor?" Cunningham said, emerging from his brooding in a confrontational mood. "I don't feel any better than I did before this session started. In fact, I feel worse. Are you going to write me a prescription for Prozac, or am I wasting my time?"

He was projecting the hostility he felt toward his father in her direction. It was an early sign of progress. She picked up her pen and made a brief notation.

"I could write you a prescription easily enough. Medication would help mask the pain of your conflict with your father." She looked up from her notes. "That would be like putting a Band-Aid on a wound without treating the wound itself. It would only hide the infection."

"The only reason I agreed to these sessions is that my family doctor said I needed to talk to you to make sure I got the right medication. Like I told you, I don't put much stock in psychiatry."

"Your skepticism is perfectly natural," Abby said. "Let me explain something. Human beings are like icebergs, Mitch. We only see a small fraction of what's really there; the greater balance is beneath the surface. Talking with a therapist is a way of exploring subconscious territory. By bringing hidden issues into the light, they can be examined and dealt with by the objective mind. The mind has a wonderful capacity for healing, given the opportunity."

"So it's all in my subconscious," he said with a smirk.

"The subconscious is where creativity and genius reside. It is also a realm of darkness. Unhappiness resides there, in the shadowy world beyond reason."

"My problem, Doctor, doesn't have anything to do with my subconscious. My problem is that I have a father who is a mean, unhappy alcoholic. He wants to make me equally miserable. Maybe afflicting me is the only way he can get relief from his demons. Or maybe he's just jealous of my happy family and wants to tear it apart. I don't know. At this point, I don't even care. All I know is that it's more than I can take. Just write me a prescription for Prozac, Dr. Bloome, so that I can go on with my life."

Abby stared at Cunningham just long enough for a crack to open in the middle of his fragile certainty.

"You have some excellent insights into the motivations behind your father's behavior. But he is not the issue: you are."

"Me?" Cunningham yelped as if he'd been pricked with a pin.

"You're a thirty-six-year-old man; you're happily married;

the father of three; successful in your profession. Then there's your father. For all practical purposes, he deserted his family when you were seven. He did not take an interest in you when you were a child, or make a place for you in his own life. And now you have children, three lovely boys, with whom he is similarly uninvolved. All true?"

Cunningham nodded.

"So why do you care what he says or thinks? Would you be so easily and deeply wounded by an old curmudgeon at the end of your street who dislikes children and thinks you do a bad job of caring for your lawn?"

"I care because he's my father."

"Is that it? You mentioned accidents of birth earlier in relation to your sister's Jewish fiancé. Isn't your father also an accident of birth? We don't get to choose our fathers. Some of us get good fathers. Some don't."

Cunningham was listening now with his entire body, like a parched plant reaching out for rejuvenating drops of rain.

"Your father is not what you need to come to terms with. Your father is who he is. You can't change him, no matter how hard you try. The real issue is you, Mitch. What is this need within you, crying out for a father's love and approval? What is the emptiness in you that forces you to submit time and again to the shame of his summary judgments, which invariably convict you as wrong and inadequate?"

Cunningham's eyes blinked rapidly. She was inside his defensive wall now, standing next to the well filled to the brim with a child's anguish.

"The answer to your happiness—and it is your happiness, not your father's—is to be found in answering questions like these, not in a pill that will only make it easier to bear being flogged with your father's emotional whip."

Abby politely looked away again to give Cunningham a chance to digest this information. He was struggling, the poor man, completely out of touch with his deepest feelings. Prozac was the last thing he needed, if he wanted to solve his emotional problems. Of course, a proponent of so-called "cost-effective therapy" would have found it cheaper to hand out pills than pay for $160-an-hour therapy sessions. The principal in her practice, Dr. Ritenour, was a "cost-effective therapy" man. So was Dr. Veena Govindaiah, the psychiatric resident practicing under Ritenour's supervision. The insurance companies loved that kind of psychiatry.

"If you will make another appointment with the receptionist, I promise to help you," she said after a bit, turning back toward her patient.

Cunningham nodded, getting to his feet as she did, their time finished.

"If you really think it will help." His voice was taut with his effort to maintain control over his emotions.

"I know it will help. And remember this, Mitch: the fact that you have a bad father doesn't mean that you are a bad son."

7

MARK MILLER SET up the camera on the fantail, aiming it toward the bow, where the moon was rising behind the bare-tree array of antennae rigged atop the bridge.

The gig was almost over.

Even if Drake sweet-talked Patricia Mobius out of more money, the filming window was shot. Everybody said the weather couldn't hold much longer. The squalls would return, curtains of darkness sweeping down on them from the horizon, turning the North Atlantic into a churning, nauseating vomit bucket.

Some of the people on the *Bentham Explorer* were depressed about the way things turned out, but not Mark. He was a realist. The odds had not been good that they could successfully raise the bow of the *Titanic* to the surface, despite the line Drake had spoon-fed his pet heiress. Besides, Mark had had his fill of claustrophobic life aboard the ship. He'd expected the sailors to be fun, but the *Explorer* had turned out to be the straightest ship on the sea. All work and no play had made Mark a very dull boy. He missed his apartment. He missed his friends. He missed *dancing*. He was ready to go home and kick back in Venice Beach until his next gig, a romantic comedy scheduled to start shooting after the first of the year in Vancouver.

Jesus Christ, he thought. Vancouver in January. Would it snow all the time or just rain forever?

At least Drake was no fool. From the start, the director had planned two endings for the documentary. While the others got drunk and felt sorry for themselves, Mark and Nick worked on the Plan B wrap-up. Earlier, he'd filmed Nick's obituary for the aborted expedition. The director had sat at the chart table, with a coffee mug (filled with a vodka martini) and a map of the North Atlantic spread out before him. Nick wore a white cable-knit turtleneck and his battered captain's hat, sweating like a pig beneath the lights, though nobody seeing the footage would be able to tell. Nick's words ran through Mark's mind as he reloaded the camera's film canister.

Maybe the Fates have decreed that the sea shall keep her dead, that the Titanic *shall remain in Davy Jones's locker for the rest of eternity. It may have been a mistake to disturb the lost leviathan's rest. Perhaps the* Titanic *holds secrets we dare not bring to light. . . .*

Such schlock! Nick was a master of the extended, grandiloquent overstatement. Little wonder television executives ate out of his hand as if his fists were filled with candy corn.

Mark had spent the evening collecting poignant footage. The tear in Melanie's eye as the makeup artist hugged Nick to console him. Patricia Mobius staring bleakly out to sea, her beautiful complexion made dark with her disappointment. They'd also filmed Nick's visit to sickbay, where the bodies of Anthony and Thomas were laid out in rubber body bags. The bags were zipped shut, thank God. Nick bowed his head over the bodies, seeming to pray, a tear on his cheek.

Doc said he was going to stow the bodies in one of the food lockers until they could get back to port. Now *that* was a disgusting idea, Mark thought.

* * *

Katie Bush gathered the soda pop and beer cans from the mess to take to the recycling bin. She'd put herself in charge of the ship's recycling program after seeing one of the *Bentham Explorer*'s crew—a muscle-bound dummy named Pete—throw a Coke can into the ocean. Thinking about dolphins and whales swimming around discarded aluminum cans almost made her sick to her stomach.

Katie was feeling a little guilty about her attitude. The others were so down about what had happened. It was almost as if their moms had died. It was a drag that the *Titanic* had gone back to the bottom and everything, but even that wasn't enough to deflate her mood.

Katie was helping make a movie!

She would be a senior when she returned to UCLA. Majoring in film, of course. Landing a job as an intern with Nick's production company had been a dream come true. It didn't pay anything, but it was her foot in the door, her first exposure to Hollywood's magical mythmaking machinery. She'd been in a state of bliss since Nick hired her. The documentary wasn't a feature, but it was still a movie. Millions of people would see it. Nothing, not even the day's huge failure, could erase her smile.

The others were sad that night, even sullen. Nobody had much to say. They sat around, quiet and glum, drinking even more than usual. Katie decided to get up and do something useful, leaving the others to their moping. They'd get over it.

Nick liked her ideas. He'd even let her rewrite a couple of scenes, though he'd ended up redoing them himself before they were shot. He'd promised her a job as an assistant director on his project next summer. And it wasn't just because she'd slept with him. Katie knew that Nick Drake respected her talents.

He'd said as much, lying beside her that morning after breakfast, when they'd made love.

Pete Frazer, a twenty-seven-year-old seaman from Maine, came off the bridge, where he'd gone to report for the beginning of his watch.

He was bored out of his skull. A month of hovering motionless over the same patch of ocean had turned most of the *Bentham Explorer*'s crew—the *real* crew, not the movie people—into zombies. The only thing to keep them from going screaming mad was the skipper's make-work details. There wasn't a square inch of the ship that hadn't been scrubbed, scraped, painted, and polished three times over.

The money be damned, Frazer thought, clanking down the metal stairs. He would have been better off staying in the Navy.

Frazer saw one of the movie people on the fantail, fooling around with a camera on the helicopter pad. Something glittered when the man turned his head. *Him,* Frazer thought, recognizing Mark Miller by his diamond-stud earring. Actually, he was surprised more of the movie people weren't like Miller. He had the impression that a lot of them were *that way*.

One of the girls—Katie—came onto the deck swinging a garbage bag filled with empty drink cans.

"Evening," Frazer said.

"Oh, hi," the girl answered. Her eyes lingered a moment on Frazer's powerful arms as she bounced past.

She had long blond hair and a nice, tight little butt, though she was too small-breasted to fit Frazer's image of a California girl. He suspected she and Drake had something going. He'd seen him come out of her cabin once during the late watch. Frazer wished she had a little left over for him. She was a cute thing, even if she was a tree-hugger who often lapsed into babbling about whales and gulls.

Frazer heard a rustling sound.

He turned and pointed his flashlight casually at the shadows. Nobody there. He started off in the direction he'd been heading—the direction Katie had gone—when he heard it again. Then a groan, soft and whispery, like a woman when a man touches her *there*.

Frazer peered into the darkness, not bothering to use the flashlight. Was somebody getting it on? If he was quiet, he might get a peek. Or maybe it was one of the women, trying to get his attention. He'd seen how they looked at him when he worked on deck without his shirt. It was crazy that he hadn't managed to connect with one of them. He was beginning to think he was losing his touch.

Frazer took a step toward where the sound had been.

Something moved from one shadow to the next. Something weird. It looked like a person, impossibly thin, only the way it moved was all wrong. It was like a marionette jerked along by an amateur puppeteer.

Somebody was playing a joke on him.

Frazer gripped the flashlight like a club and took another step forward. He'd sometimes thought the movie people were laughing at him behind his back, making fun of him because he hadn't gone to some college where they taught you how to talk fancy and treat other people like they didn't matter. It made him angry. It would have made anybody angry.

If they were trying to play a joke on him, if they were fucking with him—they'd better hope to hell he didn't get his hands on their pansy asses.

The weird figure appeared again, popping up from the shadows. It bobbed up and down, swaying back and forth at the same time, as if too drunk to balance. It wasn't a person but some kind of dummy. It looked a little like an *X-Files* alien to Frazer. The silhouette was—what was that word?—*humanoid,* with a big head and elongated arms. The hands and fingers were especially drawn out, almost like claws. Something about the thing reminded Frazer of an insect: it must have been the way it held its arms with the elbows bent far back and up high as it crouched down on spindly legs.

"Very fucking funny," Frazer said in a warning voice.

His thumb found the button that switched on the flashlight.

"Mother of God!" he gasped.

The thing flung itself almost vertically into the air. The arms flew out from its bony arched shoulders, its legs waggling loosely, scrabbling at the air as it catapulted itself toward the stunned sailor.

Mark Miller looked up from the camera. He'd seen something fly across the deck. Birds sometimes appeared out of nowhere, hovering over the ship in the middle of the ocean, though he'd never seen them at night. It must have been an albatross—huge, spooky birds. The bony specimen he'd just seen glide between the crates was almost like a pterodactyl.

" 'Instead of the cross, the albatross was hung about my neck,' " Mark said, quoting *The Rime of the Ancient Mariner* to himself. One of Mark's lovers taught poetry at Berkeley. Stephen had a terrible habit of quoting poems, and Mark had the kind of mind where things people said tended to become stuck. He could parrot dozens of Stephen's lines. Which was useful, at times. A bit of whispered poetry had gotten him into more than one pair of pants.

Patricia and Nick emerged from a door on the upper level. Nick reached for her elbow. She pulled away, angry. He followed her around the corner. She was in a snit. Poor Nick. Like every rich girl he had ever known, Mark thought, Patricia was a handful.

Mark returned his attention to the camera's viewfinder, where he found the face in the moon staring coldly back at him, leering.

It burned, it burned—even submersed in icy water, the sun's fire burned.

The shadow of the ship provided a small measure of relief. He floated there, scraping his back against the barnacles, waiting for dark. His mind was gone, his intelligence even more atrophied than his hideously shrunken body. Instinct alone guided him now, informing him to hesitate a little longer. When the sun was gone, he would at last be able to satisfy the Hunger that howled in the marrow of his decalcified bones.

Consciousness, such as it was—a sluggish, reptilian sentience limited to cerebral activity in the primitive stem area of his brain—came and went, with changes hardly perceived. The familiar sense of blankness returned, disturbed only by the terrible need, by his thirst as deep and vast as the waters in which his ruined body floated.

By degrees the greenish light ebbed from the water, daylight leeching away. When instinct at last moved him from his shelter, the light reflected off the moon was enough to sear his skin like phosphorous. He could not open his eyes against the silvery brilliance, yet he *saw* things plainly enough with his mind. He blindly found the platform that the ship's divers used to load the Zodiacs. Strips of waterlogged flesh came off his hands as he dragged himself from the water for the first time in almost a century. His bones popped out of their sockets, but the tendons and the muscles held. He hauled himself toward the deck one stair at a time, unable to stand, unable even to crawl. The greenish algae clinging to his skin lubricated his body, making it easier to move, each convulsive pull accompanied by a wet, slithering sound.

The smell of blood was intoxicating, overpowering. Yet instinct told him to husband the little strength he had until he could feed and grow stronger.

He sensed people on the deck, maddeningly near. The pulse from their hearts drummed in his ears. He felt his own heart stir, but in vain. The awful pressure in his breast! The wrenching pain as his heart tried to come back to life. It was futile. The viscous substance in his veins could no longer race hotly through his body, filled with the passion of life.

But soon.

He dropped down between a piece of machinery and a wooden crate, pressing himself into a dark corner like a spider hiding from the light.

There were footsteps.

His fingers grabbed blindly overhead until they found something to grab. He hauled himself up on his feet. The world began to move—slowly at first, then whirling faster. He could not make himself stand. His body had forgotten how to obey him. His knees buckled, and not in the direction they were designed to bend. He collapsed in a wet heap, helpless, pathetic.

"Ooooh."

He groaned with frustration and began to silently cry. The Hunger screamed in him like a demented mother berating her child, but he was helpless when it came to satisfying the cruel demand.

The footsteps came closer.

The Hunger would not accept defeat. Gasping from the effort, he somehow managed to pull himself into a partly standing position a second time. His muscles were remembering how to work together. Even without skeletal support, he stood there, grasping a strip of metal, his body defying the laws of gravity and biomechanics.

The man was so close, and the smell of blood so powerful, that the vampire nearly swooned. Yet the Hunger braced him up, focusing him on the one thing he so desperately needed. His desire was so great that for a moment it seemed that it alone would draw the blood out of Pete Frazer's body and into his, feeding cells that had been starved for so many decades. But that was even more than he could do. If he wanted the precious nectar of life, he would have to take it, which seemed patently impossible. His balance was precarious, his strength failing him with each passing second. He could never overwhelm the well-muscled man.

"Very fucking funny," the man said.

He heard the words; they meant nothing to him. He'd forgotten what they meant. There was only one language he understood now, the language of Hunger.

The sailor lifted his torch and switched it on.

"Mother of God!"

The light seemed to shatter him into atoms. His agony magnified, like the blast of supercompressed air racing out in all directions from the source of an explosion. He felt himself flying through the air, propelled by the power of intention alone, hurled toward the sailor, who dropped his torch in horror.

He encircled the man with his arms and legs, tying him up in an embrace.

The sailor staggered backward, flailing helplessly as his assailant sank his teeth deep into his neck.

The rush of orgiastic pleasure was like being struck with a bolt of lightning. The vampire trembled with bliss, but he did not loosen his grip on his victim.

Overcome with animal terror, the sailor staggered in a circle, clawing at the thing hanging on to him. He would have screamed, but the teeth buried in his neck robbed him of his voice. The hands on his shoulders belonged to a skeleton sheathed in dirty cellophane. It was amazing how quickly the sailor's strength left him, running out of him with his blood. He stumbled behind one of the lifeboats and fell to his knees. The pounding in his heart slowed to a weak flutter as he pitched forward onto the deck.

The vampire embraced the sailor in his death's grip, releasing him only after sucking the last drop of love out of his desiccated body.

He stood over the corpse, looking down on it without remorse, without any more interest or emotion than one would feel looking at a discarded shoe or day-old newspaper.

There was new strength in his muscles, and his bones were perhaps a little less rubbery now. Best of all was the heat. Although it had been years since he'd realized it, he'd been cold, so cold. The blood in his belly and smeared across his hideous face was like a warm, comforting balm. Life was slowly moving back into the cold, shrunken cells of his body.

An invisible dagger plunged into his heart, the pain dropping him to his knees, hands clutching at his naked breast. With one slow, wracking convulsion, his ancient heart began to beat again.

He gasped—too weak to scream with the agony he felt. The first ragged gasp was followed by another and then another. He had started to breathe again, irregular rasping breaths drawn into shriveled lungs, breaths that wheezed and rattled from the saltwater choking his airways.

He looked up with a dull awareness. He knew where he was. While he could not remember that the thing he was on was called a "ship," he did realize he was at sea. He looked at the electric light glowing from the rows of portholes. How strange it all was to him! He felt that he was even more of an alien than he had been when he went into his long sleep.

He was an outcast.

A monster.

And the Hunger was not finished with him. No, far from it.

He peered around the lifeboat. There was a man on the far end of the ship, standing at a device mounted upon a tripod. The vampire's old cunning returned. It would be risky to take the man in the open, but he could knock him over the railing and hold him under the water while he drained his blood.

Somehow getting back into the cold Atlantic did not seem like a good idea.

There was somebody coming from the other direction.

He turned to look, impatiently pushing back the snarl of wet, matted hair whipping across his face.

Katie.

He considered that briefly. *Katie.* What did it mean?

The young woman's blood was as fresh and flowery as new wine. She exuded a life force and a fresh, almost adolescent sensuality. She was not coming closer. She had turned and was heading toward a door leading into the ship.

He dashed out from behind the lifeboat, across the open deck, toward the concealment of the shadows.

"Katie!"

The most he could manage was a strangled whisper. Whatever the word meant, it proved an effective charm. The young woman stopped, turned.

"Nick?" she said softly, leaning into the shadows.

Mark lifted his head up from the camera. He stood to his full height, putting his hands against his hips, arching his back, stretching out his muscles.

A movement amidships caught his attention. He stared at where he'd seen a man scuttle across the deck with a peculiarly feral lope. He heard a woman sigh somewhere in the darkness. Maybe where he'd seen the man. It was hard to tell. A couple playing cat-and-mouse on the deck, Miller thought. Everybody was getting some except him. He'd have a lot of lost time to make up for when he got back to Venice Beach.

He turned his attention back to his camera.

8

✧

"**T**HERE ARE ONLY a handful of reported cases of autovampirism in the literature, so it's exciting to have the opportunity to study this extremely rare disorder."

"Auto what?" Veena asked.

"Autovampirism," Abby repeated. "The compulsive drinking of one's own blood."

"I know what autovampirism is. I simply did not hear." Veena's defensiveness was characteristic of most of her exchanges with Abby. "The myth of the vampire originates in the Indian subcontinent," she added with a certain pride.

"You manage to come up with the most interesting cases," Calliopy said, smiling at Abby.

"Kindly share the details, Abigail," Ritenour said in his vaguely condescending manner.

Dr. Peter Ritenour, Psychiatric Associates's senior partner, was at the head of the walnut conference table. By unspoken mutual agreement, that spot was reserved for him at their weekly case review meetings. Dr. Veena Govindaiah, who was one year away from completing her residency, sat to Ritenour's immediate right, wearing a sari. Dr. Calliopy Hill sat on Ritenour's left. A plump, middle-aged woman with coffee-colored skin, she was the senior psychologist at the practice. Hill directly supervised the psychiatric social workers—the MSWs—who did most of the actual patient counseling and ran many of the therapy groups under the doctors' supervision. Abby sat two chairs down, on Calliopy's side of the table.

"The patient is a sixteen-year-old female named Desiree Hohenberg. She is a high school dropout who lives at home with her mother, a single parent who works as a bookkeeper at a tire store."

Abby saw the corners of Ritenour's mouth turn downward. He preferred the term "client" to "patient," though she refused to use it.

"The patient," Abby continued, undaunted, "presents as a relatively typical teenage girl, although she affects an unmistakable outward morbidity in her dress. She admits to wanting to look like a vampire. Every time I've seen her, she's been wearing a black blouse, a long black skirt, black tights, Doc Marten boots, and silver jewelry. She has long, straight black hair, and her skin is so pale that it is almost milky. The only color on her is in her nails and lipstick—both bloodred.

"She was hospitalized two weeks ago for anemia severe enough for the resident to start a transfusion. One of the nurses observed her moaning as she watched the blood drip into her via an IV. She seemed to be deriving sexual pleasure from a procedure that most people find at the very least mildly unpleasant. A physical examination found multiple scars and wounds where she had been systematically opening veins to drink her own blood."

"The poor child," Calliopy said.

"There are maybe only a dozen cases of autovampirism in the literature. I've read what I could find on the subject. Desiree fits the pattern, which begins with a strong link between drinking blood and erotic arousal."

"She admitted that?" Ritenour asked as if finally interested.

"Desiree has been surprisingly frank about her activities. She said she first became excited with blood when she was six or seven years old and was losing her milk teeth. She said she took pleasure in the pain of working a loose tooth back and forth in her mouth with her tongue or fingers and tasting the blood, which she described as 'rich and full of life.' It was about this time that she began to be excited by the sight of blood when she or someone else got cut or injured themselves. She said she would lick the blood, under the guise of kissing the wound to make it better, if she could arrange it. She also began to be fascinated and excited by blood in movies and on television and would buy comic books simply because they were gory.

"She began to menstruate at age twelve, and this is when her vampiristic practices commenced in earnest. She would lock herself in the bathroom and smear her hands and face with blood. She also liked to taste it, masturbating at the same time."

"Good heavens!" Veena exclaimed.

"Desiree began to nick herself with sharp objects, usually a knife or razor but sometimes something sharp she found—a jagged piece of metal, a broken bottle. She says that she took no special pleasure in these acts of self-mutilation beyond making herself bleed. Indeed, she has taken special effort to cut herself in places that facilitate her attempts to hide her blood fetish from people who might notice the wounds.

"She says that the sight of blood made, and continues to make, her sexually excited. She would drink her blood and masturbate, although she says she sometimes experiences a spontaneous orgasm at the taste or even the sight of blood. Further experimentation brought her to the point where her practices were discovered. Earlier this year she began to open her arteries. The pulsing, rhythmic spurting of blood proved to be so sexually exciting that she compulsively engaged in these acts until blood loss and anemia led her to the hospital and the subsequent discovery of her autovampiristic tendencies.

"I have reviewed what little I have been able to find on the subject. She is atypical in one way: most autovampires are male. Aside from this, she otherwise fits the profile."

"Maybe she suffers gender identity problems," Calliopy said.

Abby considered that briefly, then shook her head. "Maybe, but not so far as I have been able to tell at this point. She has, however, moved to the third of four progressively dangerous stages."

"There are established stages for this sort of thing?"

"There seem to be, Calliopy. According to the Stoker syndrome paradigm, Desiree reached stage three when, about a week before she was hospitalized, she killed a stray cat and drank some of its blood."

"The 'Stoker syndrome'?" Ritenour interrupted. "As in Bram Stoker, the author of *Dracula*?"

Abby nodded. "Stage one is a childhood experience that leads the subject to equate blood with sexual arousal. Stage two is autovampirism, the drinking of one's own blood, associated with masturbation and general sexual arousal. This stage breaks down into a number of intuitively obvious phases, starting with drinking blood from accidental wounds, through inflicting wounds, to finally opening veins and arteries to free a gushing stream of hot blood. The blood is either drunk or is sometimes saved and consumed later."

"Did she save her blood in jars?"

"No, Peter. She says it isn't any good unless it's fresh."

"So stage three is killing animals to drink their blood?"

"Yes. For lack of a better term it is called 'zoophagia,' which literally means eating living animals. Sometimes this stage is associated with necrophilia or necrophagia."

Abby could tell from the expression on Veena's face that she was unfamiliar with the words. Abby treated FMGs—foreign medical graduates—as equals, but she knew that understanding the often subtle nuances of English was a definite handicap, especially for a psychiatrist.

"I think we need to take this sort of thing seriously," Calliopy said. "It's not at all unusual for us to see people here who think they've been hexed or had curses put on them. This part of South Carolina is the voodoo capital of America. It doesn't matter whether black magic is real or not. What matters is if somebody *thinks* they've had the evil eye put on them. If there is any place in this country I'd expect to find a vampire, it would be in one of those moldering old plantations outside of town."

Abby caught Ritenour's slight skyward glance. He became uncomfortable whenever their discussions strayed beyond the empirical.

"This client needs medication," Veena said, looking to her supervisor for approval.

"I've already started her on antidepressives," Abby said. "I'm going to see her daily until I have a handle on this."

"Will her mother's insurance pay for intensive treatment? I thought you said she worked at a gas station."

"The mother is a bookkeeper at a Goodyear store. She doesn't have any insurance. Desiree is a state aid patient."

"Now, Abigail," Ritenour said, adopting a fatherly tone, "you know the state won't reimburse for extended psychoanalysis."

"I'm taking her on a pro bono basis."

"This case may be personally interesting, but you must not let your enthusiasm run away with you."

"This is too rare an opportunity to pass up, Peter."

"You would be setting a most bad precedent, Dr. Bloome," Veena said. "Payment to one's doctor, even from the state, is an important incentive for the patient to take treatment seriously and work to improve."

"I'm inclined to agree," Ritenour said. "Payment implies a degree of commitment."

Abby took in a slow, careful breath, looking past Veena out the window. The thick plate glass was tinted against the glare of the hot southern sun. The tint made everything look cool, artificially deepening the colors, giving them a blue-green hue. Heat rose off the Calhoun Hospital's concrete parking lot in shimmering waves. It was windy, and the trees and bushes were bending and bowing with graceful rhythm on the invisible tide. It was almost as if they were under the sea. Of course, it was all an illusion. Abby knew it was hot as hell outside.

"*The National Journal of Mental Health* is interested in the paper I'm going to write on this case," she said with perfect detachment. "It will reflect positively on the practice. It will also reflect positively on the incoming president of the South Carolina Psychiatric Association."

She looked at Ritenour and smiled, charming him. He was like that: he responded to flirtatious women. She wasn't happy that she had to try to seduce Ritenour into taking her side. She didn't like women who played that card, and didn't often play it herself.

"Well," Ritenour huffed, "I trust this won't become a habit. Like it or not, Abigail, third-party reimbursement has relegated psychiatrists to the role of supervising medication and counseling. The old psychoanalytic model is obsolete, replaced by a more cost-effective system."

"Oh, I understand perfectly, Peter."

What she meant was that she understood that Ritenour had an inflexible, closed mind. His ego would lead him to presume agreement and future obedience, when in truth there was no agreement, Abby thought, only an invisible line drawn on the ground between them that would be the source of continued conflict.

9

✦

IT WAS NEARLY dawn when he came for the last two. They were huddled together in a cabin, the door locked, and furniture piled up against it.

Gorging on blood had nearly restored the vampire's body to its former beauty, though it remained mostly hidden. His mossy snarl of hair and beard hung nearly to the deck, giving him the appearance of a mad hermit who had just emerged after years of self-confinement within a filthy and unlighted cave.

What couldn't be outwardly seen or understood, not even by the vampire himself, was the degree to which his mind had atrophied. The long decades of solitary confinement devoid of all stimulation had erased his memory and made all but the simplest thoughts impossible. The artist's eye, the wit's tongue, the sensitive soul of the suffering poet—all were vanished. He had been immersed in the icy saltwater too long for his brain to escape undamaged. The water had permeated not only his bones, but also the deepest folds of his cortex, dulling his intelligence in the way that running a rasp against the edge of a good knife might ruin it forever. This was life reduced to its most primitive level: mute, predatory, capable of careless, even casual savagery.

The vampire reached for the door, closing his eyes as he breathed in deeply, savoring the delicious perfume of living blood, hyperaware of its closeness. When he had been an ordinary man, he had not always known what he wanted; his needs often seemed to be concealed within a labyrinth, where desire lurked like the Minotaur. Now, in this limited sort of existence, things were much simpler. He had only one desire: blood. His wanting was far more powerful than a mere physical sensation. What he felt was the all-consuming thirst for life itself, the hunger for the powerful essence that animates the living. The blood filled him with Dionysian ecstasy, a primordial passion, thoroughly intoxicating, pagan, blissful. He had long since fulfilled his mere physiological requirements. He'd warmed the thick sludge in his veins, quickening his heart with stolen life, restoring his wasted body if not his vacant mind. Now, like a Roman aristocrat whose insatiable lust will not let him quit the orgy, it was pleasure alone that drove him forward.

His yellowish fingernails were so long that they curled in on themselves. The handle would only turn a little way. It was locked. Gripping the brass lever more firmly, he forced it downward with a single sharp thrust. Metal twisted inside the lock mechanism and broke free. At first the door would only open a crack. They'd piled everything they could find against it. The vampire's eyes rolled up in his head as he sent an invisible spear of telekinetic energy to blast the obstructions out of the way.

Patricia Solberg Mobius screamed as the vampire entered the cabin. The man with her—Nick Drake—pointed what seemed to be an oversized revolver toward the door and pulled the trigger. Blinding red light and stinging smoke filled the air as the flare exploded against the vampire's hand. He held it there a moment, wondering at the pain as it seared his flesh before he clamped his hands together to smother it.

The woman had started to chant: "Oh my God, oh my God, oh my God . . ."

The vampire looked down at his burned hands, watching with almost childish wonder as the burned skin healed itself.

The man continued to point the flare gun at the vampire, though it was no longer loaded. His hand trembled. He understood the fate that awaited him. The woman did, too.

The difference between the vampire's appearance and Drake's registered in some remote corner of what remained in the vampire's mind. He saw that Drake was a good-looking man, with casual but elegant clothing, razor-cut hair, and a freshly shaved face. The silver bracelet the director wore on his right wrist caught the vampire's eye. He stared at the glittering object, mesmerized, with the same wonder he had shown while watching his burned hands heal. For all his frightening wildness, there was something innocent and even childlike about the vampire.

He grabbed Drake so quickly the man did not even see him move.

The vampire put his lips against Drake's neck so that it seemed he was kissing him. The man's body jerked, suddenly tense, then went completely slack.

The woman did not scream or try to flee. There was nowhere else to go but into the ocean. The sharks that circled the ship, waiting for more corpses to be thrown overboard, elicited an even more primal horror and revulsion in her than the monster. She and Nick were the last. They had managed to stay alive the longest, but now the end had come.

Drake continued to stand only because the vampire held him up. The cabin was perfectly quiet except for the distant hum of the ship's generator and the vampire's occasional wet, greedy swallowing noises. The director's face and arms lost their healthy tan, becoming pallid. His skin started to pucker, as if he'd spent too much time in the water. Only then did the vampire let the corpse drop to the floor with a dull thud.

Then there was only one more human left alive on the ship, one more mortal to quench the unquenchable thirst.

Patricia Solberg Mobius sank to the floor. She drew up her legs under her chin, one arm tightly wrapped around her knees, the other clasping the crystal necklace she wore for luck, as the vampire came toward her. This was not Patricia's first encounter with death, and, now that the fight was lost, she was determined to die with at least some measure of bravery.

He put his forefinger beneath her chin. She did not resist as he raised her head so she was looking at him, her eyes on his eyes, inches between them, as if she were his lover and he was about to present her with the most tender of kisses.

The vampire pushed an errant strand of blond hair away from her face with his yellowed fingernail, drawing the knuckle of his thumb down her cheek in a lingering caress. He spoke then, his first word in nearly a century, a low, scratchy, almost inaudible whisper.

The vampire said: "Lovely."

10

THE HOUSE OVERLOOKING the lake was quiet, except for the crickets and the crackle of the flames in the fireplace. The logs popped and sizzled intermittently, a smallish fire on a cool midsummer night. The smell of freshly cut hay floated through the open windows from the neighboring fields. The fire provided the only light in the room.

Dr. Richard Mobius sat in a straight-backed oak chair, his spine pressed against the ungiving wooden slats, his feet flat on the floor, his hands on his thighs. He still wore the black suit and starched white shirt he'd worn to the lawyer's office that afternoon. He sat so stone-rigid that he resembled a Puritan judge ready to condemn the Salem women to burn for being witches.

After a bit, the sound of an automobile interrupted the quiet, approaching along the private lane. It was a familiar sound: a Saab with a loose tailpipe that gave it a distinctive rattle. Richard did not get up when the doorbell rang but continued to stare at the fire. The front door opened and closed. He hadn't bothered to lock it. The alarm system hadn't been set, so it didn't go off. Richard was no longer interested in such trifling details.

Footsteps came down the dark hallway toward the study.

"Richard? Are you all right?"

"Of course," he said after a moment.

Rebecca Isaac bent down and looked into his eyes, showing her concern. His eyes moved away from hers after a moment, returning to the fire.

"What are you doing?"

"Thinking," he said.

She sat on the floor at his feet. "Everybody in the department is asking about you."

The statement didn't seem to require an answer.

"Have you thought about your classes when the fall semester starts? It might be good to take some time off."

"I'm not going back."

"What?"

"I'm not going back to the university."

"Richard . . ."

"Hobson will be glad to take over my seminar, I'm sure. He's been hoping for me to resign ever since I got married. Suddenly, there's room at the top."

"You don't want to make rash decisions, Richard. You need to take the time to figure out where you really want to go from here."

"My work isn't at the university now."

"You're going to devote all your time to the magazine?"

He shook his head.

"Writing?"

"I have nothing left to say."

"What then? The fertilizer company?"

Mobius looked as if she'd slapped him. His expression changed to anger after a few moments, but then he burst into laughter completely devoid of mirth.

"You don't understand," he said after a bit. "Everything is different now."

"But, Richard . . ."

He cringed inwardly at the dependence in Rebecca's voice.

Patricia had loved him, but not in the sense that she required him to complete herself. Mobius thought it strange that he hadn't noticed Rebecca's clinging need before. He'd been too besotted with her young body to pay much attention to what she said when they weren't in bed, too intent upon punishing Patricia for leaving him alone for the summer. Except now, of course, he would be alone forever.

"Everything is different," Mobius said, repeating his cryptic pronouncement.

"You need some time," Rebecca said.

Mobius hated her at that moment—he hated her stupid optimism, her naive hope that things would somehow work out for the best, for her, for *them*. Life was no fairy tale.

"Do you remember what the minister said at Patricia's funeral?"

"It was a beautiful service," Rebecca said. The church had been packed to overflowing. She had found an inconspicuous place in the back, sitting with Dr. Mobius's other graduate students.

"He said what happened to Patricia was part of God's mysterious plan. Imagine it: You get your throat torn out by a serial killer who drinks your blood, and it's all part of God's mysterious plan." He was smiling again, a cold, bitter smile.

"Bad things happen to people sometimes."

Mobius wanted to hit her for being so inane. She must have sensed it, for she leaned away from him a little, as if struck by the psychic force of his thoughts.

"Do you know what Epicurus says about God?"

"The classics are not my long suit."

Of course they weren't. His students were amazingly unlearned. They came to the university to confirm their ignorance, to ratify one another's shallow opinions.

"Epicurus says there is one of two possible explanations for evil. The first is that God wants to prevent evil, but can't, meaning he's weak. The other possibility is that God could prevent evil if he wanted to, but doesn't, meaning he's malevolent."

"How can this sort of talk help, Richard?"

"Because it helps define the enemy."

"God is not the enemy."

"Isn't he? I can't do anything about God, but I can hunt the monster he sent to kill my wife. The killer is just the symbol, God's tool."

"Richard, this doesn't sound like you. I think your grief and anger are running away with you. Leave it to the police. Finding Patricia's killer is their job."

"I *will* find him," Mobius said. "I have all the time in the world now and more money than I can ever spend. There isn't much you can't buy, you know, with enough money."

Rebecca got up and put her arms around him from behind, resting her face in the crook of his neck.

"I can't bear seeing you in this pain," she said quietly in his ear. "Isn't there something I can do to help, to make you feel better?"

"Everything is different now," Mobius repeated. He felt her tense against him.

"What are you saying?"

"You can't imagine what this is like until it happens to you. It's as if I went to sleep and woke up another person in another life."

She continued to hold him, but he was unyielding to her embrace. He did not even soften when she began to cry.

"Are you saying you don't want to see me anymore?"

"How stupid are you?" Mobius snapped. "Only one thing matters to me now."

Rebecca released him as if she'd been scalded. She went to

stand by the door, remaining there a few minutes, crying quietly, then retreated with slow footsteps up the hall the way she had come. Mobius heard the front door open and close. The Saab's engine clattered to life and then the sound began to recede up the long paved drive.

    Mobius continued to sit as he had been sitting, staring into the fire, watching the flames for prescient glimpses of his revenge.

11

HE STOOD AT the edge of the deadly boulevard, watching the sinister contraptions scream past, one after another, no interval betwixt and between to allow him to cross. The occupants of the bizarre contrivances—deranged with terror and anger, to judge from the looks they shot him—must have been insane. Four queues of carriages traveled left to right before him. Beyond was a grassy turf ditch cluttered with refuse, then another four queues of carriages hurtling in the opposite direction.

The carriage lights blinded him. Every third or fourth vehicle made an appalling noise as it approached him, a beastly mechanical shriek of warning. The light, noise, and motion were completely disorienting.

He made a dash at a momentary break in the traffic, nearly gaining the relative safety of the street's grassy midsection when a silver Lincoln Continental driven by an aged, blue-haired harridan spun him drunkenly into the median. He felt a sharp, brittle pain in his thigh as he slammed onto the soggy grass. He tried to get up, but his leg would not support him. The bone was broken. He nearly wept with frustration. The pain was excruciating, but it subsided after a few moments. When he tried to stand a second time, the femur had mended.

He wiped his muddy hands the best he could on his trouser legs. His arms and legs were wet, the knee torn out of the left pant leg. The canvas tennis shoes he'd found aboard the ship were soaked through with water and mud. He should have found sturdier footwear before abandoning the broken ship, but his mind was childlike in its capacity to grasp such distinctions.

He stood beside the roadway, staring angrily at the onrushing queues of carriages, waiting for another break in the traffic, the air stinking of petroleum and rubber. He was vaguely aware that he'd been out of the world for a very long time, long enough for society to have degenerated into a mechanized urban hell. The texture of life itself had altered. Everything had become coarse and common, as if the pattern sketched out in London's East End slums had been perfected and projected upon the rest of the world.

The traffic eased and he started to run. A vehicle the size of a locomotive loomed up out of the moving chaos, air horn blaring. It would have been impossible for an ordinary person to escape being run over, but a burst of preternatural speed saved him. The driver stood on his brakes at the last moment. The semi-tractor jackknifed. The truck's load, sheets of steel stacked on the trailer, sliced into the cab as it careened off the road. The air was suddenly full of the delicious aroma of blood, but not even that could induce the vampire to remain a second longer in this purgatory.

A chain-link fence divided the highway from the neighboring buildings. He leaped over it, clearing the twelve-foot barrier with room to spare. He ran down an unlighted alley, slowing to a walk as he gained the intersecting street. The buildings were of recent vintage, unadorned, stark, graceless, government-built housing. Nearly a third of the structures were abandoned, the windows and doors boarded up, the exterior walls defaced with vandals' scrawls.

A goodly number of people were out on the street taking the evening air, most of them young men in cricket caps worn backward or at rakish angles. He ignored their hostile stares. He knew nothing of Negroes or their proclivities, though he kept an eye out for cutpurses. The place he was in was a bit like the Docklands, but that was part of another life, a dream of long ago. It made his heart hurt to remember, so he did not fight the forgetting, content to leave the book of his memory blank except for those innocent recollections that did not cause him pain.

He stopped and looked up into the sky, turning up the collar of his jacket against the night.

A slum such as this would make an ideal hunting ground. The abandoned buildings afforded excellent concealment. The local environs could furnish him with an abundance of young people, whose disappearance would be scarcely noted. Yet the bleakness was oppressive. Not a blade of grass, tree, or flower to be seen, not even in the window boxes of the dispirited and sullen inhabitants. There was something about the people, an air of disappointment and defeat that hung about them even as they took their evening leisure.

"What the fuck you looking at?"

In a playground sandwiched between two buildings, groups of men had been running back and forth with a ball a little larger than the size of a man's head. One man would get the ball and attempt to bounce it past his opponents toward the far end of the playing field, where a hoop was suspended in the air. The player would throw the ball through the air, apparently scoring if he succeeded in dropping it through the iron hoop.

Another young man—not the one who had spoken to him— hurled the ball against the fence, sending a sharp rattling reverberating through the metal in both directions away from the impact point.

He did not flinch but stared back at his interrogator. His opposite's head was shaved, and he wore a golden earring, like a mariner, with heavily muscled arms sticking out of his sleeveless red Chicago Bulls jersey. He was breathing heavily from the game, the pulse jerking in his carotid artery, the ebony skin on his graceful body glistening with a sheen of perspiration. He reminded the vampire of a prima dancer at the end of a ballet, although he could not recall having ever seen a dancer with black skin.

"Leave the poor mother alone, T," another man said. He was a few years older than the others. "He just a pathetic homeless."

"Look crazy to me," T said, looking at the vampire without blinking, trying to stare him down.

"He have to be crazy, walkin' his white ass through this neighborhood," the wiser man said.

They turned away as if the vampire had suddenly become invisible and returned to their game.

Homeless. What the man said was true enough. He was homeless. But where was home? He could not say. He did not even know his own name. He was lost, more lost in the world than anyone had ever been, lost in time as well as place.

He turned away from the game and continued down the street, broken glass crunching under his damp canvas shoes.

He was now aware that people looked at him with distaste, as if he were a leper, and indeed he was a leper of sorts, but far more dangerous than the ordinary sort. His hair needed to be cut. He needed to shave. His hands were dirty, his clothing filthy. Once he'd been proud of his appearance, even a little vain, he recollected.

A baby was crying somewhere. He paid no special attention until the plaintive sound began to wear on his nerves as it grew nearer. How could so persistent a cry attract no response? It was obvious the child was hungry. Where was the wailing infant's mother?

He paused before a tenement, looking up at the building, grim and mostly dark, a mansion of despair. The tiny voice carried out an open window on the third floor. Its hunger reminded him of his own. The infant had awakened the Hunger in him. He felt a moment of dark temptation, but was completely revolted at himself. How could he have such thoughts?

"Shut up," a male voice said. The child continued to cry.

Something triggered a rage deep within the vampire. He flew angrily through the front door and up the stairs two and three at a time, sickened by the reek of urine and feces in the defaced hallway. He stopped outside a door marked with metal numerals that had been painted over so many times that the 6 and 6 were reduced to impressionistic smears that seemed to be melting into the wood. He sensed four people within: the wailing child, two men, a woman.

He smashed through the door and found himself standing in a squalid, one-room apartment. The kitchenette and dining area were to the right, the combination sitting room/bedroom beyond it, past a half wall. The couch had been folded out to be used as a bed. The crying baby was there on its back on a bare mattress, tiny eyes squeezed shut, tiny hands balled into fists, helpless in its unmet need.

In the kitchenette sat a white man in suit and tie, a skeletal black woman wearing a torn T-shirt, and a black man. The woman was holding what appeared to be a pipe made out of glass. The differences between the white man and the two Negroes—the races, their social classes—were immediately apparent. The white man wore a gold watch and diamond ring. The suit jacket hanging over his chair had been cut by a tailor from a bolt of dark blue wool, like suits that had once hung in the vampire's wardrobe.

The black man was already getting to his feet, an enormous revolver in his left hand.

The woman screamed and put her hands up as the vampire moved swiftly past her and grabbed the man with the gun by his ears. He turned the man's head swiftly to the side, snapping his spine. The gun dropped harmlessly to the floor as the man sank to his knees, the muscles in his arms and legs twitching spasmodically. His tongue, purplish, hung out of his mouth, and blood oozed from his nose.

"Take my money," the white man said. He reached for the wallet in his jacket as the vampire came for him, his blood teeth dropping from the upper jaw and locking into place.

The man did not struggle or even try to get away as the vampire lifted him into the air with one hand and sank his teeth into his throat. The vampire trembled a bit from the delirious pleasure that came into him with the blood, but it was not his intention to drain the man to the point of death. That would have been too easy, for then the man would have shared the vampire's ecstasy until the moment when his foul heart stopped beating. The vampire pushed the weakened man away without bothering to free his teeth of the man's neck. His diamond-sharp incisors tore the man's throat open from the inside out. The man tried to cover the wound with his hands, but his eyes revealed that he knew nothing could save him. He lay against the wall, staring up at the vampire, at his own death, for the half minute it took him to bleed out.

The vampire went to the baby and picked it up. The little girl was so tiny that she barely filled his two hands. He lifted the child and looked into her tear-streaked face, gently cradling her head. She was beautiful. So small, so helpless.

"Hush, little one," he whispered.

The baby caught its breath twice, made a little peeping sound, and became quiet. For a moment he stood there, cradling the baby, too enraptured to focus on the fragment of painful memory playing at the edge of his mind. He gently laid the child down. There was a small cotton baby blanket on the floor. He lovingly tucked it around the child, ignoring the woman behind him. He had a perfect sense of what she was doing: She stood with her back against the wall, trying to steady the heavy revolver with her shaking hands.

The roar was deafening when the gun exploded.

The .44 caliber slug ripped into his shoulder, spinning the vampire sideways.

He looked down at the ragged hole in his shirt. The bullet had gone completely through him, back to front, puncturing his right lung. Arterial blood pumped through the sucking hole in his chest, soaking his shirt to the belt. He gently touched the wound, but the hemorrhaging had already stopped. He took a deep, ragged breath, experiencing the pain in its fullness, and relishing it, as it quickly faded.

He slowly raised his eyes until he was looking at the woman past his glowering brow.

"You the Devil?" she asked, nearly hysterical, trying to keep the gun trained on him.

"I suppose I am," he answered.

The vampire moved toward her so quickly that she did not see his approach until he had taken the revolver from her hands and tossed it aside, fearful that an errant shot might hit the baby. He took her by the hair, pulling her face close to his so that she could see the Hunger burning in his eyes.

"Are these your chambers?"

"No." She shook her head. "It's Jimmy's crib."

"And that would be Mr. Jimmy?" He inclined his head to in-dicate the body of the man whose neck he had snapped.

"That Jimmy. The other one Jimmy's lawyer. Comes up here sometimes to smoke a few bowls. His name Aaron."

"Smoke what?" the vampire asked.

"Crack."

"I beg your pardon?"

"You know. Crack cocaine."

The vampire knew all about drugs. Or at least he had the sense that he did, though he could recall none of the particulars. It had been a long time ago. "And you?"

"Yeah."

"You have the money to purchase drugs?"

"No, at least not today. I was going to smoke some with Jimmy and Aaron. I was going to give them both, you know . . ."

"And the babe?"

"She cry all the time, man. I was going to feed her. I just wanted to get some smoke while there was still some left."

He tightened his grip on her hair until she cried out in pain.

"You don't deserve to have a child. In fact, you don't deserve to live."

"Please." She began to cry. "Give me another chance. I'll never touch another pipe. I swear."

On the bed behind them, the baby whimpered.

"Very well, then," he said, his voice still hoarse from disuse. "I will give you one more chance, but only for the child's sake. I warn you that I will know if you resort to your old ways. We know everything in Hell."

The woman shook her head, too frightened to speak.

"If you backslide, I shall rise up out of Hell and tear your heart out with my hands. Your death will not be as swift as your two friends'. Do you understand me? I have the power to make your suffering last for a week, but that will be a mere prelude for the eternity of pain you will know in Hell if you do not repent your ways."

"I swear I will do good!"

He let go of the woman and went to the dead man's coat. There was a wallet in the inside pocket. The lawyer had a money roll in his front pocket with a rubber band around it.

"There's nearly four thousand American dollars here. Would that help you and your child?"

The woman's eyes were wary. She could not bring herself to believe that a devil would spare her and then underwrite her expenses to start a new life. He threw the money onto the table and backed away from it.

"Is there somewhere else you can go?"

"My mama lives in Maryland."

"Is that enough money to get you and your baby to Maryland?" She nodded.

"Take the money and go, then. Do not return to this city ever again. Stay away from drugs and take care of your baby. Remember, I will be watching."

She didn't take her eyes off him as she bent over to pick up her baby. She grabbed the money on her way toward the door and went out, not looking back.

"You are most welcome," he said to the empty doorway.

He stripped off his filthy shirt and exchanged it for a collarless white dress shirt he found hanging in the late Jimmy's closet. He put on Aaron's jacket. It was a little large on him, but it made him look more presentable. Perhaps he should have retained some of the banknotes for himself, though he didn't think he'd have any trouble getting money when he required it.

Feeling better without knowing why, he went back out onto the street.

He found the railyard quite by chance. Here, at last, was something he recognized and understood, even though the yard was lit up like day by blazing silver lights atop tall standards. He heard the familiar rumble and hurried toward the moving freight train, which was pulled not by a steam engine but a mysterious locomotive that sent no plume of coal smoke into the night sky. He found an open boxcar and jumped inside, sitting back in the corner, where he would be out of sight from railroad bulls on the lookout for tramps.

Quickening footsteps approached the car. A duffel bag flew in through the door, followed by a young woman who turned and reached out to help her companion. It was another young woman. The first girl wore a black leather jacket and had a ring in her nose, like an Arab, although she was white. The other was younger, smaller, hardly more than an urchin, blond but for the brown roots of her hair. Both girls stank of tobacco and sweat. Even in the darkness he could see they were unwashed and almost sticky. A pair of right dolly-mops, he thought.

The surprise at finding him in the car unnerved the girls. The girl with the ring in her nose pulled a knife from her jacket.

"Good evening, ladies," he said.

"Who the hell are you?"

He considered telling them he was the Devil, but that hardly seemed the thing to do. He felt suddenly tired—not physically but spiritually tired, as if the people he'd killed since his awakening had drained some vital essence from him, even as he'd drained his victims of their blood. The train was beginning to pick up speed as it passed factories on the edge of the city. Soon they would be in the comfortable darkness of the countryside.

"I do not know," he said after considering the matter.

"What's that supposed to mean?" the girl with the knife said, putting herself defensively between the vampire and her smaller friend.

"It simply means I do not know who I am," the vampire finally said, which was the truth. He leaned his head back against the wall of the gently rocking boxcar. He wanted only to be left alone, to feel the gentle reassurance of the train's maternal rocking as it carried him away from the scene of his latest violence.

"Get up," the girl with the knife said.

The vampire complied.

"There's only room in here for two. You're getting out."

"There is ample room for us and many more wanderers."

"I said out, motherfucker!" the girl shouted.

"If you insist," the vampire said with a slight bow of the head, feeling his face redden. He had never heard a young woman use such appalling language. It shocked him deeply.

"I fucking insist," the girl with the knife said, smirking. "But before you jump, you're going to give me your money."

The ebullience the vampire had felt after helping the baby had completely left him. He felt himself collapsing inward again, a dark star, a powerful vortex of crushing depression that would drag anyone unfortunate enough to come too close to him to their doom.

"You will find my wallet inside the left side of my jacket. Shall I get it out for you?"

"Put your hands up, your lordship," the girl said with a sneer as she came toward him. She held the tip of the knife beneath his chin and slipped her hand between his shirt and jacket. Her heart was pounding with excitement from the thrill of her small crime. The vampire heard its strong, quick beat as she put her hand into the empty pocket, the pulse of his own ancient heart quickening until it was in perfect unison with hers.

12

"WHY CAN YOU not tell me your name? It seems to me you are being rather obstinate. Are you unable to remember, or are you merely being difficult?"

Dr. Abigail Bloome paused outside the door as she turned through the photocopied pages in the loose-leaf notebook, looking for the paperwork for the new patient in One North. He was a John Doe. According to the admission form, police found him sitting in the park the night before. He had neither money nor identification. He was apparently a homeless man, someone who had drifted into Calhoun, probably hitching rides on the coastal freights. The patient was unresponsive, either unable or unwilling to answer even simple questions.

"I am thinking that you are embarrassed to admit who you are," Dr. Veena Govindaiah said. "Is there some shameful misdeed in your past from which you wish to hide?"

Veena was seated in a chair at the foot of the patient's bed, dressed in a crisp white doctor's jacket, blue polyester skirt, and black flats. She gave Abby a look when she came in. It was Abby's responsibility to help supervise her, whether Veena liked it or not—and she had made it plain that she did not. Dr. Govindaiah had a year left in her residency before she could be licensed as a psychiatrist.

"Good morning," Abby said, addressing the patient. "My name is Abigail Bloome. I'm a doctor. How are you this morning?"

The patient did not respond.

"He presents as catatonic," Veena said. "I am thinking he is either a major depressive disorder or perhaps catatonic schizophrenia."

"Maybe he just doesn't have anything to say," Abby replied, smiling at the patient.

Dr. Govindaiah's style of analysis was to put patients on the defensive, forcing them to erect hasty barricades that, in theory, made it possible to identify problem areas quickly. In Abby's experience, the prosecutorial style put a barrier between the analyst and patient, making the patient resistant and resentful.

The patient was seated cross-legged on the bed, wearing the white pajamas and white-and-pastel-green-striped robe issued to every person, male or female, admitted to One North, the locked psychiatric ward at Calhoun Hospital. His posture was erect. The sharp definition of shoulders, chest, and upper arms beneath the cotton garments indicated a strong, healthy physique. That alone was argument against a diagnosis of catatonia, which tended to be accompanied by malnutrition and self-injury. The man had strong, well-proportioned, almost classic features that were not disguised by his long hair and full beard. His luxuriantly curly chestnut-colored hair had been washed and brushed back from his forehead, falling past his shoulders. His eyes were large and dark and set deep under a strong brow. He had prominent cheekbones, a sensitive mouth, and the lines of a strong chin and jaw beneath his beard. The patient's eyes were fixed on some indeterminate point in the middle distance. His expression was composed. Sitting cross-legged, his hands resting on his knees, his spine perfectly erect, he reminded Abby of the miniature ivory Buddha she kept on her desk at home.

"Do you understand where you are and why you were brought here?" Abby asked.

The patient gave no indication that he heard the question.

"That's a lovely ring you're wearing. Is it an antique?"

The patient slowly shifted his gaze to Abby. He had beautiful eyes—shimmering dark orbs that sparkled with golden highlights.

"Wearing personal jewelry is not allowed on this ward," Dr. Govindaiah said.

"You have a special attachment to this ring."

The chart said that two orderlies had been unable to get him to open his hand so they could get the ring off his finger. He was also blessed with an unusually strong constitution. They'd pumped him as full of tranquilizers as they dared, without any apparent effect.

"As far as I'm concerned, you can continue to wear your ring. I'm rather partial to rubies. Besides, the hospital rule forbidding patients to wear jewelry is rather stupid."

A hint of a smile flickered through the patient's eyes.

"Would you care to tell me your name?"

"Charles Gabriel."

Veena sharply sucked her breath through her teeth, an ugly, snakelike sound.

"You have a lovely speaking voice, Charles. Are you British?"

He nodded.

Abby crossed out *John Doe* on the admission form and substituted *Charles Gabriel*.

"You can tell me more about yourself when you are ready, Charles. I'm a patient person."

She stood and laid her hand gently on the patient's shoulder, personalizing their bond—psychiatrist and patient—and giving it physical reality. "Think of this as a first step, Charles. I can help you take others, if you will let me."

"I would like that very much, Dr. Bloome," the vampire said, returning the psychiatrist's smile.

13

BRIGHT SUNLIGHT FILTERED through tropical foliage, filling the room with green-tinted light, slanting pillars of gold falling straight to the flagstone floor in the few places where there were no plants to block the sun. The greenhouse occupied the elbow where One North, the psychiatric ward, met One East, which housed the surgery and radiology departments. Giant rhododendrons, banana plants, and potted ficus trees pushed up against the glass ceiling. Drops of moisture still clung to leaves from the morning watering, occasionally falling to the stone floor as if dropped by a passing cloud. The solarium's warmth and humidity were a pleasant contrast to the hospital, which was air-conditioned to the point of being chilly.

In one corner, beneath the gathering arms of a banyon festooned with staghorn ferns, sat two cedar lawn chairs with cushions. Between the chairs was a round cedar table holding a pitcher and two glasses of iced tea. Dr. Abigail Bloome occupied one chair. The vampire was opposite her. He sat back with his legs crossed, relaxed except for his alert eyes, which never left her.

A little work with a safety razor—with two orderlies standing close by to ensure nothing untoward occurred—had taken away his beard to reveal fully the handsome and intelligent face. His hair was still long, but he wore it now pulled back into a severe ponytail. Even in the hospital-issue robe and slippers, he looked as elegant and self-possessed as a lord.

"How did you sleep? Any dreams, Charles?"

"I do not dream, Doctor."

"We all dream. It is only a matter of remembering."

"But that is why I am here, Dr. Bloome. I have forgotten how to remember."

"True enough," she said, smiling at his turn of phrase. "I do not think your near-term memory is affected. You remember my name."

"I remember everything from when the constables brought me to the hospital."

She nodded. "Try to remember your dreams from now on, Charles. I'd like to hear about them."

"As you wish."

"How do you feel today? Any sense of confusion or disorientation? Any headache?"

"I am perfectly well, except that . . ."

"Yes?" He seemed hesitant to complain.

"I am rather hungry."

"Didn't they give you breakfast?"

"Scrambled eggs, fruit, and something called a bagel. No meat."

"You crave a proper English breakfast?"

"That would be lovely, Doctor, but what I really have a hunger for is meat. There is nothing I would like better than a big, juicy beefsteak, rare and bloody."

"I promise to see what I can do." She made a notation. "Steak doesn't often appear on the menu at Calhoun Hospital, but I think I can arrange it."

"I would be most appreciative," he said, bowing forward from the waist while seated.

It was an elegant, anachronistic gesture. Abby tried not to make assumptions about people, but it seemed evident money, education, and good breeding were part of her patient's background. Eton, Oxford, a country house—none of it would have surprised her. He seemed an archetypal English gentleman—not the stuffy, stiff-upper-lip type, but a dashing young lord, someone drawn to fast cars and horses. She sensed there was a depth to him, too. Perhaps he was something of an aesthete. He had passionate eyes and the graceful hands of an artist or musician.

"Would you mind if I asked a few personal questions?"

"I will tell you what I can, little as it may be."

"Where were you born?"

"London," he said, answering quickly. He almost came out of his chair with surprise. "Where did *that* come from?"

"It's all in here, Charles." She tapped a finger against her forehead. "Together we'll get it back."

"What's wrong with me, Dr. Bloome?"

"It's too soon to really know, but my guess is that you have what is called diminishing retrograde amnesia. That's a cumbersome term that simply means your amnesia is limited to things that happened before a certain point in time. In your case, that point in time is when you were found in the park. Your amnesia is retrograde from that point backward."

"I remember nothing before that," he confirmed.

"Your amnesia is diminishing in the sense that you will most likely gradually regain your past. The fact that you were born in London, for example. Most of it will come back, in time."

"But not all?"

"Probably, but I can't guarantee it."

"What would cause such forgetfulness?"

"There are three possibilities. The most common cause for such a condition would be something organic. We're fairly certain that is not the problem. You are in excellent physical health and the CAT scan of your brain revealed no abnormalities."

"Such as?"

"Lesions, tumors, that sort of thing."

"Thank God for that," the vampire exclaimed.

"The second possible explanation would be severe trauma. You show no signs of head injury. It remains a possibility, however, although I would say a rather remote one. The third possible cause would be psychological trauma. You may have seen or experienced something so emotionally painful that your subconscious mind has decided to forget everything rather than remember—and thereby reexperience—the traumatic episode."

"That hardly seems likely, Dr. Bloome."

"Do not be quick to discount the possibility. The subconscious mind is its own master. It can be quite elaborate in devising defensive measures to protect itself."

"How does one treat such a condition?"

"By probing the subconscious until we find the hidden root of your distress."

"What would that accomplish?"

"Everything, Charles," she said with a smile. "You would be amazed at the powerful effect of simply acknowledging a conflict. These things gain power over us because they operate beyond the light of reason. Once we become conscious of their existence and force them into the light, their power over us fades. I have every reason to be optimistic about your prognosis, Charles. We are already making progress. We know your name. We know you are from London."

"I put myself entirely in your hands, Doctor."

"You must not think it will always be easy. Delving into the subconscious can be painful."

"I am not afraid," he said bravely.

"Good. Another question, then. Do you have any sense of how long you have been in the United States?"

"I think not long."

"Excellent. I'll check with Immigration authorities. There must be a record of your entering the country. Tell me what you liked most about your favorite brother."

"My youngest sister was my favorite." Again, the startled expression came into his face, a little distrustful at first, his eyes opening wider with a look of unexpected realization, then softening after a moment almost to the point of being wistful. "You are good at what you do, Doctor."

"What do you remember about her?"

"She was a poet."

"Why do you say 'was'?"

"She died," he said, frowning. "All of my family—they are all dead but me. I am the last. Do not ask me how I know it, Doctor. I cannot remember the details, only the fact. I am alone in the world."

"But let's focus on a pleasant memory. Your favorite sister: you said she was a poet?" There was no point in dwelling on painful memories, not at this early stage; there would be time to recover them later, to identify the source of the anguish from which Charles Gabriel was trying to hide.

"She was very good. Sometimes I thought Christina was a better poet than I."

"You're a poet?"

He looked at the psychiatrist with a wrinkled brow. "I must have been, although I can't recall a single line of anything I've ever written. I do remember plenty of other people's poetry, but none of mine. Or Christina's, come to think of it. But other people's verse rattles through my head constantly."

"The mind must occupy itself with something, Charles. Yours is simply using the material presently available to it. Would you recite something for me? Anything that happens to come to mind."

He looked up at the irregular patch of sky showing through the broken foliage. The brilliant blue was lightly marbled by a wisp of cloud. He closed his eyes and began to recite:

> "Our birth is but a sleep and a forgetting:
> The Soul that rises with us, our life's Star,
> Hath had elsewhere its setting,
> And cometh from afar:
> Not in entire forgetfulness,
> And not in utter nakedness,
> But trailing clouds of glory do we come
> From God, who is our home . . ."

"Wordsworth," Abby said. How many men—how many *people*, she amended her thought—could quote Wordsworth?

The pneumatic cylinder on the door whooshed. One of the high school volunteers who worked at the hospital came in with an arrangement of roses, putting it on the table between them.

"Poor Mrs. Martinson," the candy striper said, oblivious to the fact that she was interrupting therapy. "Someone sent her these beautiful roses, not knowing she's allergic to them."

"What is it, Charles?"

Her patient, deathly pale, stared at the flowers, on his face an expression of mute horror.

"Would you excuse us, please?"

The girl looked from Abby to the stricken man and back. She

only then appeared to realize the man was one of the mental patients from One North and seemed to be on the verge of a fit. The crepe heels of her shoes squeaked against the wet flagstone as she turned and fled the room, almost running.

"What is it about roses, Charles? Why are they so upsetting?"

The vampire did not answer but fell back in his chair in a dead faint.

14

"DO YOU HAVE it?"

The man across the table patted the cheap vinyl briefcase on the seat beside him by way of answer.

"I'll take delivery, then," Dr. Richard Mobius said. He held out his hand.

Coast Guard Chief Petty Officer Paul Seiver didn't move. His eyes scanned the room, looking for Naval Intelligence officers lurking in the shadows, ready to clap handcuffs on him the moment the transaction took place. The only other people in the lounge were the bartender and a hopeful-looking, thirty-something woman seated at the bar, chain-smoking Virginia Slims and nursing a margarita. Neither seemed likely to be participants in a sting to arrest the chief petty officer for selling evidence from the Coast Guard's inquiry into the *Bentham Explorer*, lost with all hands.

The lounge overlooked the harbor. Outside, silhouettes of sailboats and yachts bobbed in the water. The commercial harbor was beyond the pier, where fishing boats were tied up at the docks or riding anchor, nets hanging from booms for drying and repair.

Seiver wore civilian clothes, a green polo shirt, Levi's, and sneakers. As for Mobius, he no longer looked as if he'd stepped out of the pages of an L.L. Bean catalog. He was dressed entirely in black—black T-shirt, leather jacket, chinos, and cowboy boots. After going a week without shaving, he'd trimmed his beard into a Vandyke that made him look more like a biker than an English professor.

"I could get in lots of trouble," Seiver said.

Mobius picked up his drink. The glass was cold from the ice, and the chill went into his fingers, up his arm, and into his smile.

"Don't fuck with me," he said.

"I'm not," Seiver said. "But this would cost me my career, if I got caught."

Mobius studied the sailor. His head was narrow and wedge-shaped, with a smudge of chin over a bulging larynx. He'd grown a sparse mustache to make himself look mature, but he'd always look like a punk, even in middle age.

"If you think you can back out on me and not have them find out, you're mistaken."

Seiver blinked, his mouth coming open a little.

"You're being well paid for your trouble," Mobius added.

"I don't understand why you're in such a rush. You could have a copy for the asking, if you'd wait thirty days for the review hearing."

"It sounds as though you're trying to talk yourself out of a thousand dollars."

"I'm just trying to think this through."

"I'm an impatient man. I don't want to wait. I'm conducting my own investigation. I want to evaluate the evidence. And now, not in thirty days."

"And you think you'll see something they'll miss at Quantico?"

"Your faith in the feds is touching," Mobius said. "I think they're utterly incompetent. It's preposterous to think terrorists are responsible. Libyans, Iranians, IRA gun-runners—the usual suspects. They haven't a clue. It may fool some people, but not me."

"What do you think happened, Dr. Mobius?"

"I don't know, but I assure you I am going to find out. And when I do . . ." Mobius let his voice trail off.

"I'm sorry about your wife."

Mobius made a curt nod.

"Why do you think she was the only one they found?"

"I suspect they considered holding her for ransom. They must have been too busy trying to save their own skins, once the storm drove the ship onto the rocks, to get rid of her body the way they did with the others."

Mobius picked up his glass and drank off the rest of the martini, not tasting the gin. When he was finished, he held out his hand. His drink was finished and so was his patience.

"You brought the money, like we agreed?"

Mobius reached into the inside breast pocket for his billfold. The one-hundred-dollar bills clung to each other with the sticky tension of new money. Turning sideways in the booth, he counted out ten of the bills and passed them to the sailor under the table. Seiver snatched the money and stuffed it into his jeans without counting it. The bartender asked his woman customer if she wanted another margarita. She glanced over her shoulder at Mobius and nodded. The music on the house stereo was a New Age jazz CD, synthesized and ethereal; it grated on Mobius's nerves.

"Is it a good copy of the original?"

"I made it myself," Seiver said, nodding as he passed the videotape under the table.

"Nice doing business with you," Mobius said. He stood up and threw a twenty-dollar bill onto the table.

The woman at the bar was smiling hard at him as he headed for the door, but he never even looked in her direction.

* * *

Mobius went straight to his room and popped the video-cassette into the player he'd bought that afternoon. He pulled a chair up in front of the TV and sat holding the fast-forward button, his face awash in harsh white light, advancing the tape to the part he wanted to see.

The video was a copy of the film recovered from a camera found in the wreckage of the *Bentham Explorer*.

Mobius took his finger off the fast-forward button as the full moon rose up over the ship's bow on the screen. He leaned forward in the chair, his shoulders tensing with the same preternatural dread he'd experienced the first time he saw the ghostly image.

It lasted only about two seconds. A figure materialized beside one of the lifeboats, humanoid yet strangely inhuman, a twisted form that crept across the deck with a feral, sidling motion. The FBI's experts studied the tape and declared the presence to be a man's shadow, one of the crew, someone utterly unconnected to the mystery surrounding the crew's disappearance and Patricia Mobius's murder. Dr. Richard Mobius knew different. The figure on the tape, the "shadow," was no ordinary man.

Mobius rewound the tape and watched it again. Burning tears began to move down his face. When he'd seen it a second time, Mobius rewound the tape to watch it again, and then again. He watched the same short clip more times than he could count, oblivious to time and discomfort as he saw the demon slink repeatedly through the shadows. The insubstantial, flickering ghost captured on the video lacked distinguishing characteristics, yet there was no mistaking one thing.

Whatever it was Mobius was watching, it wasn't human.

15

"YOU NEEDN'T FEEL anxious. The staff has been given instructions. No roses will be brought here or on the ward."

He stared down at the flagstones and said nothing.

"I want you to feel safe. It is important that you have a sense of security during your visit with us," Dr. Bloome said, speaking as if he were a guest at a country estate rather than an inmate in an asylum. "Do you understand?"

Her voice called him up out of himself, forcing him to respond. It would be unforgivably rude to refuse to answer, especially since he knew that she feared their previous meeting had driven him deep back into his catatonia.

"I understand," he said finally, breaking his silence with a deep sigh. "I thank you for your concern on my behalf."

He'd spent the morning sitting in the common room with the lunatics. It had been amusing for a time, observing the variety of mental infirmity among the inmates, but he tired of it easily. Like a baby, the light and sound fascinated but quickly left him overstimulated and mentally exhausted.

He lifted his sad eyes and looked slowly around. The solarium's intimacy reminded him of a walled English garden, where one was surrounded by well-manicured and tamed nature, insulated from roving dogs, passersby, and other annoying distractions. The fecund atmosphere—smelling of freshly turned dirt, vegetation, and dampness—was primordial. He felt a certain animal stirring deep in his stomach that made him turn toward the lovely woman seated to his right. His energy came back suddenly, driven by his desire. At moments like this it was almost impossible to think of Abigail Bloome as a physician, as a psychiatrist.

Their eyes met.

She was particularly lovely that afternoon. Her skin was almost translucent, green eyes bright with the cool fire of her considerable intellect. She wore a simple white blouse, a string of small freshwater pearls around her neck. Her blue skirt—he dared only a brief glance at the place the skirt stopped just above her knee. He was both titillated and scandalized by the amount of female leg modern fashion daringly displayed. Still, nothing could have prepared him for the shock of seeing women in trousers!

"If it isn't too upsetting, I'd like to discuss your reaction to the roses the girl brought in during our session yesterday."

"I am at a loss, Doctor," he replied. "I cannot explain the horror I felt."

"Perhaps they remind you of someone."

A twinge of pain closed his eyes momentarily.

"I do not think that at all likely."

He did not care for the way she was looking at him when he opened his eyes. Although she was careful to disguise it, he recognized her pity easily enough. It made him a little angry. He was not some weakling, some mentally deficient lunatic; he remained in hospital only because it provided a comfortable refuge while he regained his bearings and remembered who he was. He had no doubt *what* he was. And he could show Dr. Bloome easily enough. Still, he did not wish to assert himself in that way with her. He felt a curious affection for Abigail Bloome that made hurting her the way he had the others unthinkable.

"Allow me to propose a simple experiment," he said, giving her a bold look. "Call for roses. Let us see if they affect me again in such an extreme way. Perhaps we shall learn something."

He could hardly believe his own words. And yet, for some reason he did not understand, he felt the need to prove himself to Dr. Bloome, to stop her from looking at him as an object of pity. Besides, he was relatively certain he could control his reaction, given the opportunity to steel himself against the shock.

"I admire your courage, Charles. Not many people would willingly repeat so unpleasant an experience."

"That which does not kill us makes us strong. Someone said that. Forgive me if I fail to cite the source, Doctor. My memory is not what it might be."

"I believe it was Nietzsche," she said with a smile. "Let me think about your idea, Charles. Perhaps we shall try it sometime."

One of the billowing cumulus clouds that had been building since late morning moved in front of the sun. They both glanced up at the same time, past the greenery, through the glass ceiling. The cloud was charcoal-gray, the outer edges a nimbus of white against what remained of the robin's-egg-blue sky.

"Any dreams last night, Charles?"

"You were dead on with that, Doctor. I *do* dream, or at least I did last night. I would not have remembered but for the fact that I made a conscious effort to fix it in my mind upon awakening."

"People often have trouble remembering their dreams. You might consider keeping a dream journal."

"My dreams are hardly worth recollecting."

"Dreams are important, Charles. They are the windows into our subconscious minds, expressions of our unedited emotions, desires, and fears. They paint pictures of your secret self. It's hard to see this because the language of dreams is largely symbolic. Tell me about the dream you had last night, and I will help you interpret its meaning."

Thunder rumbled in the distance. Light faded in the solarium as the dense storm clouds shouldered out the remaining scant patches of blue overhead.

"It is too unpleasant to relate," he said.

"Do not be embarrassed," she said with a dismissive gesture. "I have heard everything. Was it an erotic dream?"

"No," he replied, shocked that she would suggest such a thing.

"Well, then, what is there to be embarrassed about?"

"What if my dreams—my amnesia—hide some monstrous secret?"

"I will help you come to terms with it, Charles. I'm here to help, not judge." She took the cap off her fountain pen. "Now, tell me about your dream."

He leaned back with a sigh, his eyes on the almost black bellies of the ragged clouds. She was relentless! There was the sound of thunder, closer this time. The storm was drawing near.

"I was on a ship. It was a schooner, one of those sleek vessels that used to run passengers back and forth between Europe and America during the nineteenth century. I was alone. The crew and passengers were gone—dead or taken away. The ship pulled up off the shore of a wild country, lush and tropical but forbidding, a jungle. It was night. One of the boats lowered itself into the water, directed by the invisible hands of spirits. I climbed down into it and took my seat. The cutter moved toward shore, propelled by the same mysterious force that put it into the water. I climbed out onto a beach of sand. The sand was black and very fine. I had the impression it was made from some sort of volcanic rock, as black as obsidian, thrown up from the bowels of the earth and reduced over the eons by the wind and rain and pounding surf. My footprints were the only footprints."

Fat tears of rain began to fall on the solarium's glass rooftop, breaking themselves against the barrier.

"I crossed the beach and went into the forest. I had no fear. I knew it was impossible for me to die. Even if I wanted to, I could not die. If there were savages and tigers lurking in the forest, they were the ones with reason to fear, for I was the immortal predator. It made me a little afraid of myself, realizing I was the beast the others must flee. I had no rival or enemy in that savage garden except myself.

"I wandered through the wilderness a long time. I kept thinking that morning was about to break, but it never did. I had come to a land of forever night. I eventually found myself climbing the side of a heavily forested mountain. Although I did not notice it immediately, there was something peculiar about the trees that grew on the slopes. Each tree grew out of the earth in the shape of a crucifix, with a stout center trunk and two limbs jutting out at right angles. The rough, leafless bark was covered with an intricate growth of thorns, each needle five or six inches long and wickedly sharp.

"It was only when I paused to study the bizarre trees that I realized the thorns were covered with blood that seemed to ooze from within. The crucifix trees bled on me. At first it was a few drops, a sprinkling of crimson dew, but as I continued toward the summit, I became soaked in blood. It matted my hair and ran down my face. My clothing stuck to my body. It even got into my shoes so that every step I took was accompanied by the unpleasant sensation of blood squishing against the soles of my feet."

He looked at Dr. Bloome and blinked, as though emerging from a trance. A lightning flash illuminated her face.

"And then I awoke. That is all there is to tell. I warned you it would be unpleasant."

The laggard thunder shook the solarium. The storm unleashed its full fury at that moment, rain and wind lashing the trees.

"Would you prefer to go inside?" she asked.

"No, thank you. I rather like the storm."

Dr. Bloome made a small note on the pad fastened to the clipboard on her lap. "How did you feel when you were walking through the surreal forest?"

He thought for a moment before answering.

"I was happy to be off the ship. It was almost as if I had arrived home, although at the same time I knew there was no home for me in that strange land, that ultimately there could be no home or even destination for someone like me."

"How did you feel to have blood dripping on you?"

"It warmed me. I forgot to mention it, but it had been cold on the ship."

"So there was physical sensation to having the blood rain down on you," she said.

"It made me feel . . ." He looked up at the storm. ". . . exultant. I luxuriated in it. Being soaked in blood made me feel as if I were a god. Which is rather sick, is it not?"

He looked across at her. She was being true to her word. She was not judging him. His confession did not make her loathe or fear him. But that was because she was convinced that the dream was symbolic. And it was, in part, but certain aspects were perfectly literal. In the vampire's dream, blood was blood.

"I love blood," he said. "I crave it."

The interest in her eyes was so intense that her glance was almost fierce. It was better than pity. Anything was better than that. He could not bear to be pitied after the evil he had done.

"Explain exactly what you mean when you say you 'crave' blood."

"I thirst for it. Drinking it fills me with bliss beyond anything you could imagine."

She slowly brought the tip of her pen to her mouth and tapped her pursed lips.

"I have another patient, a girl, who was discharged from One North this morning," she said after a long pause. "She fantasizes about drinking blood. I wonder if you might have spoken with her. She might have said something that influenced your dream. Your condition makes you extremely susceptible to suggestion. In a sense, amnesiacs are blank slates waiting to be written upon. You are in a very vulnerable state, Charles. We must be careful that you are not unduly influenced."

"I have spoken to no one but you."

"Perhaps you overheard her in the day room."

"I have seen no girl during my time here, Doctor."

"All right," she said after a pause.

"Can I trust you, Dr. Bloome?"

"Absolutely."

"And anything I tell you falls under the aegis of doctor-patient privilege? Like a priest at confession, you cannot violate the bond?"

The doctor nodded.

"If you're interested in the real truth, I will share it with you."

"Of course I am."

"You answer too quickly, Doctor. Consider carefully before you answer me a second time. There are things in this world undreamed of in your medical texts. And though you will doubt the veracity of what I have to tell you at first, in time the truth—my truth—will force you to rethink many preconceptions you have about the way things are in this life."

"I have an open mind, Charles. If what you have to say forces me to look at things in a new light, then better that I do so sooner, if I have been operating under false assumptions."

"Wisely said, Doctor." He leaned forward on the arm of his chair. "I know you look on my compulsion as some sort of delusion, but I can assure you my need has a terrible reality. That being said, I hope the girl you mentioned is merely deranged and not a creature of my own race."

"And what race is that, Charles?"

He met her level stare. The two of them were alone in the solarium, the last place anybody would visit in the thunderstorm. He could do whatever he wanted, even if the Hunger was not presently strong in him. He studied the scintillating pulse of blood in her carotid artery, contemplating how sweet her blood would be in his mouth.

"I belong to the *Vampiri*, Dr. Bloome. I crave blood because I am a vampire. Scoff if you like. I will not become angry. I invite your disbelief. It changes nothing."

But she did not scoff or even smile. The doctor's countenance did not so much as flicker at his claim—a claim he knew her medical training left her little choice but to regard as preposterous.

"How do you feel about being a vampire?" she asked in the same tone she might have used to ask him how he felt about being in America.

"To tell you the truth, it means nothing to me one way or the other. There is nothing I can do about it. What concerns me at this point, Doctor, is not my peculiar need, but rather whether it changes the nature of my soul."

"I'm not sure I completely follow you, Charles."

"It is simply a question of good and evil. There is danger in that, in the possibility that I am a creature of evil."

"Oh, I see that clearly enough," she agreed.

"I wonder if you do, Doctor. If I am evil, there is no power in the world that can stop me from leaving a trail of death and misery in my wake as I wander the earth for all of time."

Dr. Bloome reached across and touched his hand. Her grip was warm, firm, dry, reassuring. Her touch quickened his preternaturally slow pulse. The intoxicating perfume of her blood was suddenly maddening. The Hunger began to shriek within his soul, a thousand razors threatening to shred his paper-thin resolve the way the lightning slashed the darkened summer sky. She gripped his hand as thunder shook the solarium, but not because she was afraid.

"I have not the slightest doubt about the matter," she said, speaking in a warm, reassuring voice. "In your heart, in your soul, at the deepest foundation of your true self, Charles, I know that you are good."

16

✧

"YOU'VE DISCOVERED *ANOTHER* vampire in Calhoun?" Ritenour asked. "Why, it's almost an epidemic."

"It is surprising, considering the statistical probability," Abby said.

"Maybe autovampirism is not nearly so rare a condition as you initially believed."

"I'm not sure the new patient qualifies as an autovampire," she replied, ignoring the sarcasm in his voice. They were seated around the big walnut table in the conference room at Psychiatric Associates, conducting the weekly case review. Ritenour was in his usual spot at the head of the table. Dr. Veena Govindaiah, the psychiatric resident, sat to his right. To his left were senior psychologist Dr. Calliopy Hill and Dr. Abigail Bloome.

"What makes the new vampire different?" Calliopy asked.

Abby knew her friend was trying to save her from having an open confrontation with Ritenour.

"Autovampires drink their own blood. Charles Gabriel exhibits no signs of self-mutilation."

"Unlike Desiree," Calliopy said, more for Ritenour's benefit than Abby's.

"Exactly," Abby said. "Desiree's arms are crosshatched with scars."

"Are you suggesting Gabriel drinks other people's blood?" Ritenour asked.

"I'm not sure what to think at this point. It's too early in his analysis to know."

"Analysis!" Ritenour exclaimed, jumping on the word. "This is not prewar Vienna, Abigail. The state of South Carolina does not pay us to delve into the deeply buried trauma of our clients' childhood toilet training. I recommend that you make a diagnosis according to *DSM* and prescribe the recommended medication, like every other psychiatrist in this state."

"I have no problem with that," she said brightly. She waited a beat then added, "As soon as I've made a proper diagnosis."

"Sometimes I feel like I'm talking to myself," Ritenour said in an aside to Veena. His subordinate nodded in eager agreement.

"I fully understand your concerns, Peter, but you can understand that I don't want to cut corners."

"Nobody is asking you to," he replied crossly.

"How are you coming with Mr. Gabriel's amnesia?" Calliopy asked, interrupting to muddy the water and defuse Ritenour's mounting temper.

"Immigration has been unable to trace him. Their best guess is he's been in the country longer than he thinks. There's no record of a recent arrival."

"I would think they are able to do a routine computer search."

"You would think so, Veena, but apparently there's a problem with the mainframes where they keep the data. It seems the information goes in more easily than it comes out. They promised to keep trying."

"Could he be in the country illegally?" Veena asked hopefully.

"It seems unlikely. He gives every appearance of belonging

to an upper-class British family. I hate to stereotype people, but he hardly fits the profile of a typical illegal."

"We need to stick to particulars," Ritenour said in the manner of a wise and benevolent father bringing focus to a family discussion. "The client's central problem is amnesia, not this business with vampirism. Electroshock therapy can be effective in treating amnesiacs."

"Just as I was thinking," Veena said.

"If you pursue that course, Abigail, I'd suggest bilateral placement of the electrodes. I've found it is preferable to the nondominant unilateral arrangement."

Abby was careful not to challenge Ritenour's authority too directly. Although she was appalled at his suggested treatment, she did not want to push him into a corner, tempting him to make an ultimatum.

"As you know far better than I, Peter, psychogenic amnesia most often clears itself without any treatment whatsoever," she said with her most charming smile. "The most advisable course for us may be to provide emotional support to Charles Gabriel while he decides on his own when to lower his barriers and recollect the lost details of his life."

"Very well, then," Ritenour said sourly, pushing himself back from the table. "You may continue to have it your way for now, Abigail. Only don't be surprised when you get called before the hospital's Health Care Utilization Review Board to explain yourself."

"I always welcome the opportunity to speak out on behalf of responsible psychiatric care."

"As do we all," Ritenour snapped. He stood, signaling the conference was over. "I should have known better than to hire a Jungian," he muttered to Veena just loudly enough for them all to hear. Veena pulled the door shut behind them with a small but unmistakable slam.

"I refuse to let him bully me," Abby said to Calliopy.

"Stick to your guns, girlfriend. But what about Gabriel? Is he dangerous?"

"I don't think so."

"And Desiree?"

"You know Desiree," Abby replied with a sad smile. "She's not dangerous to anybody but herself."

17

HE WAS STRETCHED out on his back in bed, hands behind his neck and ankles crossed. He patiently watched the new day being born, the light crawling slowly across the ceiling, driving the shadows back into the angles. The smell of blood continued to linger in the air. Now more memory than sensation, it was still strong enough to hold off sleep, denying him new dreams to share with Dr. Bloome.

The surgeons and operating theater nurses were the first to arrive for work at Calhoun Hospital. They came before first light, early morning being the most propitious time to cut into a living body and have it remain living. He reached out with his preternatural hearing, listening to them in the multistory concrete carriage house beside the hospital. Their ringing voices were bright and cheerful. No doubt they would have been more somber had they been the ones about to go under the knife. It excited them to hold lives in their hands. It was the purest sort of power one could know, like being God—a feeling the vampire could well appreciate, though he had been but little predisposed of late to indulge the merciful aspects of divinity.

Outside his own closed door, down the corridor and around the corner, the day nurses chatted with the night crew. The murmured conversation was about Louise Godwin. "Poor, pathetic girl," they said over and again, as if the words were part of the ritual for the dead. She'd been popular in high school, a cheerleader and a member of the homecoming court—whatever that was. She later was a Tri Delt at the University of South Carolina; apparently Tri Delt was a prestigious social group, like the dining clubs at Oxford. That was before schizophrenia blossomed in the young woman like a poisonous flower. She came home to live with her family then and had been in and out of One North ever since.

And now she was dead, the poor, pathetic girl.

Miss Godwin tried to kill herself just after midnight. After her wounds were dressed, she was sedated and strapped to her bed with heavy leather arm and leg restraints. Her psychiatrist—a Dr. Ritenour—had not come to the hospital during the night, telling the night nurses it could wait until morning rounds. The staff was harshly critical of Ritenour, calling him "imperious" and "unconcerned." What other kinds of doctors were there? the vampire wondered. All physicians were tinhorn idols, in his experience, Dr. Bloome being the sole exception to the rule.

It had only been a halfhearted suicide attempt, a few scrapes across the wrists with a piece of jagged metal worked loose from her bed frame. Perhaps Dr. Ritenour had been correct in electing not to interrupt his evening's pleasure. Miss Godwin had hardly bled, though enough of the rich red wine of her life had spilled to release an intoxicating frisson of blood into the still air.

The temptation was simply too much to resist.

The nurses watched the sedated woman closely through the night, but the vampire possessed far too much stealth for that to stop him. He had not cared a fig whether Miss Louise Godwin lived or died, such moral distinctions continuing to remain beyond the limits of his conception. His sole concern was that he not compromise his friendship with Dr. Bloome.

He had crept into Miss Godwin's room and cut her throat

with a sharp piece of plastic before having his usual way with her. He even managed to stop himself after a few modest swallows of blood, proving he did possess some tiny measure of self-control. He got what he wanted, and so did Miss Godwin, the poor, pathetic girl.

The kitchen staff began to deliver food to the ward at seven-thirty. He breathed in deeply, savoring the mingled aroma of Miss Godwin's blood and the stronger smell of fresh coffee, eggs, warm bread, bacon, and sweet fruits. Patients were expected to serve themselves from a big folding table across from the nurses' station. He did not join the others, but stayed in bed, staring at the ceiling, feeling as if he were about to remember something significant from his lost past.

Dr. Bloome would be there in a few hours. She would want to know whether he was aware of the tragic death in the ward. She would worry that the death might traumatize him. He was as impressionable as a child, a blank slate for the world to write upon in all its coldness and cruelty.

"Poor, pathetic girl," he said quietly to himself, rehearsing his reaction when Dr. Bloome told him of the suicide.

His thoughts passed on to other things.

He'd remembered his name during the night—a part of it—as he'd slowly, almost daintily, sipped a mouthful of Miss Godwin's blood. His namesake was Dante, the great poet. And he had been a poet himself, during his natural life. A poet and an artist, before the change came upon him.

He attempted to follow this strand of memory, pulling himself up into the more complex web of recollections comprising the greater part of who he was, but it was mostly useless. The memories floating on the surface of his mind were delicate as soap bubbles. He could observe them, if he left them to drift

languidly by, but if he reached for them, they burst at first touch.
He did, however, recollect a few lines.

> Afar from mine own self I seem, and wing
> Strange ways in thought, and listen for a sign:
> And still some heart unto some soul doth pine,
> (Whose sounds mine inner sense is fain to bring,
> Continually together murmuring,)—
> "Woe's me for thee, unhappy Proserpine!"

Proserpine—the queen of Hell, the vampire remembered. His
mind conjured the image of Miss Godwin as the queen of the
underworld, sitting on a throne surrounded by the gibbering,
mournful souls of the dead. For the first time since his awakening, he felt the impulse to draw—to create. He had neither
pencil nor paper in his room, but he was certain Dr. Bloome
would happily get him some supplies if he asked.

The door to the room opened and closed. A woman entered
on sandal-clad feet, pushing a mop bucket on rubber rollers
across the linoleum floor. He did not take his eyes off the ceiling. Something else was there in his head, something just beyond remembrance. There was another Proserpine. This was not
Miss Godwin but *his* Proserpine. But the woman's face—he
could not make it out. The memory pulled away the moment he
reached for it, receding before he could possess it.

"Get yo' crazy ass up outta that bed."

He slowly turned toward the voice, feeling the anger move
through his body, setting his nerves afire. It was a black-skinned
woman, tall, thin, long-boned, with big eyes. She reminded him
of a heron. She wore a housekeeping staff uniform, a cheap blue
dress made from cheap synthetic textile, held together in front

with a row of metal snaps. The plastic name tag pinned over her right breast informed him that her name was Dorian.

"Did you hear? Get yo' ass up so I can make up yo' room."

He moved so quickly that he was standing in front of her before she could realize he was no longer in bed. Her brown eyes shimmered with fear, but he held her with his mind so that she could not cry out or flee. He squinted a little as he pushed past her weak will, entering her thoughts. She'd grown up dirt poor and mostly illiterate, her mind filled with superstitions: witches; "haints" as ghosts were called in the southern dialect; graveyard dirt sprinkled on the front steps after midnight.

But there was something else—someone else. There was another One North patient, a girl, of whom Dorian was terrified. It took him a moment to realize that it was the girl Dr. Bloome had asked him about, the one who shared his passion for blood. Though his attraction to Dr. Bloome had led him to leave the girl out of his immediate calculations, it now seemed impossible to ignore the fact that there might be someone else like him, a fellow member of the *Vampiri*, in the sleepy southern town.

"There was a girl discharged from hospital recently. She drinks blood. You know the one I mean."

Dorian nodded.

"Tell me about her." There was no question that she would answer. He had her completely, effortlessly, in his power.

"Her name is Desiree Hohenberg."

"Is she a local girl?"

Dorian nodded. "Everybody in town know Desiree. An' everybody stay 'way from her. She a witch. She got the darkness in her. I don' think even Dr. de la Croix want to cross her path."

"Who might he be?"

"The mos' pow'ful root doctor in these parts."

"What, pray tell, is a root doctor?"

"Part witch, part doctor. They can make you well when you sick, or make you sick when you well, if somebody don' like you pays them to."

"They traffic in both white and black magic?"

"One ain't no good without the other."

He placed his hand gently on her trembling arm.

"Do not fear me."

"I'm not afraid," Dorian said, suddenly relaxed with her new friend.

"I want only the smallest taste. I just need enough to take the edge off the Hunger. You see, my dear, I am trying to regain some measure of my old self-control."

"I glad to help with that, sir."

She put her hands on the upper part of her dress and pulled, popping open the cheap metal snaps. The dress slid off her narrow shoulders and fell around her feet. The underpants that were the only thing Dorian wore under the dress were all the more white against her ebony skin. She went to the bed and sat down so that he could stand between her legs.

"You the Devil?" she asked.

"You are not the first to suggest the possibility," he answered in an equally pleasant tone.

She lifted her chin and turned her head to the side to make it easier. He put his hand behind her neck and brought her lips to his. She moaned and put her hand on his shoulder, pulling him closer.

His lips escaped hers, dancing kisses down her cheek and along the soft skin of her neck. Her heartbeat was suddenly loud in his ears, the blood rushing through her arteries a torrent of ecstasy he yearned to have drown him.

Dorian's breath started to come in quick gasps. She clawed

him as they fell onto the bed together. She bit his ear with her small white teeth, biting him even as he bit into her deeply, passionately, and almost—yet not quite—savagely.

18

MEMORIAL GARDENS CEMETERY stretched across five hills overlooking the slow-moving Senatee River.

The road entering the cemetery was paved with cobblestones, passing between tall wrought-iron gates, dividing around the statue of Robert E. Lee, seated astride Traveller. Surrounding the bronze equestrian was a circular garden of geraniums and fiddle-headed ferns. At night, the general and his horse were bathed in colored lights from fixtures hidden in a low bank of evergreens.

At the crest of the first hill, a bluff overlooking the opposite shore, was the section where veterans of the Army of the Confederate States of America were buried. Six hundred bone-white tombstones stood queued in neat ranks, as orderly and quiet as soldiers at attention on a parade field. This was the high ground in Memorial Gardens, which the soldiers' graves held long after the soldiers themselves had turned to dust.

The old section of the necropolis was next, a display of almost rococo mortuary art. Angels wept, lambs mourned, stone hounds stretched themselves across the graves of lost masters—elaborate expressions of grief from a time when death was never very far away. A mausoleum on an outcropping of limestone at the top of the second hill was patterned after the Temple of Nike on the Acropolis. On the terraced slopes beneath it, entire families were buried together, gathered around obelisks and massive stone monuments, rectangles of shared eternity fenced in marble beneath pines and old oak trees.

The farther from the cemetery gates, the more recent the graves. Though the markers became generally smaller and more restrained, a certain standard was upheld. Even the graves from the present decade had marble tombstones, but it was no longer fashionable to fence in family plots with stone borders, the clannish styles of the past giving way to a more egalitarian openness among the society of the dead.

The cemetery was neatly maintained. The cinder paths drawing away from the cobblestone drive were raked, the yews trimmed, the flower beds tended.

The sun slipped toward the horizon, washing the western sky with purples and reds as the light hit the atmosphere at increasingly oblique angles. The light breeze made the pines sigh, setting the Spanish moss swaying elegantly in the wind.

A young woman sat on a sepulchre halfway up the hill, leaning heavily on her right arm, her feet hanging over the side. She was dressed entirely in black, wearing a long-sleeved man's shirt, ankle-length skirt, and Doc Marten boots. Her hair appeared black, but it gave off weird highlights that showed it had been in fact dyed a dark shade of purple. Her thick hair, in which she wore an antique silver comb, was long enough to reach to her waist. Her fingernails and lips were painted bloodred, and her eyes were deeply shadowed with mascara. Her anemic pallor made her seem a likely candidate for permanent residency at Memorial Gardens. Her skin was so pale that it had an almost translucent quality; here and there blue arteries ran close to the surface.

An angel's image had been carved into the top of the tomb she was sitting upon, the once-crisp lines softened by time. No grass grew around the tomb. The dirt was loose, as if it had been spaded and raked for planting flowers.

"Good afternoon."

Desiree Hohenberg looked up, surprised she had not heard the visitor approach.

"I know you," she said. "You're from the hospital."

"Charles Gabriel, at your service," he said, making a small bow.

Desiree studied him with interest. He was plainly dressed in a dark suit and white shirt with a band collar. His clothing looked expensive. It was. It belonged to a doctor. He'd taken it from one of the lockers in the shower room adjacent to the physicians' lounge.

"Where are you from, Gabriel?" she asked, smiling a little.

"London."

"How did you get out of the hospital? Run away?"

"Good heavens, no. I checked myself out. I fear you Americans have rather lax policies governing the detention of the insane."

"Are you insane?" Desiree asked, grinning now.

"Of course not. I suffer from a touch of amnesia."

"Better now?"

"I am as cured as I wish to be. An excellent memory is not necessarily a boon to us. Not when the past is filled with pain and suffering."

"True." Her eyes narrowed slightly. "You came for some of Michelle's dirt, didn't you?"

"I am afraid I do not understand your meaning."

"Michelle LeClaire was a famous *gris gris* woman. This is her tomb," she said, patting the stone. "The Yankees hanged her for a witch after their officers started to mysteriously sicken and die after raping our town. You're too early, you know. Graveyard dirt only has power if you dig it a half hour before midnight. That's if you want it for white magic. If you plan to do evil, you need to dig it the first half hour after the witching hour."

"To be completely honest, Desiree, I came here looking for you. I thought of asking Dr. Bloome to introduce us, but I know she would have refused. Patient confidentiality and all of that rot."

"I suppose she wouldn't want her patients comparing notes. What do you want with me? Most people are afraid of me," she said, and smiled.

"I can't imagine why. You are not at all what you pretend to be."

"What do you mean 'pretend'?" she said, becoming a little angry.

"You claim you are a vampire."

"I *am* a vampire."

"My dear girl—"

"You don't know me. Nobody knows me. Not even Dr. Bloome."

"There is no cause to upset yourself."

"Upset this, motherfucker," she said, and made an obscene gesture. "You don't know what it's like to crave blood every waking minute. I drank so much of my own blood that I ended up in the hospital, but even that wasn't enough to ease my thirst."

"You drink your *own* blood? How satisfying can that be?"

"It is deeply satisfying." She looked at the inside of her wrist, studying the purple scars.

"Show me," he demanded. "If you really are a vampire, prove it."

She needed but little encouragement. Desiree found a razor in her beaded bag and pushed up her sleeve. Her fingers were trembling with excitement as she opened a vein with a tiny, expert motion. She stared raptly at the blood trickling along the stark whiteness of her outstretched arm. She used her tongue to find the precious elixir. The first taste made her gasp. Her shoulders trembled as she traced the free-flowing blood path toward its source.

She looked up at him, her eyes nearly as hungry as his, her lips, now smeared with her own blood, smiling. She held out her arm, offering to share.

He grabbed her hand roughly—her skin was cool—he began to suckle at the wound. The blood was sweet as new wine, yet it was only a trickle, barely enough to whet his prodigious thirst. This was no way to feed when the entire explosive torrent of bliss could be his in a few practiced motions.

He released her arm and met her smile, noting how the light-headedness amplified her sense of excitement.

"How would you like to fuck me and drink my blood at the same time?"

"I believe you are the most wanton little hussy I have ever known," he said, drawing back his lips to reveal his blood teeth as they came down from the recesses in his upper jaw and locked into place with the dull click of bone and cartilage.

"Oh my God, you're a—"

"Yes, dear child, I am. You are about to embrace the true exemplar, an authentic specimen of the creature you dare to imitate."

Desiree slipped off the tomb in what he took to be a swoon until she grasped at his feet, groveling worshipfully. It was hardly what he'd expected, her subservience making him angry and excited in equal measures.

"Make me your slave, master," she begged, and pressed her lips against the toes of his stolen shoes. "I will serve you in all ways, body and soul, if you will grant me one small favor."

"And what might that be?" he asked, knowing even before she answered.

"Make me like you," she pleaded. "Turn me into a vampire."

19

THE VAMPIRE WAS trying to act cool, but Desiree could see the excitement burning in his dark eyes. He stared at the diner's jukebox as if it were a miracle. His mouth nearly fell open when a man at the counter took a ringing cell phone out of his pocket, pulled out the antenna, and began to talk.

"All of this amazes you, doesn't it?" Desiree asked.

He did not answer.

"How long have you been asleep, Gabriel?"

His glance became cold, like a snake sizing up a small animal. "You are a rather perceptive young woman," he said after a moment.

She leaned toward him across the table, her long purple hair nearly spilling into her coffee cup, and touched his hand. His skin was feverish, but that was normal for him, he'd said.

"What is your story, Gabriel? I know you've led an amazing life. Tell me everything. Your secrets will be safe with me."

"I would greatly prefer to let the past remain past."

"Can't you remember?"

"Perhaps I do not wish to remember."

"I can wait," she said with a toss of her head. She leaned closer, dropping her voice to a whisper. "Tell me what it feels like to sink your teeth into the soft skin of someone's neck and have their blood spray into your mouth."

He gave her such a look!

"Pray do not play these games with me, Desiree."

"But I want to know what it's like, Gabriel," she said, almost begging. "Can you feel the Hunger now?"

"Yes," he sighed, "but only because you are trying to provoke me."

"You would never hurt me."

"Do not take too much for granted, my dear."

She touched the place where he'd bitten her neck. The memory of the bliss she'd felt then made her want him all the more. There were no words to describe what it had been like. The vampire's embrace was the best sex in the world multiplied a thousand times.

The waitress—a woman in her early twenties named Sandi Watt—came with more coffee. Sandi looked from Gabriel to Desiree and back. Desiree could see the wheels turning in the other woman's head: Why was somebody so handsome and rich-looking having coffee with Desiree Hohenberg?

Desiree put her hand over her cup. "No more, thanks," she said, and gave Sandi a significant look. "We have more important things to do."

"I am afraid I am in a rather embarrassing position," Gabriel said when the waitress went away and he'd patted the jacket's empty pockets.

"I've got this one," Desiree said, tossing two one-dollar bills onto the table. "Come on. It's almost eleven. That's when the shift changes."

He followed her outside toward Jackson Park. The moon was nearly full, a bright light surrounded by a glowing corona of white haze that hinted of the thunderstorms that would come before the dawn. A dappled lunar light spread across the park, bright enough to read by, bright enough even to bring the color back into Gabriel's ruby ring. The night breeze whispered through the trees, making a sound like water running over rocks in a stream.

He did not resist when she took his hand, feeling the arc of electricity that attracted them to one another. She led him into a shadowy stand of pines.

"We'll wait here. Sandi, the woman who waited on us in the diner, will pass by just over there. She lives in the trailer park on the far side of the park. She takes a shortcut home through here."

"I do not need it tonight," Gabriel protested.

"I always need it," Desiree said with a giggle. She put her free hand on his stomach, sliding it lower. "It feels like you do, too."

He caught his breath when she touched him.

"If you don't want her, don't take her," she said, whispering now. "I only hope she's alone. You probably saw the way Mr. Cell Phone was staring at her tits. Sandi Watt is only about the biggest slut in town."

She felt Gabriel's body tense next to her, his chin coming up, his face turning. He'd sensed the approaching woman's presence before she had. Desiree looked through the boughs and saw the silhouette of the waitress walking toward them.

"You have waited here for her before," he whispered.

"Yes," Desiree confessed. "She's so careless, walking through here alone at this time of night."

"Yet you lacked the courage to go through with it. Watch and learn how simple it is," Gabriel said harshly.

He moved from the shadows with what seemed to be a single quick, fluid motion. He did not pursue the woman but stood watching her back.

Sandi stopped abruptly after a few more footsteps.

Desiree could see Gabriel's dreamy expression in the moonlight. His head was tilted back, his lips slightly parted, his hands folded behind his back. His dark eyes glittered with silver light.

Sandi slowly turned to face the vampire.

"My beloved," he said.

Sandi ran into Gabriel's waiting arms. He held her tight against him, turning her so that he could look over her shoulder at Desiree. There was triumph in his eyes and an expression of merciless glee. He began to kiss the other woman. She wrapped one arm around him as his face moved into the hollow of her neck, becoming lost in the tangle of dishwater-blond hair. Sandi's entire body convulsed, as if she'd touched a power line. He was in her. Sandi's hands closed and opened, her entire body quivering in Gabriel's embrace of love and death.

Sandi's feet went out from under her. She fell backward, Gabriel falling with her, his teeth locked onto her throat. He broke their fall at the last moment, catching them effortlessly with one hand, as if their bodies had no more substance than two leaves floating to earth. He lay to one side of her, gently suckling at her neck, his hand idly caressing her breast.

Desiree's feet pulled her toward the mortal act playing itself out on the moonlit grass, drawn the way a moth is to a flame. If the vampire was aware of her approach, he gave no sign. Gabriel's unfocused eyes stared up at the night sky, the pupils reduced to pinpricks. He was fastidious: only a small trickle of blood showed in the corner of his mouth. Sandi's eyes were open wide, the pupils rolled up in her head, her breath coming in short little gasps, like a rabbit about to die.

Seeing Gabriel drinking the blood sent a gush of warmth flooding through Desiree. She dropped to her knees, laying her head upon Sandi's breast, covering Gabriel's hand. He pulled his hand free and began to caress Desiree's face.

"Drain her, my darling," she purred.

Gabriel let out a low, guttural groan as Desiree began to fondle him through his trousers. He began to tremble, shaking Sandi by the throat the way a dog shakes a squirrel. The neat holes in Sandi's neck became ragged tears. Blood spurted into the air, splattering the vampire's face, raining red down upon the three of them.

Desiree found her razor and cut a quick, careless slash across Sandi's limp wrist, pulling it toward her mouth, the spurting arterial blood hitting her full in the face. Wave after wave of bliss coursed through Desiree's body. She was sharing just a small measure of the ecstasy Gabriel felt every time he drank blood. What must it be like for him? she thought deliriously.

Gabriel prolonged their pleasure as long as he could, but soon the blood was gone and he rolled onto the grass, his unfocused eyes looking past the moon.

Desiree sat up, smiling to herself as she wiped the blood off her face with the back of her sleeve. It was a shame to waste it, but now that she had become Gabriel's apprentice, there would be oceans of blood for her to drink.

She crawled over the corpse on her hands and knees, like a wanton moving from body to body at a Roman orgy. Gabriel was insensate, drunk from the immortal elixir he'd consumed, blood smearing his face. He did not resist as Desiree opened his pants. She squatted over him and lifted her skirt, lowering herself onto him.

Gabriel moaned as she began to rock herself back and forth and took his face in her hands. She did not kiss his lips, however, but began to lick him, cleaning the blood off his face with her tongue.

It was delicious.

Michael Kimball

Michael Davis said, looking at his watch.
"Then, I have to ask you—"

Robin interrupted, half pleased, as if in spite of himself. "I said go on or hit him back." "Why do you have the book?"

"The book was left there for us—" And it no longer was beyond question.

"I'm the author, the preliminary warning feels to be given permission...

DR. RICHARD MOBIUS was reading a copy of *Moby Dick* with "Property of the Nantucket Library" marked on the spine in indelible ink. He'd visited Nantucket to see what was left of the wrecked *Bentham Explorer* after it broke up on the rocks. It was a grim place, no longer famous for whalers so much as for its high incidence of heroin overdoses. Melville's book hadn't been checked out of the library since 1987, so Mobius told himself it wouldn't be missed and took it with him when he returned to Boston.

Sitting in his hotel room, Mobius read:

Now, three to three, ye stand. Commend the murderous chalices! Bestow them, ye who are now made parties to this indissoluble league. Ha! Starbuck! But the deed is done! Yon ratifying sun now waits to sit upon it. Drink, ye harpooners! Drink and swear, ye men that man the deathful whaleboat's bow—Death to Moby Dick! God hunt us all, if we do not hunt Moby Dick to his death.

It was his favorite scene from the book, Captain Ahab exhorting his men to join his obsessive hunt for the monstrous albino whale. He snapped the book shut as the telephone began to ring.

"Mobius," he said, picking up the receiver.

"This is Medgar Ronson."

Mobius reached for a legal pad and the Mont Blanc pen his wife had given him on his last birthday. "What do you have for me, Mr. Ronson?"

"A body in South Carolina. I'm faxing you the police report and copies of some autopsy photos."

The fax machine gave the preliminary warning beep to signal an incoming transmission.

"And?"

"The M.O. is similar. This may be our guy."

"How sure are you?"

"It's a young woman with her throat torn out. I'd say there's a fair chance the person we're looking for is responsible. A lot of blood is unaccounted for, even considering what soaked into the ground. Police think the killer and his accomplice drank it on the scene or else collected it and took it away with them to drink later."

"Accomplice?"

The first page dropped into the plain-paper fax machine's tray.

"The killer wasn't working alone on this one. There's no way to know yet whether the second person was on the boat when your wife was killed. If not, it's somebody he—or she—joined up with after the *Bentham Explorer* broke up on the coast."

"She?" Mobius said skeptically. "I've always assumed the killer was male."

"That's a safe bet with serial killers, since most are male. But there was a male and a female involved in the South Carolina deal. The police know from the footprints. The woman wore a pair of Doc Martens. It's all in my fax. Also, there was a strand of hair on the body that didn't belong to the victim—long and dyed purple."

"Purple?"

"Yep. And there were also smears of semen and vaginal fluid on the victim's clothing."

"The victim was raped?"

"The vaginal fluid didn't belong to the dead woman. The killers apparently had sex almost on top of the body. They used the victim's dress to wipe up afterward."

"My God," Mobius said.

"God doesn't have anything to do with something like this, Dr. Mobius."

"Yes, he does," Mobius snapped.

The second page dropped into the fax tray.

"There were bite marks on a wound to the victim's wrist, which has been slashed with a razor. The dentition is small, probably from the female. If the suspects are apprehended—"

"*When* the suspects are apprehended."

"When they're apprehended," Ronson said, backtracking, "the bite marks and DNA evidence from the body fluids should make the case easily."

"And tie them to my wife."

"I would hope so."

"Where exactly did this latest murder take place?"

"Calhoun, South Carolina."

"That's a long way from Nantucket."

"Yeah, Dr. Mobius. Our man is on the run. Chances are he'll keep running. We need to move quickly."

"Get on the next plane for South Carolina."

"I already have my ticket, Dr. Mobius. I leave from O'Hare in two hours."

Mobius looked at his watch. It was nearly ten P.M. "I wonder if I can still get a flight. Maybe I can charter a plane."

"Fly down tomorrow. The trail has already had a week to get cold."

"Fuck."

"I'll call when I get to a hotel and let you know where I'm staying."

"Reserve a room for me."

"Sure thing. You'll have FedEx copies of the pictures first thing in the morning at your hotel in Boston. I don't need to warn you that they're gory. Even the faxes will be hard to look at."

"It's nothing I haven't seen with my own eyes, Mr. Ronson. Goodbye."

Mobius hung up the telephone and sat back in his chair. He'd had to identify his wife's body in the Boston hospital where the autopsy was conducted. He would have nightmares for the rest of his life about the way she looked.

Outside his hotel window, the offices of the neighboring buildings were dark except on the floors where cleaning crews were busy. Nobody worked late on Friday nights, especially not in August, when people loaded their families into Volvo station wagons and left for vacations on Cape Cod or in Maine. How pleasant still to be one of the deluded masses, one of the herd who thought life was calm, orderly, and rational. Mobius knew life as it really was. Evil walked the Earth, the misshapen child of creation's malevolent side, evidence of God's hatred for man.

The fax machine beeped twice, the end-of-transmission signal.

Mobius picked up the stack of documents. The police reports came first, after Ronson's fax cover letter on agency letterhead. He scanned for salient information; he would go back over the pages dozens of times later, committing details to memory, searching for anything the police might have overlooked.

The dead woman's name was Sandi Watt. She was twenty-two

and single. The cause of death was blood loss—the technical term was hypovolemic shock—due to massive neck trauma. She lived in a trailer, where police had been twice on domestic violence incidents. Her former live-in boyfriend might have been a suspect, but he was in jail for driving while intoxicated the night of the murder.

Mobius got to the crime scene pictures. Even with a top-quality fax machine it was no better than looking at middling-quality photocopies. Still, the savagery was plain enough. Sandi Watt and Patricia Solberg Mobius had been killed by the same monster.

Mobius pulled open the drawer and took out a magnifying glass to examine the wrist wound pictures. The razor cut was encircled by a deep oval bite mark. He couldn't be sure from the fax, but he thought he could see discoloration where the capillaries in the skin were broken from being sucked.

The second killer—the female in Doc Martens boots—had needed a razor to open the waitress's veins. The fiend who ripped open Sandi Watt's throat—and Patricia's—hadn't used a razor. He hadn't needed to. God had equipped him with the means to kill with an animal's predatory savagery.

Mobius threw the papers down, got up and went to the window, staring up past the glittering skyline toward the night sky above Boston. At least he knew what he was up against now. The woman with the razor—she was probably a garden-variety psychotic killer. She may or may not have been aboard the *Bentham Explorer*, but Mobius tended to doubt it.

The other one, the killer whose fangs cruelly tore out women's throats, was the primary killer. He was the one—the vampire—Mobius would hunt to his death.

21

✧

DR. ABIGAIL BLOOME closed the unread file and turned her chair away from her desk to look out the window. In the garden between the office and hospital, immaculate beds of flowers shimmered in the afternoon heat. It was after four. The stereo was on, Mozart playing softly in the background, but she had ceased to hear the music almost as soon as she turned it on.

Worrying was a waste of mental energy, Abby told herself.

The telephone rang. Someone at the front desk wanted to see her.

"Is it a British gentleman, by any chance?"

No, it was a woman named Jennifer Avery. She was not one of Abby's patients.

"Send her to my office," Abby said.

Abby had been counseling a rape victim in the emergency room when Charles Gabriel checked himself out of One North. They'd tried to alert her, but the battery in her pager had gone dead. By the time she found out, he was already gone. A week had gone by without word from him. Charles was an intelligent, apparently educated, high-functioning man. If he wanted to disappear, he'd disappear.

It was unfortunate that Charles had bumped into Desiree on the

132

ward, though he'd denied it. Nature abhorred vacuums, including psychiatric ones. Lacking his own identity, he was adopting bits and pieces from other people. There was a chance, statistically remote, that Charles was truly fixated with blood, but it was far more likely he was echoing something that he'd heard Desiree talk about. Authentic cases of vampirism were extremely rare.

As for Desiree, Abby had reason to be concerned about her, too. She'd failed to keep her afternoon appointment. Abby left a message on Desiree's answering machine, asking her to call and inquiring whether she'd happened to run into Charles Gabriel.

Abby wanted to keep those two apart.

Someone tapped on the door.

"Come in," Abby said, standing to greet her visitor.

Jennifer Avery was about thirty and model-thin. She had a confident, practical expression in her eyes and a mass of curly red hair tied in back. Abby liked her immediately. When she reached out to shake Abby's hand, her blue suit jacket fell open, revealing the gun on her hip.

"Special Agent Jennifer Avery," she said, speaking with the sort of southern accent that only the very poor and the very rich seemed to have. She showed Abby an FBI badge.

"I'm Abby Bloome. Let's sit over here."

She motioned for Jennifer Avery to take the couch. Abby sat in one of the two easy chairs positioned on either side of the coffee table. There were flowers from her garden in a cut-crystal bowl on the table—wild flowers, rather than her roses, in case Charles Gabriel turned up for a visit.

"I appreciate your taking the time to see me, Doctor."

"That's quite all right. I keep this time of the day free for unscheduled meetings, Special Agent Avery."

"It's a mouthful, isn't it? You can call me Jennifer."

"Is this an official visit, Jennifer?"

"Yes, it is," the FBI agent answered, looking past Abby. "I like your Cassatt poster. She's one of my favorites."

"Thank you."

"I came down from Charlotte this morning—I work out of the field office in Charlotte—to talk to the local police about Sandi Watt's murder. I'm sure y'all are familiar with that crime. She was the waitress killed walking home from work."

"I saw the headlines in the paper. I didn't read the stories."

"The police didn't give the newspaper most of the details anyway. They never do."

Abby nodded.

"There's a chance a serial murderer might be involved. There are similarities between the Watt murder and some crimes that took place in New England and aboard a ship in international waters."

A warning went off in the back of Abby's mind, but she didn't think Charles Gabriel could have been involved. Immigration officials were still looking for information about when he entered the country, but the chances were it wasn't recently.

"Were these other crimes committed recently?" she asked.

The FBI agent nodded. "I need y'all to keep this confidential, of course."

"That goes without saying. But how can I help?"

"I thought you might have some insights into what goes on inside the mind of somebody who could commit crimes like these."

"Doesn't the FBI have specialists who know all about these sorts of people?"

"We do, Dr. Bloome. I just thought it might be worth my while to talk to a local expert face-to-face before driving back to

Charlotte. I hear there's a lot of voodoo in this part of the state. There were certain ritual aspects to the Watt murder that might indicate an occult angle."

"Such as?"

"The killers have a special interest in blood."

"Could you be a little more specific?" Abby asked, careful that her expression remained neutral.

"The killers seem to have drank a substantial quantity of the victim's blood. How would you explain that kind of behavior, Doctor? Is it at all common? Could it have something to do with local black magic?"

"I'm fairly new in town and not at all expert in local activities. I can tell you that cases of clinical vampirism are extremely rare."

"Clinical vampirism," the FBI agent said, repeating the phrase, seeming to test it against her ear. "What sort of things do you look for in somebody you would diagnose as a vampire?"

"It's hard to say. The condition hasn't been studied enough to be able to talk authoritatively about broad behavioral patterns. As I understand it, the attraction to blood usually has an erotic component."

"It excites them."

"Exactly. There is a strong arousal factor. I would expect a history of childhood abuse; there usually is with anyone who is pathologically violent. I'd also look for past instances of abuse to animals and ritualized self-mutilation. They might start out cutting themselves to drink their own blood. That's known as autovampirism. I suppose the level of involvement could escalate into attacks on other people, at least theoretically."

"Is Desiree Hohenberg an autovampire?"

"I wondered if you were setting me up for that," Abby said

with a cool smile to show Special Agent Avery that she hadn't been caught off guard.

"Is Desiree an autovampire?"

"I can't discuss my patients."

"Not even one who is a murder suspect?"

"Not even then."

"I thought it was worth a shot, Dr. Bloome."

Abby shrugged. "So you think Desiree is involved in Sandi Watt's murder?"

"I don't know. That's what I'm trying to figure out."

"Desiree has never been out of Calhoun, as far as I know, if that's of any use to you."

"That rules her out in the other killings, then. I don't suppose you'd know where I can find the girl? Her mother hasn't seen her in a week."

Abby shook her head.

"Be careful if she turns up, Dr. Bloome. The people who killed Sandi Watt were both sadistic and savage."

"I haven't treated anyone in Calhoun I believe is capable of committing a sadistic killing. You said two people were responsible?"

"Yes, but I'm afraid I can't tell you any more than that. You don't think Desiree is capable of this sort of thing?"

"No, frankly I don't."

"It'll probably end up being a drifter with a history of sex crimes or a couple of teenagers whose role-playing games got out of hand. If there really is a link between Watt and the murders in New England, it would argue against Desiree's involvement."

The FBI agent stood up and handed Abby a card.

"If y'all hear from Desiree or think of anything you want to tell me, give me a call. My home number is written on the back."

Special Agent Jennifer Avery gave Abby a close look before turning away, leaving her wondering how much of what she'd said the FBI agent believed.

22

✦

"IT IS CALLED scotch," the vampire said, holding the amber liquor up to the lamp. The gentle vibration inside the speeding limousine made the liquid tremble in the crystal tumbler as if possessed with a life of its own. Unfortunately, Dante's own metabolism put him beyond the reach of alcohol and other social poisons.

"More," Desiree said, holding out her glass. "With lots of ice."

"Ice," the vampire said with a sigh.

"Another American abomination," the girl said. "Like flying. You know, it would have been a lot simpler for us to have just hopped on a jet."

"The notion of hurtling through the troposphere in a metal tube strikes me as unnatural in the extreme."

"It's a hell of a lot faster than driving, Gabriel. Not that I mind the limo."

"What is the hurry? We have all the time in the world."

"You do. I'm still mortal."

"And rather lovely, too, my dear." He was in a satisfied, almost mellow mood. The trip had been a complete success. At his feet in an aluminum Zero Halliburton briefcase were crisp new banknotes in neat packets. He had all the capital he needed for the foreseeable future. And when the money ran low, there would be more where that came from.

"This music sucks."

"Hush," he said, putting a forefinger to his lips. Mozart's Jupiter symphony was playing on the limousine CD. The stereo was the one modern invention he could embrace without reservation.

The vampire and Desiree had arrived in Atlantic City with less than twenty dollars. It took a little more than an hour at the casino to build that modest stake to $10,000. The next day, he took Desiree on a spree, spending half the money in the shops. Desiree bought a skirt and an intricately woven Gypsy shawl, three silk blouses, and some naughty underthings from a scandalous women's store named Victoria's Secret. Dante bought himself an elegant Armani suit, a half-dozen collarless white shirts with a golden pin to hold them closed at the neck, and handmade Italian shoes.

He patronized a different casino the second night, finding a seat in the high-stakes baccarat room. He was up nearly a half-million dollars when he decided to call it a night. The casino management invited him to stay on as their guest in their finest penthouse, hoping he would lose back the money. He obliged, intentionally losing more than $100,000 to satisfy them.

They stopped at a jeweler on the way out of town. Desiree wanted a silver bracelet; he bought her two dozen, twelve for each wrist, and an emerald to replace the stud she wore in the upper part of her right ear. He bought himself a Breitling timepiece—they were called "wristwatches" nowadays, he learned.

"Why do we have to go back to Calhoun? I've spent the past sixteen years waiting to escape that burg."

The chauffeur on the opposite side of the opaque, soundproof divider kept his eyes on the road. The vampire had forgotten how pleasant it was to have servants. He would be sad to see the man and the sleek black car go.

"I have unfinished business there," he answered.

"With Dr. Bloome?"

He glanced sideways at the girl. She was sprawled in the corner, her bare feet pulled up beneath her on the leather seat, the tumbler of scotch and ice held in her lap in both hands, the new silver bracelets glittering on her arms.

"You're not going to hurt her, are you?" Desiree asked.

"Would you care if I did?"

"I think I would. I like Dr. Bloome. She's always been nice to me."

"I have no intention of being anything but a gentleman with the good doctor. I only want to speak with her again."

"Do you think she'll help you remember?"

"To be perfectly honest, I could care less whether I recollect the arcane details of my past. However, there are a few things about it that affect me in a way I do not understand."

"Like fainting when you saw the roses."

"We made rather merry with the courtesans in Atlantic City," he said to change the subject. "We shall have to behave more responsibly when we return to your native city."

"What? No blood?"

"Oh, there will be plenty of that, dear girl." He reached across and stroked her face. She was a perfectly loathsome little dolly-mop, yet he had become fond of her, in spite of his better instincts. "However, we must be more prudent about whom we invite to join us in our pleasure and be careful to clean up after ourselves when we are finished. We must choose people who will not be missed as our playmates. A clever vampire can remain in the same place almost indefinitely, but one who behaves recklessly runs into complications almost immediately."

"I like being reckless."

"I know you do," he said. "I think it's what I like best about you, my dear."

"Tell me about the casinos. That wasn't just luck, was it? You read the other gamblers' minds."

"And the dealers' minds. A gentleman does not cheat, but I was mostly cheating the casino. I do not feel too badly about that. Casinos tilt the odds heavily against the individual player. Still, there is no thrill in winning when there is no chance you might lose."

"Can you read my mind, Gabriel?"

"If I wish. It is a power one can turn on and off. It is far less intriguing than you might imagine to know what people are thinking. People's heads are typically filled with banal, disordered nonsense."

"People are fools, aren't they?" she said with a sneer. "They are so weak next to you. I envy your power. Somebody once said power is—"

"The ultimate aphrodisiac," he interrupted, finishing her sentence.

"You knew what I was about to say."

He nodded. "And what you are about to do."

Desiree put down her empty glass and slid across the leather seat until she was kneeling between his legs.

The noise increased inside the limousine as it passed a semi-truck traveling next to them on Interstate 95. The vampire looked out the window as they moved by the huge steel beast. There was a sign on the side of the road. It said: WELCOME TO SOUTH CAROLINA.

He switched off the lamp, leaving them in darkness in the back of the limousine, alone with each other and the sweet music of Mozart.

23

✧

"TROUBLE?"** MEDGAR RONSON asked, holding out his hand when Dr. Richard Mobius came in, looking hot, tired, and irritated.

"I sat on the runway at Logan most of the day. Fucking weather. You said you had news."

"Let's get a drink in the lounge and talk." The private detective tipped his head in the desk clerk's direction. The clerk was looking down at some paperwork, but the unmistakable alertness in the man's face confirmed he was eavesdropping.

"Mind your own damned business," Mobius said.

"Excuse me?" the clerk asked, looking up from his stack of room charges. He was a gangly young man, with watery eyes and jug ears.

"You heard me," Mobius said.

"Come on," Ronson said, touching Mobius's arm briefly and starting for the leather-upholstered lounge door.

Mobius detested piano bars, but at least it would be noisy enough for them to talk without being overheard. Two traveling salesmen sat at the table by the door, the small cocktail table between them crowded with their catalogs and planners as they plotted the next day's strategy. A boisterous party of a dozen people crowded around the piano, most of them already drunk.

The pianist was a man about sixty in a pink sport coat, his hair an unnaturally uniform shade of dark brown.

Mobius went to the table farthest from the music.

"Number twenty-three," one of the drunks cried, a fifty-something man in a loud red plaid jacket with a toupee that was so artificial-looking it made Mobius want to laugh. The singers all had photocopied books, the song request list.

The pianist lifted his right hand with an effeminate flourish. "Number twenty-three it is," he proclaimed, then launched into the theme from *The Flintstones*. The drunks roared with laughter as they tried to sing along.

"Does it bother you to be the only black man in a barroom full of liquored-up southern rednecks?" Mobius asked.

"Not particularly." Ronson shook his head. "This place is too white even for most white people."

"I wouldn't give any two of these crackers odds against you, even if you didn't have a revolver on your hip."

"And what about you, Dr. Mobius? You get a license yet for that cannon under your arm?"

"Damn right."

"You okay?"

"Certainly."

"You seem tense."

"I'm pissed after getting jerked around by the airline and the weather. A drink will set me right on my rails. Actually, I'm happy as a fucking lark to be closer to catching up with the son of a bitch who butchered my wife."

The waitress interrupted for drink orders. Ronson asked for a bottle of Heineken, Mobius a Tanqueray martini, up with two olives.

"I have a report on another murder," the retired policeman said. "A double homicide, in fact."

"A modest day's work for the bastard."

"They were teenage girls. Runaways, found dead in a box-car in some backwater burg called Noll, Georgia. Near the Florida border."

"Florida?" Mobius clenched his fist and brought it down to the table, stopping himself just before he hit it. Nobody noticed. The others were too busy launching into an enthusiastic rendition of "Cabaret."

"Steady, my man."

"Steady, my ass. How am I going to get my hands on the bastard if he keeps moving?"

The waitress returned with their drinks. The bartender had made the martini with ice. Mobius flew into a rage, stopping the singing and drawing stares. The waitress was almost in tears when she went away to get him another drink.

"You got to chill, man. You're going to blow a gasket. Besides, you're missing the point. The report on the runaways is old and cold. Noll, Georgia, has one policeman and no computer. The report didn't pop up on-line until it was mailed into the capital and keyed in by the state."

"Meaning?"

"These girls were killed a few days after your wife. Your next question should be . . ."

"Where did the train come from and did it pass through here?"

"Bingo." Ronson pointed his index finger at Mobius and fired it like a gun. "The train came out of Maine, through Boston, bound for Orlando. The tracks are about two miles from where we're sitting right now."

Mobius's laughter had a jagged, manic quality. "So he jumped off the train here. He stayed in Calhoun at least long enough to do the waitress. He could still be here."

"No reason to think that he isn't. Lots of tourists moving through here. The ocean is nearby, and there's a big ol' swamp inland a few miles. It's the kind of place people could easily disappear without anybody noticing."

"The perfect hunting ground for a predator."

The waitress came back then with Mobius's martini on a tray, careful not to make eye contact as she put it on the table. She was about to retreat to the safety of the bar when Mobius stopped her.

"Just a minute, miss."

She stopped backing away, but she seemed to shrink under his stare. He picked up the martini and took a sip.

"That's much better," he said.

The waitress visibly relaxed.

"I didn't mean to be rude a few minutes ago," Mobius said, reaching into the inside pocket of his black raw-silk sport coat. "We martini lovers tend to be particular about the chemistry of our drinks. Besides, I've had a hell of a day."

"No problem, mister," she said.

Mobius took a hundred-dollar bill from his wallet and handed it to the woman.

"This is for the drinks. Keep the change."

"Thank you, sir!" she gushed, almost melting where she stood. "Is there anything else I can get you?"

"Not right now, thanks."

"If you need anything—"

"Run along now," Mobius said, his smile fading.

The waitress turned quickly away.

"I have a question for you, Dr. Mobius."

He took a long taste of his drink, holding the stem of the martini glass between his thumb and forefinger. The pianist was playing an extended flourish leading into "Love Is a Many Splendored Thing," good old number 184 on the song list. The drunks were looking misty-eyed, couples putting their arms around one another.

"What are you going to do if we catch this creep?"

"Turn him over to the police, of course," Mobius answered.

The detective's eyes dropped to the bulge under Mobius's arm.

"We're going to have a heart-to-heart about how we're going to handle things, when the time comes."

"Oh, absolutely, Mr. Ronson. You have my word on that. My absolute fucking word."

Mobius turned sideways in his chair to survey the room. It could be any of them. He was out there somewhere. Not in the piano bar, but somewhere close. Deep down in his bones, Dr. Richard Mobius knew that his wife's killer was very close indeed.

24

✧

"THERE ARE A lot more people on the street in this part of town."

"That's because it's hot as hell and nobody has air-conditioning," Desiree said.

She and Gabriel were riding in the black Lexus LS400 he had bought that afternoon. Desiree was driving. The vampire didn't know how to drive.

Gabriel had been a complete jerk about buying the car, not even haggling, paying full sticker price when Desiree was sure he could have gotten a better deal. The salesman's eyes had practically fallen out of their sockets when Gabriel opened his aluminum briefcase and began tossing packets of new one-hundred-dollar bills on his desk.

"Why did you want to come to this part of town?"

"Simply for a lark, my dear. Please turn."

Desiree made a left. An angry-looking man on the sidewalk stared at the expensive sedan.

"We're going to get fucking shot."

"I sincerely doubt it," the vampire said.

"They call this part of Calhoun 'Buck Town.' "

"Roll down my window, please."

Jesus. He didn't even know how to roll down a car window.

147

She stabbed a red fingernail against the power button and the window disappeared silently into the door. The car was flooded with air that was hot, damp, and smelled of hickory smoke.

Gabriel leaned his head out of the car and took a deep breath, smiling as if the night air were fresh and sweet with rare perfume. There were people sitting on the picnic tables outside Green Front Bar-B-Q, eating and laughing. Some checked out the Lexus, others studiously avoided looking at it, pretending the white people were as invisible as *they* were in the white part of town.

Desiree pushed another button and the electric door locks snapped into place with a reassuringly solid and secure sound.

"You will find hunting is best where life is hardest," Gabriel said. "In London that is, or at least it used to be, the Docklands, a gurgling sewer of humanity where life was very cheap indeed. Human affairs are conducted along more casual lines in the slums. People come and go without anybody much noticing."

"You prey on the weak," Desiree said, nodding. "You're the lion that culls the sick and the weak from the herd."

"I am nothing of the sort," Gabriel said, sounding offended.

Three prostitutes outside the down-at-the-heels Hotel Calhoun perked up when they saw the Lexus. They stepped toward the curb, primping their wigs, straightening tight, short skirts over their hips, precariously balanced on spiked heels.

"Where else but in the demimonde could one find women so welcoming of strangers?" the vampire said. "Certainly not near our new home in the Garden Terrace district."

"Do you want me to pull over?"

Desiree felt the familiar excitement in her voice. She wanted blood so badly that she ached. She could not imagine what it would be like to feel the Hunger with the full frenzy she'd seen possess the vampire.

Gabriel's eyes became hooded as he seemed to sniff the air for danger. "No. This is far too public. People will remember the car. We should have purchased something more nondescript."

Desiree exhaled loudly.

"If I can wait, my darling, you certainly can." He reached for the stereo, pushing his new Mozart CD into the player. She *hated* Mozart.

"When are you going to transform me?"

The vampire continued looking out his window. "When I am ready."

"When will that be?"

"When you are ready."

"You make me so fucking mad sometimes, Gabriel."

"You should learn to express yourself properly. What is this place?"

The vampire pointed toward a cinder-block building with big plate-glass windows that had been painted black from the inside. The parking lot was filled with cars and pickups. Young black men, some in sunglasses despite the darkness, loitered around the cars, drinking from bottles held in paper bags, listening to the low rumble and thump of rap music playing on competing stereos.

"It's a nightclub called Mother Jam. I think it used to be a grocery store. They have illegal gambling in a back room. They must pay off the police."

"Interesting," Gabriel said, drawing out the word.

"Don't even think about going in. We'll get knifed."

"You have nothing to fear with me as your protector. Turn in, please."

"My guardian angel," Desiree said in a mocking tone. "My Gabriel."

"If an angel of death can serve as a guardian, then you can say I am yours."

The men loitering in the parking lot seemed a lot more interested in the Lexus than in Desiree and Gabriel. She locked the doors and pushed the remote control that armed the alarm system.

The air inside Mother Jam was blue with smoke. The music was loud, the heavy beat making the floor vibrate, the rhythm entering her body through her feet, making her feel the bass pulse in her stomach. A table of old men looked up at them with startled surprise. Desiree followed Gabriel as he pushed through the crowd, past the people writhing on the crowded dance floor. He made straight for the red metal fire door in the brick wall. Two enormous men in tank tops that showed off their heavily muscled arms blocked the door.

"They'll never let us in," she shouted in Gabriel's ear, rising on her toes to get closer to matching his height.

The vampire nodded at the bouncers. They stood aside, one of them pushing back the metal door, which slid easily on roped counterweights.

The atmosphere of the makeshift casino was subdued compared with the front room. To Desiree's amazement, nearly a third of the customers were white, which put her more at ease. There were banks of slot machines along the outside walls where the players—mostly women—stood with plastic cups filled with coins, feeding the chirping machines. The blackjack tables were in the middle of the room, the roulette wheel and craps table against the far wall.

The vampire made his way toward the nearest blackjack table, leading Desiree by the hand. A tall, skinny black woman looked up at them from the slot machines. She did not seem able to take her eyes off Gabriel. Desiree recognized her. She worked at the hospital.

The vampire took a seat at the table and handed a wad of bills to the dealer, who gave him back a stack of red chips. "Ignore her," Gabriel said to Desiree as the dealer put out his first card.

"Don't tell me that you had *her*," she whispered in his ear.

"A momentary indiscretion. It was she who told me how to find you. Pray do not concern yourself. She remembers only what I want her to remember."

"Then why is she touching her neck like that?"

"Perhaps it is with the sweetness of anticipation. A card, please," he said to the dealer.

The stack of chips in front of Gabriel grew until he'd won nearly ten thousand dollars. A crowd gathered around the table, watching him beat the house. A man came to the table and handed the dealer a piece of paper with something written on it in pencil.

"I have to go on break now," the dealer said, gathering up the cards.

"They closing you out 'cause you hot," said a disappointed bystander.

"It is just as well," Gabriel said, handing his chips to a smiling girl in a fringed red dress.

The thin woman emerged from the margins of the crowd. Desiree could see terror in her eyes, yet she seemed unable to keep herself from approaching the vampire.

"You remember me?"

"How could I possibly forget," Gabriel said gallantly, bowing until his chin touched his chest. "Enchanting to see you again, my dear. I believe you know my friend, Desiree. Desiree, wish a good evening to Dorian."

Dorian didn't seem aware of Desiree's presence. She stared at Gabriel, scared of what might happen if she took her eyes off him.

"You left the hospital."

"I found it to be a tedious place, Dorian."

"The doctors didn't fix your mind?"

The vampire laughed. "No, I suppose not."

"Maybe you didn't see the right kind of doctor. I know someone special, if you not afraid."

"Gabriel," Desiree warned.

"It seems a meeting has been ordained or we would not have run into one another tonight," he said to Desiree.

The girl who had taken his chips returned with his winnings. He tipped her enough to get a kiss in thanks.

They drove to the edge of town, Dorian giving directions from the backseat, and turned down a sandy patch of road. At the end of a dead-end street was a saltbox house a little bigger and better kept than the others in the neighborhood. On the front porch was an old-fashioned overstuffed sofa.

"That it."

Desiree parked in front of the house and turned off the motor. Dorian got out first and went toward the house.

"I've never gotten up the nerve to come here before," Desiree said. "This is Dr. de la Croix's place. He's the most powerful root doctor in South Carolina."

"Oh, really?" Gabriel said, sounding not particularly impressed.

Dorian waited on the porch for them to catch up, then knocked. A girl opened the screen door without a word of greeting. It took Desiree a moment to realize the girl wasn't white, though her café au lait skin and straight hair would have let her pass for Caucasian. She was barefoot and wore an old-fashioned cotton dress. The girl looked closely up at Gabriel, making no secret of the fact that he alone interested her. Her expression seemed to say that she knew—or pretended to know—something secret about him.

"Welcome, friend," she said to Gabriel with a smile, speaking with a French accent. "Come in."

The house was almost completely dark, the air heavy with the aroma of candles and incense mingled with the smell of dust and unwashed dishes. The girl led them into the back bedroom, holding the door open while the visitors filed past into the room.

Dr. de la Croix filled an easy chair facing the door, an enormous presence who seemed to leave no air in the room for Desiree to breathe. De la Croix leaned heavily forward, propping himself up on a gold-headed cane. He wore white shoes, white trousers, a white short-sleeved shirt, and red suspenders. The panama hat on his shaved head was perched at a rakish angle. His eyes were hidden behind sunglasses. It was impossible to tell his age in the dim light. He might have been in his thirties or even forties, yet the exhaustion evident in the way he held himself suggested he might be much older.

In the corner was a voodoo altar—red candles, bones, rum bottles, rags, jars filled with graveyard dirt. The altar wasn't the center of attention, though.

The girl gave Gabriel another significant look, nodded at de la Croix, and went out, closing the door behind her.

"That him," Dorian said, pointing to Gabriel. "He the one I told you about. He the demon."

Dr. de la Croix began to nod his head, slowly, with tremendous deliberation.

"I can see that, Dorian," he said in a deep, lugubrious rumble. "I knew you would come." He touched the deck of tarot cards on the ratty card table beside him, his small hands surprisingly graceful. "Whenever I look at the cards, monsieur, I see the same thing over and over again."

"And what would that be?" Gabriel asked.

"Death crawling his way up out of a tomb after nearly a century of imprisonment."

Desiree thought she saw a flash of anger in the vampire's eyes, but he continued to smile at Dr. de la Croix with apparent amusement.

"You may call me Gabriel."

"You have a delightful name, Monsieur Gabriel. Like the angel. But I do not think you are an angel."

"No," he agreed.

Gabriel pulled back his lips just enough to reveal his distended blood teeth. The fangs were gone in the next instant, retracted into their cavities in his upper jaw. The display startled Desiree, and excited her. She later regretted having not looked at Dr. de la Croix. She wondered how he'd reacted to the vampire's display, whether he'd been frightened or satisfied to be face-to-face with such a being.

"I have a proposition for you, Monsieur Gabriel. I hope a being as magnificent as yourself is not above an arrangement that will benefit us mutually."

Gabriel nodded for him to continue.

"I have a—"

Dr. de la Croix began to cough, a terrible wracking cough that made it sound as if something was torn loose deep inside his lungs. He bent over, hanging onto the gold-headed cane as if it were the only thing keeping him in this world. The girl came into the room and held a cup to de la Croix's mouth, helping him drink a few strangled swallows. The coughing subsided, leaving Dr. de la Croix gasping for breath. He sat opening and closing his mouth like a beached fish, gripping the cane with one hand, the other resting on the girl's ass.

"Thank you, Marie," de la Croix said finally, and the girl went away. He took several gulps of air. "I would like to propose an arrangement between us."

Gabriel drew up a battered Windsor chair with most of the varnish worn off and sat down.

"You see, monsieur," de la Croix continued, "I have a rival. In my business, rivals are deadly." He wheezed, managing to stifle another bout of coughing. "She did this to me—my rival. I would like you to help me take care of her."

"I would think you are capable of that yourself."

"Ordinarily, yes, but she caught me off my guard. Now I am weakened, as you see, and so are my powers."

"You want me to kill Mama Coretta."

Desiree knew the name—but how did Gabriel? The old *gris gris* woman was reputed to be almost as powerful Dr. de la Croix.

"You are an individual of rare ability," de la Croix said to the vampire. "You will have no trouble disposing of her. Dorian can take you to her."

Dorian had been standing silently in the corner, so that Desiree had almost forgotten the woman was in the room. Dr. de la Croix's words had an electrifying effect on Dorian. Her shoulders jerked back and her arms flew up.

"I won' never go there!"

"You don't have to go in, foolish girl," de la Croix said. "Just point out the house."

"And what do you bring to the bargain?" the vampire asked.

Dr. de la Croix pulled off his sunglasses, revealing pale, almost white eyes that reminded Desiree of a dead dog she'd once seen. He studied Gabriel, looking inside him. Like Gabriel, he had the ability to *see* into the heart of things, peering all the way into the soul.

"People come from all over to consult Dr. de la Croix. If some of my clients disappear from time to time, who will be the wiser?"

"I imagine some of them do anyway," Gabriel said.

"Only the ones with more money than sense and nobody waiting for them at home. If you help me, I will send you someone every month to help satisfy your needs."

Gabriel looked at de la Croix and said nothing. Desiree was sure he was going to reject the proposition, but he held out his hand.

"That would be a suitable arrangement," he said as he and de la Croix shook hands. "There is only one additional thing I will require."

The vampire continued to hold de la Croix's hand as the man's face became wary.

"Name it, monsieur," de la Croix said, looking as if he wanted to pull his hand away.

"Marie."

"I beg your pardon?"

"The girl, Marie. I want her."

"My apprentice?" he sputtered.

"I thought she was your servant."

"Oh, no, monsieur. She was born in Haiti, like my own *grand-mère*. She is powerful for someone so young."

De la Croix began to cough again.

"Mama Coretta put the snake eggs on him," Dorian said to no one in particular.

"Those are my terms, de la Croix. Take them or leave them. I advise you to take them, since we are not leaving here without Marie, and you are scarcely in any condition to protest."

Dr. de la Croix hauled himself back up in his chair as the fit passed. He put his sunglasses on again and sat with his fist in front of his bluish lips, as if to hold down the coughing.

"I should have known better than to deal with a devil," he wheezed.

"Faustian bargains are prone to hidden pitfalls," Gabriel agreed. "Come now, ladies," he said, getting up from his chair. "It is time to collect our new friend. I have work to attend to this evening before we can turn to pleasure. Wish us Godspeed, de la Croix," he said, going through the door.

Dr. de la Croix said nothing. He was still leaning forward on his cane when Desiree glanced back, his forehead pressed against the golden knob, lost in anger, helplessness, or prayer. It was impossible to tell.

25

NUMBER 13 GARDEN Terrace sat in the middle of the antebellum neighborhood where the money in Calhoun had collected during the nineteenth century. The Georgian-style mansion previously belonged to Howard Mosely, a lawyer now retired to Palm Beach. Mosely's decision to sell the family home stunned his neighbors, though he and his wife had no children to turn the sprawling home over to, with its formal gardens and expensive upkeep.

The houses in Garden Terrace were owned by Calhoun's leading citizens. The next house to the south, number 12, belonged to Edward Stapleton, president of the First National Bank of Calhoun. To the north was number 14, the residence of Dr. Richard Williams, chief of staff at Calhoun Hospital.

Number 13 sat on a spacious lot filled with mature, well-tended trees, the perimeter of the property neatly delineated with a spike-topped, wrought-iron fence. Behind the house was an English-style garden, with trellis-lined brick walkways. There was a low marble fountain in the center of the garden, the focal point of a geometric arrangement of low hedges. In the fountain, golden carp swam among the lily pads. A gardener and his helper came by three days a week to maintain the garden and lawn.

At the back of the lot, a carriage house with room for six cars adjoined the alley. It was empty except for the black Lexus.

Four broad columns in front held up number 13's white portico. The double front doors opened into a spacious formal entry. There were parlors off to either side. A broad staircase climbed the right wall, sweeping upward past the second floor to the attic, where the house slaves were once quartered. There was no furniture in the foyer or either of the two front parlors.

The solarium in the back of the house at the far end of the hall was the only room with anything in it. Angled into one corner of the sparsely furnished room was an antique four-poster bed. Piled high around the bed were teetering stacks of books. In front of the fireplace was a single leather club chair and ottoman surrounded by still more heaps of books—novels, histories, biographies, heavy art books. In the center of the room, a long formal dining table sat at an angle to the walls. There were still more books on the table, plus miscellaneous art supplies—tubes of paint, a box of pastels, brushes—and a Waterford decanter of port and a glass.

The western wall was a series of French doors opening onto a limestone balcony and steps leading down to the garden. The heavy curtains were pulled back on either side and tied open. An easel sat near the windows, angled to take advantage of the natural light when the sun was up. The canvas was new, its blank surface awaiting the artist's touch.

Dante sat at the table with his sketch pad propped on the knee of his crossed leg. Oak logs crackled in the fireplace. How he loved a fierce fire! It was the perfect antidote to years spent trapped in the dark, frigid waters. Fires, Mozart, and art—they were the only three nexus points with the past that didn't make Dante's head whirl. He smiled inwardly at the feel of charcoal in his fingers, familiar and comfortable, a tool he knew how to use that brought him pleasure. Dr. Abigail Bloome's face looked back at him from the pad. Beauty, intelligence, and self-possession combined in her face, haunting his art.

Behind him, Desiree made a small sigh to remind Dante of her existence.

She sat on the floor in the corner, her feet drawn up under her chin and her arms around her knees. Dried blood was matted in her hair. She'd thrown herself on Mama Coretta with a savagery that had both impressed and appalled the vampire. She slashed the old black woman's wrist open with a razor, sucking what blood she could before Dante drained her dry to satisfy his own greedy thirst.

Dante could *feel* the hatred in Desiree's eyes as she looked at Marie. The Haitian girl was stretched across his bed, delirious with fever, her body caught in a tangle of silk sheets. She was lying on her stomach, naked, one small, well-shaped breast visible, an arm dangling over the edge of the bed. Her breath came in quick pants, as if she were exhausted from running or making love. Two tiny discolorations on the side of her neck were all that remained of the wounds Dante had made. The punctures were healing with unnatural speed. By morning, no outward sign of their passion would remain.

Dante had taken her gently, even tenderly, weakening her enough for the mysterious *Vampiri* bacillus to enter her blood. She would become the same sort of creature he was, if he took her two more times in the same way, reintroducing the immortal infection at fortnightly intervals.

"Do you really think she could make a better partner than me?"

Dante lifted his hand and let it fall in a gesture of not knowing. He took a sip of port, wishing it still had some power over him. He could not explain why he'd given to Marie the thing Desiree so desperately desired. Maybe it was because Desiree disturbed him in a way he was only beginning to understand. The madness for blood was the one immutable landmark on a vampire's horizon, but there was something unnatural and off-putting about its powerful hold over the eccentric young mortal.

"Are you going to keep your promise and change me?"

"Have I said that I would not, Desiree?" he answered with the patience one would use to deal with a persistent child.

"And what about her? Will you change Marie, or are you just playing with her?"

"I am not sure myself."

"Why give the gift to her but not me?"

"There is no real reason. I can be impulsive. It is not a good thing."

"But why did you give it to her before me?"

"Good God!" Dante exclaimed, instantly regretting the outburst. A gentleman did not express impatience, no matter how sorely he was tested.

Desiree began to cry, which only served to deepen Dante's shame and discomfiture. The Hunger spoke to him in his weakness, telling him to fly across the room, sink his teeth deeply into her neck and be done with her. And yet he didn't. Something made him force the Hunger's voice from his head. He did not really want to kill Desiree. For better or worse, she was the only friend he had—she and Dr. Bloome.

"Perhaps I did it because I sense a kindred darkness in her," Dante said, trying to explain his actions to himself as much as to Desiree. "Marie may be a lovely young girl, but there is a familiar nothingness in her eyes. Maybe she comes by it naturally, or maybe it was bred into her by generations of forebears who worshiped the darkness. De la Croix saw it, too, a deceptive, dangerously subtle evil."

"If it is evil you want, Gabriel, I will give it to you!"

She ran from the room, crying bitterly. A door slammed. A few moments later he heard the automobile come to life. Dante told himself he should be concerned about where Desiree was going and what she might do, but he could only feel a vast relief that she'd gone away and left him in peace.

Marie L'Enfant kicked at the covers, fighting them. Her breasts were completely uncovered now, revealing the delicate curve running from her ribs to her belly.

Dante threw the sketch pad onto the table and went to stand over her, looking down on her body, seeing the sweat glisten against the satin smoothness of her unblemished skin. He could barely restrain himself from falling on her. He wanted to press himself against her feverish skin, crushing his mouth against hers, pushing himself into her the way a man does with a woman. And then, at the perfect moment, he would feel the bliss explode within him as his mouth filled with her sweet blood.

Why should he care if he killed Marie L'Enfant? She had no real role to play in his future. He'd taken her from de la Croix simply because he wanted her. Now that he'd had her once, what was to stop him from indulging himself again? She had tasted delicious!

Dante stood looking hungrily down on the insensate girl, wondering what held him back. There was a tiny, almost inaudible voice in his head, the same one that had kept him from killing Desiree earlier. The voice confused Dante. What was its nature? How could something so soft compared to the Hunger's shrieking hold him back? It was a miracle he could hear it at all.

Then it came to Dante—a realization that was like the first opening of enlightenment but that quickly turned itself upside down, plunging him more deeply into despair. The unexpected rebirth of his conscience brought no relief after the things he'd done.

Dante spun away from Marie, wanting to scream to relieve the anguish that came with recognizing the depth of his guilt.

He strode to the fire, thinking furiously.

Why regret the mortals he'd killed? Perhaps an invisible Rubicon divided mortal and immortal morality, defining right and wrong in contradictory terms for the two races. What was a vampire besides a predator? Maybe Desiree was right in describing him as a lion living off the human herd. What purpose could there be to a vampire's existence if not to gorge upon mortal blood? It seemed absurd to argue that something that brought such transcendental pleasure could be somehow wrong.

Yet Dante sensed it was wrong—the savage bacchanal that had been his life since his awakening. A vampire did not have to kill to get what little blood he needed to keep the Hunger at bay. Why kill at all? And yet why not? It was maddening! he thought, striding back and forth in front of the fire. Which of the two opposing voices in his head spoke the truth: his conscience or the Hunger?

Something was missing in him. There was a lost piece of the puzzle that was his life. He had to recover it and fit it into place if he ever hoped to know the truth, if he ever hoped to be whole again.

Dante stopped and looked into the fire, watching the flames flicker and jump, as ephemeral and elusive as the answers he sought.

Dr. Bloome was the only person who could help him.

26

❖

IT WAS NEARLY nine o'clock before Dr. Abby Bloome's obligations to her patients were discharged, freeing her to go home, take off her work clothes, and curl up in an over-stuffed chair with an out-of-print book that a rare-book dealer had found for her, *The Paris Acid Murders*.

The dusty hardbound had a red, water-stained cover, its dust jacket long gone. She skimmed through the pages quickly, her green eyes running over the details of the Acid Murderer's career. Few books directly addressed her present field of interest. The Acid Murderer was not a classic type, but he exhibited behaviors that were very much of interest to the psychiatrist.

The reading lamp was the only light on in the bungalow, a smallish brick house among larger residences on a street where most of her neighbors were lawyers, accountants, and other doctors. Abby spent her free time in the yard, which was mostly given over to flowers. Gardening was one of her hobbies, an inherited trait. The women in her family had been passionate gardeners going back at least as far as her great-great-grandmother, Lisbeth Bloome, an early Freudian psychoanalyst whose life inspired Abby in her own choice of careers.

Claude Guimard, or the Acid Murderer, as he had been known in the popular press, was born in Paris during World War I in a house on a narrow side street not far from Notre Dame off the Boulevard St. Michel. His parents were solid middle-class citizens. Guimard's childhood was bland even by the standards of the petite bourgeoisie. He sang in the church choir and raised pigeons as a hobby. After earning his baccalaureate—Guimard was an average student—he became a minor bureaucrat in a minor department of a minor ministry. He married at twenty-nine, remaining in the house he'd inherited from his parents.

Guimard's only outward peculiarity was that he disliked violence of any sort. He refused to go to the cinema if the film dealt with war or subjects he deemed unpleasant. He kept a succession of pets as an adult, including a parrot that he'd had since he was a boy, and was known in his neighborhood as a man who loved animals. He drank little and didn't gamble, go to the cabaret, or express an interest in women other than his wife. Those who knew him described Guimard as a sober, predictable, even plodding man.

When Guimard was thirty-seven, his wife divorced him.

According to Madame Guimard's testimony during the divorce proceedings—which did not become publicly known until after his later arrest—Claude Guimard had an unnatural obsession with blood. Years earlier, when Guimard was still a student, he cut himself badly with a penknife. The wound had taken a long time to heal, perhaps partly because he got into the habit of breaking it open and licking it as it bled. His obsession gradually intensified over the years, though Guimard was careful to keep the habit—which he described as "disgusting"—secret. He'd been married nearly two years before Madame Guimard discovered his peculiarity.

Madame Guimard testified at her divorce that she tried to convince her husband to give up his unusual habit of wounding himself so that he could drink his blood. He promised to comply, but it was impossible for him to conceal the fact that he continued to indulge his unnatural obsession. Like many a sensible wife, Madame Guimard said, she decided the best way to deal with the situation was to ignore it. Except for this one small thing, she was entirely satisfied with her marriage.

Then something happened that upset the balance of their marriage.

One night in a café, the Guimards witnessed an argument between a man and a woman that culminated with the woman being stabbed. Guimard's morbid interest soon overtook his initial revulsion to the violent scene. He became so excited at the sight of the bleeding woman that Madame Guimard could not get him to leave the café until the police arrived and forced everybody out. Later that night, Guimard tried to convince his wife to allow him to open one of her veins so that he could drink her blood. The perverse request proved to be more than Madame Guimard could take. She packed her bags and left the next day while her husband was at the office, shortly thereafter filing a petition to have their marriage dissolved.

At the time of the divorce, the court instructed Claude Guimard to seek professional treatment for his "strange perversion," as the magistrate described it. Guimard saw his physician twice, but there was no record that he sought psychiatric therapy.

Claude Guimard's life appeared to return to its low-key, dull routine after the divorce. He continued to work for the same ministry and to live in the same house. He maintained his old affection for animals, keeping his parrot, two cats, and a dog.

Ten years after the divorce, a police informant reported seeing Guimard talking to a young schoolteacher, who later disappeared, outside the St. Michel–Notre Dame Metro station.

When police searched Guimard's house, they discovered a

necklace that belonged to the teacher. Other women's jewelry was found in a cigar box in a kitchen cabinet. Guimard claimed it belonged to his ex-wife, but some of it matched descriptions of property belonging to other women who had been reported missing in Paris.

Claude Guimard was extremely cooperative after his arrest. Almost without prompting he confessed to killing the missing teacher, adding that he'd killed eleven people during the past four years. Police first took the milquetoast Guimard as a lunatic confessing to his fantasies, but he said he could prove his claims if police would accompany him to the small warehouse he rented near the Orsay train station.

Abby closed the book on her forefinger and closed her tired eyes. The Orsay train station was now the Musée d'Orsay. She'd visited it two summers earlier to view the magnificent Impressionist collection.

Police found a half dozen noncorrosive metal drums in the warehouse, some empty, some filled with sulfuric acid. There was a pump and protective rubber gloves, some ropes, and a heavy wooden mallet. While police scraped together enough evidence to send Guimard to the guillotine, they told the author of *The Paris Acid Murders* that they never would have caught Guimard, much less convicted him, if he hadn't delivered his own head to them upon a platter.

At his trial Guimard said he'd abandoned his habit of drinking blood after the humiliation of his divorce. He'd considered himself cured until a few months before the first murder, when, purely by chance, he was the first person to come to the aid of a couple severely injured in an automobile accident on the Ile de la Cité. In the course of trying to help—the driver and his female passenger both died—Guimard's hands became covered with blood. Overcome by his old compulsion, he retreated to a washroom, where he could not restrain himself from tasting the blood on his fingers.

If fate hadn't put him on the street where the accident occurred, Guimard told the judge, he never would have become a killer.

The night of the accident, Guimard dreamed blood was dripping into his mouth from the ceiling as he slept.

Haunted again by the strange desire, Guimard made careful plans. He took some of the money he had saved—he had always been frugal—and rented a warehouse near the train station and stocked it with supplies. His first victim was a porter from Orsay hired to collect a trunk at the warehouse and carry it back to the station. Guimard hit the man in the head with a heavy wooden mallet, spilling his brains all over the floor.

Guimard cut the man's neck with a straight razor, collected blood in a wineglass, and drank it off quickly. He said drinking his victim's blood made him feel relaxed, easing what he described as an almost unbearable pressure that had been building up in the base of his skull since the day of the automobile accident.

Guimard dumped the man's body into one of the drums and proceeded to pump acid over the body to destroy the evidence of his crime. It was only then that he discovered that the porter was still alive, that neither the blow to the head nor having his throat slashed had succeeded in killing him, although either certainly would have proven fatal with time. Guimard had cried in court when he told about the suffering the porter experienced as the acid ate into his body.

Guimard resolved to be more humane the next time.

As soon as the acid bath had done its work, he rinsed the sludge down the floor drain, using a hose to wash up the blood and brain tissue that remained from his clumsy first effort.

Guimard went back to his job the next morning, thinking the porter's blood might be enough to satisfy his craving. For a time he seemed free of his compulsion. Several months passed before he experienced again the dream of blood trickling into his mouth. The pressure, as he described it, began to build in him. He tried to fight it, but in the end it was too powerful to resist.

Guimard's second victim was a plain-looking but pleasant widow who had designs on him as a potential new husband. He lured her to the warehouse and struck her in the head with the mallet, careful not to hit her too hard. He tied her to the rafters by her arms. She woke up as he cut her throat, struggling so much that he had trouble collecting a proper glassful of blood.

Once again the blood made Guimard feel better, immediately relieving the pressure. He enjoyed the woman's blood so much that he drank a second glass, more slowly this time, savoring it, he told the court, like fine brandy.

After she'd bled to death, he disposed of the widow's body the same way he'd gotten rid of the porter.

And so it went for four more years. Guimard would feel fine for months at a time before the pressure would start to build. After the porter, he told the court, he was always extremely careful to make sure his victims were dead before putting them into the acid bath. Some of his victims bled to death; the others he strangled with a length of leather from a discarded buggy harness.

Guimard lured his victims to the warehouse by telling them he had something rare and potentially valuable he wanted their opinion about. His demeanor provided perfect camouflage. He was a smallish cipher of a man. Even relative strangers found nothing threatening in his person or his request.

Dr. Otto Schendel, the author of *The Paris Acid Murders*, had several interviews with Guimard as the killer waited for execution. While the condemned man exhibited no readily identifiable psychiatric disturbances, Schendel noted that Guimard seemed to have a poorly developed sense of self. Unfortunately, the psychiatrist did not have time to develop more fully his observations before the sentence was carried out.

Guimard was a favorite with the guards, Schendel reported. Despite the notoriety of his crimes, the killer was a good conversationalist and sympathetic listener. Indeed, Guimard seemed to blossom in prison. Schendel attributed the change to the beneficial effect of the "de facto analysis" Guimard had undergone with the police and later in court. Talking about his obsession and what it led him to do had freed Guimard from his neurosis, Schendel believed. Guimard had an extensive repertoire of anecdotes and stories, and a beautiful singing voice he used to entertain his jailers, who were sorry to see him executed in spite of the horrific crimes he had committed.

Schendel differentiated between vampires and vampirists in the final chapter. A vampire is a mythical creature, while a vampirist is a disturbed person compelled by his neurosis to drink blood. Vampires don't exist in the real world, Schendel concluded, but vampirists do, and can be just as dangerous as their mythical counterparts.

Abby closed her eyes and leaned her head back against the chair. It was difficult to say which of her two patients most closely resembled Claude Guimard. Desiree's self-mutilating behavior was similar to Guimard in his earlier years. On the other hand, what better way to describe an amnesiac than as someone who lacks a solid sense of identity? Still, she could not imagine either of them going to Guimard's extremes.

The doorbell rang.

Abby tightened the belt around her red silk dressing gown as she turned on the hall light. Charles Gabriel was at her front door, his face framed in the window like a portrait. His eyes were sadder than she remembered them being.

She smiled through the glass and unlocked the door.

27

⟡

THE COUCH AND easy chair in the study were covered in brown leather and heavy, more suited to a man's comfort than a woman's. A Chippendale writing table sat at an angle on a blue Oriental rug, the darkened garden behind it through the windows. A grandfather clock in the corner quietly ticked away the minutes.

The walls were lined with built-in bookcases. A survey of their spines provided an overview of the psychiatrist's interests. One bookcase was reserved for books by and about Carl Gustav Jung. The second wall—the longest in the room—held volumes relating more generally to Dr. Bloome's profession, books about psychiatry, medicine, and pharmacology. The third wall seemed devoted to her personal interests: gardening and Impressionist art. One shelf was reserved for contemporary novels, some of which Dante Gabriel Rossetti had read to catch up with eighty-five years of missing culture.

The vampire pulled down a book, a thick, oversized volume with a maroon jacket. He hefted it in his hand, as if to judge its substance by its weight, before flipping through the *Diagnostic and Statistical Manual of Mental Disorders, Fourth Edition*, his eyes flying over the pages—he could scan an entire book in a few minutes—until he found what he wanted. The manual said amnesia could result from drug abuse, injury, or a medical condition. Often, there was damage to the diencephalic and mediotemporal lobe structures—whatever they were—from a closed-head trauma or "penetrating missile wounds."

He closed the book as Dr. Bloome came into the room. She had put on a blouse, trousers, and deck shoes. He had never seen her casually dressed and was still having trouble becoming accustomed to women in trousers. She came into the study carrying a silver tray with two mugs of steaming coffee.

"Interesting reading, Charles?"

"I was just discovering that I am subject to diagnosis number 294.0."

"That's amnesia due to medical conditions. I presently have you down as 294.8, 'Amnestic Disorder Not Otherwise Specified.' "

"Meaning?"

"It's the category we use when the cause of memory loss has not been identified."

"Diagnosis 294.8: it sounds very logical and precise. Does science truly have the power to dissect the human psyche with its infinite intricate variations, categorizing and cataloging the misery and madness of the mind as easily as one might a broken bone or goiter?"

Dr. Bloome smiled at him over her coffee. "In a word, no. The *DSM* is a starting place, a way to project an artificial pattern of diagnostic uniformity on a very difficult subject. The human mind is too complex to be reduced to an exact science."

She paused a beat.

"I was wondering if you would come back to see me, Charles."

"I apologize for the lateness of the hour."

"I'm here for you anytime. I need to tell you that I'm always disappointed when my patients check out of the hospital without consulting me."

"I felt bad about it, Doctor, but it was something I had to do. I had an epiphany of sorts: my memory returned, or at least the better part of it did. To that point, I had not minded being in asylum. After all, what is an asylum in its truest sense but a place one goes for safety and respite? However, almost from the moment I remembered who and what I was, being in hospital became unbearably oppressive. You understand how being surrounded by the insane makes you uncertain about your own sanity?"

Dr. Bloome nodded.

"I had the sense that maintaining my equilibrium depended upon my getting out of hospital and returning to a reasonably stable, quiet life. I wanted to come here tonight to explain that. And to ask you to forgive me for the rudeness and abruptness of my departure."

"I understand perfectly, Charles." She put down her coffee and leaned back in her chair, looking him up and down, appraising him. "So tell me a little about yourself. I've been as anxious as you to know who you are."

"I am an artist and a poet."

Her eyes widened a little. "I can't help but note your suit and watch. You must be very good at what you do."

"I have had my successes, though I have worked as hard as any man ever has."

"Some people mistakenly think art is easy," Dr. Bloome said agreeably.

"Yes, but it is not. I have been on what you might call a sabbatical. That is why I came to the United States. I needed a change. I had become tired of the same subjects, the same London light in my studio, the same friends. The edge was gone from my art.

I decided to go to New Orleans. I had never been there, but it seemed like it would be a place I could work. I was not in New Orleans very long, unfortunately."

"What happened?"

"I will tell you what I can, though I cannot recollect all the details," he said, pushing back his long hair, making up the story as he went. "I do not think I was in New Orleans long enough to rent a flat or a studio. I remember checking into a hotel. The next thing I know, I was riding a bus, unsure of who I was or where I was going. I ran out of money and found myself in Calhoun, not knowing what to do next. The rest you know."

"You have no idea what caused your amnesia?"

"I have not a clue."

"Maybe an accident? Or you could have been robbed and hit in the head."

Dante pretended to try to remember. He shook his head. "I am sorry, I remember nothing."

"Is there a friend or acquaintance in New Orleans we could contact who might know something?"

"Part of the Crescent City's charm for me was the fact that I knew no one. I wanted to escape the endless socializing of London, which only distracted me from my work. I came to America to be alone and to concentrate on my art."

"Have you notified your friends and family in Britain? They will be worried."

"I have no family, no friends who would have known I was missing."

"Your wife?"

He looked from Dr. Bloome to the grandfather clock, his hands opening and closing against his thighs.

"Charles?"

He did not answer. He was too intent upon the outline of

something perfectly horrible rising up out of the shadows that held his lost memories.

"Charles?"

"My wife is dead," he said in a wooden voice.

"What happened to her?"

He gave the psychiatrist a blank stare. He had not expected Dr. Bloome to ask him that. The answer did not come immediately to mind, and when he tried to think about it, the pain made him wince.

"I do not remember."

Dr. Bloome looked at him with the same expression. Her eyes were alert, her countenance patient, interested—and determined.

"Some rather prominent pieces of your past remain missing, Charles."

"So it seems," he said, his voice quiet, uncertain, almost frightened.

"What happened to your wife?"

"Leave it, please," he said, and closed his eyes as if to shut the memory out.

"You can remember, Charles."

"No," he said, his voice filled with anguish.

"You must make yourself remember."

"I don't want to remember," he said, suddenly angry. "I don't want to remember how she . . ."

His voice fell off as something gave way inside him. Somewhere deep in his heart, the dam holding back his despair crumbled, releasing a flood of emotion. He buried his face in his hands, but the tears would not come. Crying would have brought some measure of relief, and he would not grant himself that. His guilt was too great. He deserved no mercy.

"Let it rise to the surface, Charles," Dr. Bloome said, her voice gentle and encouraging. Her small hand was on his shoulder.

Firm. Warm. Filled with friendship. "It will hurt until you acknowledge it. It's the first step to healing."

"She killed herself," he said, whispering the terrible words as the memory of that black time pressed down, a mountain of grief.

"I am afraid, Dr. Bloome," he said, his face still in his hands. "I am afraid of things I do not remember, of terrible acts I may have performed in the past—or may yet do in the future."

"This is perfectly natural. It is always frightening to lose one's way. Think of how much more frightening it is to lose one's self."

He looked up at her, wanting to take comfort in her words, ignoring the seductive song of blood rushing through Abigail Bloome's veins.

"Your amnesia is a defense mechanism," she continued, "a strategy your subconscious mind devised to give you time to regroup yourself. You must come to terms with whatever you are hiding. You must make your peace with the past."

"Do you think evil exists, Dr. Bloome?"

The question seemed to catch her off guard. "Evil is nothing more than the wrong choice. If we choose good over evil, we have nothing to fear. Think of it this way: the consequences of choosing good are invariably positive, the consequences of choosing evil invariably negative. Therefore, it is always logical to choose good. An act of evil is by definition irrational."

"Am I not irrational, Dr. Bloome, with pieces of my past missing? Am I not a walking example of irrationality?"

"That hardly means you are predisposed to evil."

"But what of my urges?"

"Are you talking about your earlier claim to being a vampire?"

He could not think of how to answer that. Dante did not merely "think" he was a vampire, yet it would be impossible for

Dr. Bloome to accept the truth about what he was. She did not believe in vampires.

"We all have impulses," she said after a moment. "Some of our impulses are irrational and inappropriate. Our impulses are not important, but how we deal with them is. I can control my irrational impulses. I know you can, too. I have faith in you as a human being. I have faith in your ability to choose good over evil, Charles."

"Will you help me, Doctor?"

"Of course I will. But how long will you be in Calhoun? Aren't you going to return to New Orleans?"

"I will stay, if you agree to see me. This place is as good as any."

"Very well, then." She stood to signal the meeting was over. For a short time she had been a friend, but now they were returning to their former relationship of doctor and patient. "Come to my office at three tomorrow afternoon and we will begin anew."

He followed her toward the door.

"By any chance have you seen Desiree Hohenberg?" she asked with elaborate casualness.

"Who?"

"Never mind. Good night, Charles."

28

✧

DANNY RICE WAS sitting on the hood of his car, drinking a quart bottle of beer, talking with his friends. The boys were quick to spot her, using the sixth sense boys have about girls, but they couldn't make out who she was until she walked into the lights near the basketball court.

"Scag."

"Freak."

"Slut."

"Witch."

Desiree could only hear selected words. She was used to it. In a way, she liked it. The disparagement gave her a feeling of power. Even the hoods in Calhoun were a little afraid of her.

"Watch your fuckin' mouth," Danny said.

The cruel laughter died. Danny's unlikely chivalry caught the others off guard. There weren't too many people in town ready to cross Danny, one of the toughest boys in Calhoun.

"Hey, Danny," she said, ignoring the others.

A boy called Piggy snickered.

Danny grabbed Piggy by his flannel shirt. "What's your problem, fuckface?"

"No problem," Piggy said, holding up his hands.

Danny shoved Piggy backward.

"Come on, guys," a boy named Emil said. "Let's scare up more beer."

Doors slammed and engines started with the rumble of poorly muffled horsepower. A Lynyrd Skynyrd tape began to blast as the first car shot out of the cul de sac with screeching tires.

"Assholes," Danny muttered. He took a big drink from a Budweiser bottle. Danny held his liquor well, but the unsteadiness in his eyes told Desiree he was drunk.

Danny and his friends hung out in the Plantation Park cul de sac as part of their weekend ritual. They drove up and down Main Street, "dragging the strip," until the police ran them off around ten, when they retired to the park to drink beer and smoke pot, if anybody had some. Later, around midnight, there would be drag races on the Lennox blacktop north of town.

Danny was sitting on his car, an old Camaro with a chrome racing tachometer bolted outside the windshield and huge rear tires that made it look as if the car's nose would dig into the pavement at the smallest bump. The body was painted with flat brown primer. It was noisy and uncomfortable to ride in. Danny had ripped out the carpet, and instead of a backseat there was a roll cage to keep the top from caving in if he crashed during a race. The Camaro wasn't much to look at, but it was the fastest quarter-miler in Calhoun, a fact that solidified Danny's status as king of the local greasers.

"Where you been, Des?"

"Around."

"New shoes, huh?"

Desiree wiggled the toes of the black Converse basketball shoes. "I ripped them off from Wal-Mart."

"I liked your boots."

"Boots are too hot in summer. I got a new bag, too." She

turned in profile to show him the knapsack she carried slung over one shoulder. She was glad she wouldn't have to lug it much farther; it was getting heavy.

"It's working," Danny said in a low voice, even though there was no one else there to hear. "Jimmy got fired. He made a pass at Eddie's daughter."

Desiree snorted. "She must be all of twelve."

"Jimmy was pretty drunk. I've almost—*almost*—got Eddie talked into fucking letting me drive!"

Danny's dream was to become a NASCAR driver. He worked at Calhoun Auto Salvage, where he'd spent the past year trying to convince his boss, Eddie Fritz, to put him behind the wheel of the junkyard's dirt-track racer. Unfortunately, Eddie had no interest in letting the untried novice replace Jimmy Cherry, his longtime driver. In desperation, Danny had asked Desiree to use witchery to get Cherry out of the way. She'd sprinkled graveyard dirt on the stoop of Jimmy Cherry's house. She didn't let on, but she was almost as surprised and impressed as Danny that it had apparently worked.

"You been to church, Danny?"

"No, ma'am." He'd been raised Southern Baptist, same as Desiree.

"Nothing will dissolve the spell faster than you letting your mama drag you back to Reverend Hock."

"I done everything just like you told me," Danny said.

She took a step closer, moving into his space, smiling to hear the breath catch in his throat. Boys like Danny didn't get many dates, even if they did own the fastest car in town.

"Eddie hasn't asked you to be his driver because somebody's blocking you. I can feel it in my bones."

"What can I do?"

"You really want this?"

"More than any fucking thing in the world."

"We need to go visit Michelle LeClaire again. We need to raise your power. You're not afraid to do me there again, are you?"

"Fuck, no," he said, leaning more heavily against the car. She could tell he was lying.

"We need to take things to the next level to overcome whoever is blocking you."

"Whatever it takes," he said, smiling, showing her his bad teeth. "Plus I'm gonna get some."

"You're going to get all the pussy you can handle."

Danny had already drank half his quart of beer by the time they pulled into the cemetery with the Camaro's lights off.

"Who's that over there?"

"Dr. de la Croix."

"Oh, Jesus," Danny whispered.

"He's got what he's come for. Don't worry about him. It's not like he's going to call the cops."

The fat man with the cane moved quickly, even spryly, up the hill and disappeared. He seemed to be doing a lot better than when they'd visited him a few nights earlier.

Danny took an old sleeping bag with a broken zipper from the back of the Camaro and spread it across the white sepulchre engraved with the name LECLAIRE. While he was busy with that, Desiree pulled on a pair of rubber gloves and picked up the unopened quart of beer Danny had given her. As he kneeled on the tomb, smoothing the sleeping bag, she took a quick step forward and smashed the bottle against his head before he had time to react. The bottle exploded against Danny's skull, spraying them with glass and beer.

Danny sprawled on his face, his arms and one leg hanging over the tomb.

Desiree grabbed him by the back of the hair and jerked up his head. His eyes were closed, his mouth slack, open. He was still breathing. His hair was wet with beer and blood.

"Danny? Danny, can you hear me, you stupid fuck?"

He was out cold.

Desiree rolled him onto his back and straddled him, kissing him softly on his unresponsive mouth. She moved her lips to his cheek, then his neck, the way she'd seen Gabriel nuzzle his victims. She forced herself to linger, savoring the moment the way the vampire usually did. Then, when she couldn't make herself wait any longer, she bit into his neck with all the savagery she could muster.

The experience was oddly disappointing.

The skin and muscle in Danny's neck were pliant, even rubbery, and mostly resistant to her teeth. The small amount of blood that trickled into Desiree's mouth was a far cry from the powerful torrents Gabriel's wicked teeth released.

Danny groaned weakly and began to move beneath her. His hand came up to her shoulder, but there was no strength in his arm when he tried to push her away.

Desiree jumped down and opened her knapsack, digging for the box cutter.

Danny muttered something incoherent. He'd pushed himself up on one arm by the time she turned around with the razor. He looked at her dumbly. He didn't seem to recognize her, but then he called her name.

"Desiree," he managed. "Help."

Danny wasn't even smart enough to know that she'd broken a bottle against his thick skull! People were stupid, Desiree thought, as stupid as cattle. No wonder Gabriel killed without remorse. She thew herself at Danny, knocking him flat against the sepulchre, dragging the razor across his neck with a slashing backhand. Blood sprayed into the air—hot and sticky, steaming in the cool night air.

"Oh," Desiree moaned, opening her mouth wide to catch the precious liqueur.

Danny thrashed beneath Desiree, trying to close the wound with his own hands, but it was futile. After a few more seconds his body went slack when he passed out from the bleeding. She pressed her mouth to the open gash in Danny's neck. She could feel the pounding of his pulse against her lips, a sensation so intimate that it sent a trembling orgasm through her body. She found the opened artery and slipped her serpentine tongue into it.

She would show Gabriel that she, not Marie L'Enfant, deserved to become his immortal lover.

Danny's body convulsed with death tremors. Desiree kept her blood-smeared face against his neck, gorging on his blood. Her stomach felt heavy and distended, the hot blood sitting in her belly with an almost greasy sensation. She barely had time to turn her head before she vomited.

"Too much," she said, but she went back and drank more.

Desiree never imagined she could get enough blood to slake her thirst, but now, finally, she was satisfied—more than satisfied. She would no longer be constrained by pathetic human limitations once she'd been transformed. She had seen Gabriel effortlessly drain three prostitutes in Atlantic City, one after the next. Soon she would do that and more!

Desiree vomited a second time, then got the hatchet out of the knapsack. It was old and rusty and didn't look very sharp, but it would do the job. She'd found it in the carriage house behind the mansion. Holding it in both hands, she raised it high, then brought it down hard on Danny Rice's neck.

"Shit!"

Desiree squinted against the spray of blood and splintered bone chips. She had to wipe her eyes on her sleeve before she could see the wedge-shaped wound in Danny's neck. It would take some hacking to get the head off. She went to work in earnest, shutting her eyes with each chop, irritated at how difficult it would be to get the gore out of her hair. She should have thought to wear a hat. It would have made cleaning up lots easier.

The chop that severed the head sent it rolling onto the ground. Desiree picked it up by the hair and deposited it into a garbage bag she closed with a twist tie. She put the first sack inside a second and tied it shut, too, so it wouldn't leak. She fished the car keys out of Danny's pocket, holding her nose against the stink: his oily Levi's were wet with urine.

Desiree carried her knapsack, now even heavier, to a marble tombstone with the name SOTHBY inscribed in its face. She sat down and took off the basketball shoes and rubber gloves, then stripped off her blood-soaked clothing. When she was naked, she stood with her arms out, turning slow witch circles in the soft grass. She had wanted to kill someone and drink their blood for a long time. Now that she'd finally done it, she wondered why she hadn't killed sooner. It had been so *easy*.

Gabriel would be impressed. He would see that she was evil, that she was the one who deserved to be made immortal, not that nigger.

Desiree put on the spare clothes from the knapsack, pulling on her Doc Martens last. She bagged the other clothes and put them into the knapsack with Danny's head. She'd burn the clothes in the incinerator in the basement of Gabriel's house. The knapsack was stuffed, with Danny's head in it, along with the bag of sodden clothes; she could hardly zip it shut.

Desiree climbed into the Camaro, laughing at the sound of the powerful motor when she turned the key. She hated noisy cars and was going to drive Danny's Camaro into the river and watch it sink.

Oh, yes, she told herself, she was going to enjoy being a vampire.

29

MEDGAR RONSON SAID he could handle the police better without his client tagging along. Mobius doubted it, but he'd deferred to the former Chicago policeman and watched him go into the station house alone.

Mobius sat on a park bench in the public square outside the station and lit a Cohiba. He was toying with adding cigars to his repertoire of vices. Cigars were all the rage at the university with tenured professors, who had the income to indulge in meaningless luxuries. He exhaled a lazy plume of blue smoke and watched it dissipate into the purer blue of the summer sky.

Mobius wondered how Ronson would handle the redneck southern police. Maybe the brotherhood of the badge superseded skin color. Race was a complicated thing in the South. Threads of misunderstanding, resentment, and hostility were woven into the social tapestry. Mobious thought of Faulkner, who'd been haunted by faded glory and enduring blame, the stain of guilt as indelible and powerful as an Old Testament curse.

Mobious took the cigar from his mouth and gave it a sour look. He didn't give a damn about Faulkner anymore.

The police and fire departments shared a vaguely Art Deco building constructed of brick. The big garage bay doors were open. Inside, Mobius could see the gleaming brass pole the firemen slid down when the fire bell rang, their boots and coats waiting next to a pair of shiny red trucks that stood with their doors open, everything at the ready. Distant music played in a tinny loudspeaker outside the True Value hardware store. It was almost noon. People were emerging from the offices and shops for lunch. It was a *tableaux vivant* of small-town life. The sentimental American scene would have attracted Norman Rockwell, Mobius thought, although he wasn't sure how the artist would have suggested the presence of a monstrous killer lurking somewhere just out of sight, watching the innocents go about their business from behind a cracked shade in a darkened attic window.

The police station's double doors swung open and Ronson emerged. The leather attaché case with his initials stamped in gold made him look more like a lawyer taking care of business than an ex-homicide cop.

"You feel like getting some lunch, Dr. Mobius?"

Mobius wasn't hungry, but one of the good things about having Medgar Ronson around was that he reminded him to eat.

The café was crowded, but there was a room in the back where Mobius and the detective had some privacy. Ronson ordered the meat loaf, a Diet Coke, and apple pie for dessert. Mobius ordered the same. He didn't like meat loaf, but ordering what Ronson did saved him from having to think about it.

"I don't think this last murder is our guy. The victim was a kid, a gearhead named Danny Rice who liked to drag-race a souped-up Camaro. They fished his car out of the river outside of town. Whoever killed him took his car and dumped it."

"Was the throat ripped out, like the others?"

"Hard to say. Chopping off somebody's head with a small ax tends to obscure the forensic evidence. The killer took the head with him. The chief thinks the kid was some kind of sacrifice. He was killed in a cemetery on the grave of a woman who was supposed to have been a witch back during the Civil War. This looks like an occult crime. This is voodoo country."

"Come on," Mobius scoffed.

"For real. Old traditions die hard in the rural South. I know. I'm originally from Georgia. There's voodoo in Miami, New Orleans, even on my home turf in Chicago. But this is the heart of it, right here in the Carolinas, the soul of the old Confederacy. There are a lot of down-home, uneducated, ignorant people in these parts. It's mostly harmless, but not all of it."

"What if our guy is just trying to make it look like somebody else is responsible to throw us off the trail?"

"Killers don't change their M.O., Dr. Mobius. There was a hell of a lot of blood. Our guy doesn't leave much blood behind."

"Did you get the pictures?"

"They wouldn't let me look at them. And the detective in charge of the investigation wouldn't have time to talk to me for a few days. I ended up talking to the chief. The local law are in panic mode. There hasn't been anybody murdered here for ten years. Now two murders, one right after the next, and not just run-of-the-mill murders where somebody shoots or stabs a spouse or friend in a drunken argument. They're freaked."

"The police?"

"They act plenty tough, but they're freaked just like everybody else. It's always hectic working a homicide, especially with a geek killing. There's a missing head out there somewhere. The local boys in blue are wondering if it's going to turn up on the altar of the local Baptist church or get stuck on top of that flagpole in front of the police station. We need to leave them alone for a couple of days to let them do their jobs."

"I want to see the crime photos and reports. Go around the locals, if you have to. Talk to your state contact."

"It will still be a few days before we see them. In a deal like this, paperwork is the last thing the detectives catch up with."

"Grease the wheels. The chief of police in a burg like this can't pull down much salary."

"I don't think that's a good strategy."

"Don't get squeamish on me, Ronson."

"I'm not squeamish, Dr. Mobius. I don't mind pushing the envelope when it's doable, but the vibe isn't right to throw your money at this one. I can charm most people, but Chief Miller clearly isn't a member of my fan club. I'm from the city. I'm from the North. I'm black. That's not a combination that works with his kind of guy."

"Do southern whites tend to be racist, in your experience?" Mobius asked as he raised a forkful of apple pie.

"All whites tend to be racist, in my experience."

"Even white Yankee liberals?"

"They're the worst."

"How so?"

"They pretend they love you, but deep down they're as afraid of you as an unreconstructed cracker. Plus they think the black man can't make it without the white man's help. It's actually easier to deal with old-fashioned, send-them-back-to-Africa racists. You can fight that kind of ignorance." He reached for his Diet Coke. "Do you really want to sit here and have a colloquy about race in America?"

"No, but I was wondering earlier if there would be complications with you dealing with the police here. I certainly don't fault you."

"That's a tremendous relief."

"Don't get touchy, Ronson. What do you think about me taking a run at the chief?"

"It might work, if you tell him about your wife and get him feeling sympathetic. His name is Charlie Miller. I still don't see the point. There doesn't seem to be a connection between the headless kid and the waitress."

"You think this Charlie Miller is more approachable than the detective in charge of the case?"

"Most definitely. The man working the case is going to be busy and running on no sleep. He'll be a lot more prone to get angry. Trust me. I been there."

"Chief Miller it is, then," Mobius decided.

"You'll know him when you see him. He looks exactly like you'd expect a southern police chief to look."

"You're letting your prejudice show, Mr. Ronson."

"I don't really give a damn. I'll be back at the hotel working the phones. Call if you need me to bail your sorry white ass out of jail."

30

DESIREE WAS SITTING cross-legged on a blanket on the floor, listening to a Marilyn Manson CD, when she saw the oval brass doorknob start to move.

Desiree had appropriated one of the second-floor bedrooms as her personal space. None of the other rooms on the second story were occupied. The room, like the rest of the mansion except for the parlor that was Gabriel's lair, was devoid of furniture. Clothing and trash were thrown about. The vanity in the adjoining bathroom held the supplies Desiree required to maintain her look: white pancake makeup, bloodred lipstick, heavy black mascara and eyeliner, which she used to paint her eyelids in the exaggerated fashion favored by ancient Egyptian priestesses. The light in the room came from a dozen candles. Desiree loved candlelight, with its flickering otherworldly glow.

The doorknob had a decorative rim of pearl-like bumps cast into its surface around the outer edge. Desiree watched it turn as far as it could, then stop. She'd locked the door from the inside. The knob reversed direction. Whoever was on the other side seemed to think she wouldn't notice.

Desiree turned off the CD.

"Gabriel?"

He hadn't been home when she came back from the cemetery

with Danny's head. She'd waited up past dawn, but the vampire had stayed out all night. He still wasn't home when she woke up late that afternoon. He'd been gone long enough for her to begin worrying about whether he was coming back. It awakened painful memories of an earlier abandonment, although Desiree could hardly remember the father who had left her when she was a little girl.

Desiree got up and moved toward the door. Footsteps receded down the hall. Someone was running barefoot down the staircase by the time she got the door unlocked and opened it.

"You fucking bitch!" Desiree screamed.

She went back into her room for the box cutter and flew down the stairs. It was nearly midnight. Moonlight poured in through a multipaned window at the end of the foyer, casting a spiderweb shadow across the floor. Desiree crept to Gabriel's chamber and peered in through the crack in the door.

Almost everything was as he had left it—the single lamp burning, the Jean Paul Sartre book facedown on the table, the half-consumed glass of port. Marie L'Enfant was no longer sprawled, naked and unconscious, in Gabriel's bed, moaning piteously. Desiree had hoped the girl would die from the fever, but no such luck. Now she thought she should have strangled Marie while the girl was helpless and Gabriel was gone.

Desiree slipped into the kitchen, looking for her rival. Marie was watching her from the doorway when Desiree turned.

"How dare you skulk around *my* house," Desiree said, the box cutter hidden within her hand.

The girl was wrapped in a sheet, naked under it, like a corpse wound for burial. Her eyes still burned with fever, but there was something else there—the Hunger. Marie lifted her chin a little, sniffing the air. Desiree realized Marie was smelling her blood.

The Hunger was already calling to her, singing what Gabriel called its savage song.

Desiree raised the box cutter. "You're smaller than I am, and weaker, and you don't have any real powers. If you try anything cute, I'll slit your throat and drink *your* blood."

Marie took a tentative step into the kitchen, her eyes locked on the box cutter. Desiree sensed the calculation in the other girl's mind. Marie was trying to decide if she could get the box cutter away from her, so that she could use it the same way Desiree had put it to work on Sandi, Mama Coretta, and Danny.

Desiree felt a draft play around her ankles, ghostly fingers brushing her skin.

The front door closed.

Marie disappeared into the darkened hall. In the next instant, Gabriel appeared in the doorway, seeming to materialize the way he sometimes did.

"What have you done, you little fool? You have brought death into our home."

"I told you I was evil," Desiree bragged.

He moved past her to the refrigerator, knowing what was inside.

"Why would you do something so foolish?"

"To prove I am worthy."

The refrigerator swung open, touched by invisible hands. The cold had not entirely arrested decomposition of Danny Rice's head. The lips were drawn back in a leer, exaggerating the size of his crooked, stained teeth. The eyes were sunken and almost shut, small half-moons of white. The skin had turned a yellowish-brown, black on the tip of the nose and chin, which was pulled upward, nostrils flaring, as if the head were recoiling from the stench of its own decay. On the glass drip panel at the bottom of the refrigerator, a puddle of black goo had congealed.

"Give me the immortal kiss, Gabriel," Desiree begged, holding her hands out to the vampire. "I am the one who deserves it, not *her*."

Marie had returned. She cowered in the doorway, as if afraid to come in and risk the vampire's wrath.

"You know nothing of what this infernal life is like. If you did, you would never make such a request of me."

"What price is too great to pay for life eternal?"

"You may as well ask for damnation eternal. To live forever—unable to die, unable to put the pain behind you, unable to know the simple peace of the grave. Immortality is a curse."

"Then I happily doom myself to be cursed."

Desiree saw some of the pain go out of the vampire's eyes, replaced by a hard, almost cruel look. A small movement in her peripheral vision made her glance toward the refrigerator. It was the head.

"Remember me."

The voice, a wet, gurgling whisper, came from the refrigerator. An involuntary shudder shook Desiree, as if a centipede had started crawling down her spine. Black-purple bubbles swelled on the lips, popping to form a long, viscous drool that flowed down the chin and into the drip pan below.

"Desiree," the severed head said. "Remember me."

It was a trick, of course. Gabriel was trying to frighten her.

"Do you like it in Hell, Danny? What did Michelle LeClaire think of us fucking on her grave?" She turned to Gabriel. "Your little performance does not frighten me."

The vampire's eyes narrowed.

"Don't become angry, Gabriel. How can you hate me for wanting to be like you, for wanting to be with you, forever?"

He softened a little.

"I only want to follow you, my love. I want to become a virtuoso artist, using eternity for my canvas and blood for my paint. I want to learn the most intimate secrets of your race. I promise to become very good at killing. Some I will kill in the blink of an eye, others slowly and languidly, draining the last drops of suffering from them along with their blood."

"Enough," Gabriel said, closing his eyes and holding up a hand. "You misunderstand everything. You are completely around the twist."

"You used to like me being kinky."

"You are mad."

"You should know. We were both locked up on the same mental ward."

"I mistook your craving as a bond between us. Now I realize it is nothing more than an outward sign of degeneracy."

"If you don't like what you see, Gabriel, change me. Make me into whatever kind of vampire you want. Mold me. I will be your slave in all things, in all ways, forever."

"I don't want a slave. I am not so wicked that I would give you the power of the *Vampiri* and set you loose upon the world."

"You *are* a coward," Desiree said, spitting the words. "You're afraid I'll be as powerful as you. No wonder you surround yourself with girls. You think we wouldn't dare challenge your authority. Maybe that's the way it was in whatever century you crawled out of, Gabriel. Did you push your women around then, too?"

Desiree cried out as he grabbed her hair and cruelly pulled her to him, forcing her head to one side. The light from the open refrigerator reflected on his glimmering blood teeth as he swiftly brought his open mouth toward the small of her neck. Desiree heard footsteps retreating up the hall—a terrified Marie L'Enfant running for safety lest the vampire next turn his wrath on her.

Desiree expected her union with the vampire to be filled with bliss, a smooth, gliding, erotic stab. Instead there was a terrible, searing pain as he sank his teeth into her, as if red-hot nails were being driven deep into her. Desiree pushed back, instinctively fighting her attacker although she had wanted this more than she had ever wanted anything else. His arms wrapped around her like adamantine chains, holding her close as her blood gushed into his ready mouth, at long last making them truly one.

The pleasure started to flow into Desiree's body, moving up and down her neck, running through her like an injection of the purest morphine. When the rush reached her head, it touched off an orgasmic explosion that radiated out into her arms and legs. This was everything she had imagined, an ecstatic transport to a blissful realm transcendent to anything that could be experienced in the gray world of ordinary mortals.

Desiree's head fell back as the muscles in her body went slack. What she did, what he did—nothing mattered but the warm, blissful vibration humming between their bodies and souls.

The last thing Desiree saw before losing consciousness was the rotting head, staring at her stupidly from the refrigerator shelf. She wondered if Danny Rice was somehow watching from wherever he was, watching and wondering if she were about to join him.

31

✧

FBI SPECIAL AGENT Jennifer Avery nearly collided with Abby as she was going out the doctors' entrance at Calhoun Hospital.

"We need to talk," Avery said. Her eyes were tired and red. Abby guessed Avery had been up all night, running on caffeine and adrenaline. She looked as if she'd put on her makeup in the rearview mirror while waiting at a stoplight.

"I have some calls to return but nothing urgent."

"Any place to get some coffee? The cafeteria open?"

"Let's go to the doctors' lounge. It was empty a few minutes ago, and there was a pot of fresh coffee."

"I'm sure you've heard the news. There's been another murder."

"It's all anybody is talking about this morning," Abby said.

The housekeeping staff was busy going from room to room, emptying wastebaskets and changing linens. A tall black woman stood behind her cart for protection, watching them with wide eyes.

"Good morning, Dorian," Abby said as they went past.

The housekeeper nodded.

"We try to insulate the One North patients from this sort of news."

The FBI agent gave a curt nod.

Abby held her key card in front of the sensor on the wall outside the doctors' lounge, and the electric lock clicked open.

"How do you take your coffee?"

"Black, thanks."

Avery sipped her coffee and looked at Abby. She was using a technique Abby often employed with patients. Sometimes the most effective way to find out what was on a person's mind was to sit back and wait to see where the other person directed the conversation.

"Is there a connection between the two crimes?" Abby said after a moment, deciding there was no harm in accepting the gambit, since she understood it for what it was.

"You mean the blood thing? Maybe. It's hard to tell. The victim's head was chopped off and removed."

"My God," Abby said, not trying to disguise her shock. "It didn't say that in the newspaper."

"No," Avery said with a tight smile. "Sometimes things go as planned. Have you talked to Desiree?"

"Do you think she's involved?"

Avery gave her a sharp look. "You do remember you were supposed to call me if you saw her."

"Of course I remember. And no, I haven't talked to her."

"There were ritualistic aspects to Danny Rice's murder that might tie in with the others. I understand Desiree Hohenberg is a practicing Satanist."

"I don't want to talk about a specific patient, but the first thing I would wonder with an adolescent is whether a professed interest in the occult is sincere or merely an attempt to express contempt for authority."

"Chopping off somebody's head in a graveyard is sincere enough for me." Avery fished a roll of Tums out of her jacket pocket. She pried a tablet off the end and popped it into her mouth.

"Coffee aggravates stomach acid," Abby said, nodding at the cup the detective held in her other hand.

"I don't know what's wrong with kids," the FBI agent said, ignoring Abby's comment. "They just get weirder and wilder."

"Kids see so much violence. Some of them have trouble discerning the boundary between reality and fantasy. They cross over."

"Do you think Desiree crossed over?"

"It's a possibility, but I doubt it."

Jennifer Avery took the notebook out of the inside pocket of her blazer, giving Abby another glimpse of the gun she wore. She'd prepared a list of questions for the interview.

"For the record, Dr. Bloome, when did you last speak to Desiree Hohenberg?"

"The day she was dismissed from One North. I can get you the exact time and date."

"And she has not telephoned or otherwise contacted you?"

"No."

"I need you to understand that you could be charged as an accessory-after-the-fact to capital murder if you're lying to me."

"Does intimidation work with most people, Special Agent Avery?"

"Don't spar with me, Doctor."

"Then don't threaten me." Abby drew in a slow breath and forced the anger from her mind. "I haven't talked to Desiree. I don't know where she is. She has not kept her therapy appointments."

"Her mother said she'd been back to the house at some point and had taken her portable stereo and a few personal items. Any idea where she might be hiding out?"

"Not really. Desiree is a loner. She didn't have any close friends, not anybody she could stay with."

"What about Danny Rice? Did she ever mention that she was sleeping with him?"

"No. Was she?"

Avery began to smile. "I guess you don't know as much about Desiree as you think. She and Danny had a thing going. Nothing serious, I gather, but off and on. She was the last person seen with him while he was still alive. Are you still confident Desiree's violent impulses were directed only at herself?"

It was galling that an FBI agent from Charlotte, someone who had never even met Desiree, knew things about her patient that she didn't know. But that was just her ego goading her, Abby realized; she wasn't foolish enough to listen to its petty carping.

"I would have thought so," Abby said with a shrug, "but I don't claim to be infallible."

"It's probably all the result of the way Desiree was toilet trained."

"Don't try to bait me into losing my temper, Jennifer," Abby said, intentionally using Avery's first name to defuse some of the FBI agent's tactical hostility. "It won't work. If I hear from Desiree, I promise to convince her to talk to you so that you can resolve whether there is any basis for your suspicions."

"I'd be more inclined to believe you if you'd told me about the second vampire. There was another patient on the ward, a drifter suffering from amnesia, who shared Desiree's delusion that he was a vampire."

"You've been talking to Dr. Govindaiah."

Avery didn't deny it.

"Veena should have told you their stays at the hospital barely overlapped. They had no contact, as far as I know. Believe me,

I've checked. Sorry as I am to say it, I think it's actually more likely that Desiree is involved than Charles Gabriel."

"I'll buy that," Avery said, and snapped the notebook shut. "I'd like to talk to him, too."

"May I offer you a piece of advice?"

"Medical or psychiatric?" Avery asked with a grin. They were back on a friendly basis, or at least the FBI agent meant for it to appear so.

"Both," Abby said. "Get some rest. You're obviously exhausted."

"You think I tried to bully you."

"I doubt it's your normal technique. It is not extremely effective."

"Thanks for the advice and the coffee," Avery said, standing. "You going to bill me?"

"No, but if you ever want to talk about things, give me a call. I'd be happy to sit down with you as a professional courtesy."

She handed Avery her card. The special agent looked at it as if trying to decide whether to hand it back, but she put it into her jacket pocket the way she would any bit of seemingly inconsequential material that might turn out to be evidence.

"Maybe I will," Avery said, "but unless it's business, I would tend to doubt it."

Abby nodded. She doubted it, too.

32

HE STOOD AT the window in Dr. Abigail Bloome's office, watching the bird glide toward him, spreading its wings wide to brake its flight. The creature settled onto the branch of a locust tree and looked brightly about, turning its head with small, precise motions, as delicate and exquisite as an intricate clockwork fashioned to amuse an emperor. It made the vampire think of Keats's nightingale.

Away! Away! for I will fly to thee . . .

Keats's poem was one of Dante's favorites.

But here there is no light,
Save what from heaven is with the breezes blown
Through verdurous glooms and winding mossy ways . . .

"What are you looking at?" Dr. Bloome asked, coming up beside him.

The bird launched itself into the sky as he pointed.

"The blackbird."

"Grackle," she corrected.

"I thought it was a blackbird."

"A grackle is a type of blackbird."

Subtle distinctions were important to Dr. Abigail Bloome. Logic and reason ruled her Apollonian mind. His own soul was ruled by Dionysian passions that made him subject to extremes of emotion, dizzying flights of creative expression and, at times, a reckless surrender to pleasure—a derangement of the senses, Rimbaud called it. Like Keats, Dante Gabriel Rossetti had lived a life of sensations. It was part of what made him an artist, even though it had brought him to grief.

"What is it you dislike about grackles, Dr. Bloome? I thought you treated all things with perfect equanimity."

"I'm afraid I don't know what you mean."

"You are frowning, Doctor. You obviously dislike the humble grackle."

"That's very perceptive, Charles. Last week I put a suet cake in my garden to attract woodpeckers. The grackles devoured it in a day. There was no point in putting out another."

"The world is filled with rapacious creatures," Dante said. He caught himself starting to frown, but Dr. Bloome was too observant to let the transformation pass.

"I apologize for letting my negative associations spoil your mood, Charles."

Ah, the vampire thought, she is not infallible. His sudden darkness of mood had nothing to do with Dr. Bloome's harmless dislike of grackles.

"Shall we start our session?"

"We already have, Charles."

"Is that how therapy works, Dr. Bloome, with talk of grackles and whatever random thoughts leap off the tip of one's tongue?"

"In essence, yes," she replied as they were seated. "We begin with the ordinary, with everyday impressions that sit on the surface of the mind. From there, we patiently work our way downward, mining our way to the significant, the subtle, the secret."

"It is a bit like archeology."

She favored him with one of her easy smiles.

"But perhaps it is not always a good idea to dig too deeply into the past."

"When you were a child, were you ever afraid of the dark? Humor me with an answer."

"Every child is afraid of the dark at one time or the other, Doctor."

"But do you have a specific recollection of being afraid of the dark when you were young?"

The vampire looked up at the ceiling as the memory took shape in his mind's eye.

"I remember there was a wardrobe in my bedroom. It was a big, hulking thing, much larger than I, constructed from heavy, dark wood, with copious scrollwork around the top that struck me as especially sinister, although I cannot explain why. It reminded me of an ornate wooden coffin. I was convinced the wardrobe harbored some monstrous evil. I was certain that it—whatever the formless *it* was—would emerge one night when I was alone in the dark and devour me."

"Did you tell anyone?"

"My mama."

"What did she do?"

"She turned up the lamp and opened the wardrobe so that I might see there was nothing inside that could harm me."

"Was there a demon hiding inside the wardrobe?"

"Of course not. There were only the things one would expect—jackets, trousers, shirts."

"Were you able to sleep in the dark without being afraid after she showed you there was no monster?"

"She had to show me several times before I was fully convinced," he said with a laugh. "But yes, I was no longer afraid."

"I propose we do the same sort of thing. We'll shine a lamp into the dark corners of your past, illuminating the things you have trouble thinking about and episodes you cannot consciously remember. There is nothing there that can harm you; I will help you prove that to yourself. The past has no power over us, Charles, although we sometimes convince ourselves it does."

She opened the notebook on her lap.

"Are you ready to open the first closed door to your past?"

The vampire gave a tentative nod.

Dr. Bloome opened a drawer in the table beside her chair and reached inside. When she brought out her hand, she was lightly holding a single rose. The bud at the end of the long green stem was the color of blood. Dante felt himself recoil as she offered it to him. He did not take it. He did not seem to be able to do anything but stare into the inwardly turning crimson spirals, which seemed to draw him down toward the depths of despair.

"Why do you find this flower so disturbing, Charles?"

A wave of nausea rose up in his stomach. He was going to be sick.

"Say the first word that comes into your head. Don't think, Charles. Just say it."

"Elizabeth."

"Who is Elizabeth?"

He did not want to answer, but she made him, using her force of will to drag the words out of him.

"My wife," he said.

His heart pounded in his ears. Or was it her heart? He closed his eyes against the sound of blood pounding in his head.

"Try to control your breathing, or you will hyperventilate."

He heard the drawer close as she put the rose away. He felt a small, inexplicable degree of relief at that. He heard Dr. Bloome stand and cross the room. Ice clinked in a glass. Water poured. She came back toward him.

"Drink this, Charles. It will make you feel better."

He opened his eyes to accept the glass. His strength seemed to have left him, the tumbler almost too heavy to lift. He was as drained as the poor souls he'd forced himself on, listening as their hearts fluttered to a stop while he sucked out their last few precious drops of blood.

"I'm sorry to shock you like that, Charles. You see how much power the unconscious mind has over us. What do roses and your late wife have in common?"

"They were her favorite flower." His voice sounded distant in his own ears, distant and weak. "Lizzie—Elizabeth—had a passion for roses. I buried her with a bouquet in her arms."

"What happened to her, Charles?"

"She died."

"You told me that before. You haven't told me how Lizzie died."

"I cannot remember."

"You can if you try."

"No," he said sharply. "It is impossible. I cannot remember. Let us speak of other things."

He wanted to stop Dr. Bloome when she reached for the rose a second time, but for some reason he could not make himself move. A terrible paralysis came over the vampire, making it impossible for him to do anything but sit and stare in horror as the psychiatrist held the rose out to him again. She'd pricked her thumb on a thorn, he noticed sickly. A crimson bubble the size of a freshwater pearl glittered against her skin.

"It becomes easier each time, doesn't it, Charles? Remember

the hospital? You fainted when you saw a rose. Now, you're only trembling."

The rose, the blood, the howling Hunger—the three powers warred against one another for possession of Dante.

"You have trouble with roses because they subconsciously represent your late wife. Look at the flower—look at it, please, Charles. You must!"

Though the air was so thickly perfumed with her blood that he started to feel intoxicated, the vampire did as he was told.

"This rose symbolizes Lizzie. This rose *is* Lizzie. Look at it closely. Let it fill your mind. Stop fighting it, Charles. The only way to win some battles is to surrender."

The room began to shift. Dante pushed himself back against his chair, trying to maintain his equilibrium. He felt the blood teeth coming down. He somehow managed to will them back into their cavities in his upper jaw.

"What happened to Lizzie? I want you to remember."

"She was sick."

"Sick from what?"

"She wasn't sick. She was pregnant."

"What happened?"

"She lost the baby. Our daughter was stillborn."

"And?"

He opened his mouth to speak, but that was as far as he could get. The words refused to come.

"What happened to Lizzie after she lost the baby? Were there medical complications? Did Lizzie die in childbirth?"

He shook his head.

"Then what?"

"She killed herself."

"Why?"

His eyes filled. A tear ran down his cheek; it burned like fire.

"That question will haunt me as long as I live. I loved her so very much."

That was as far as he could go. He buried his face in his hands.

"That's remarkably good progress, Charles." Dr. Bloome's hand rested briefly on his shoulder. "We'll stop here for today."

The psychiatrist went to her desk and picked up a file folder, giving him time to compose himself. He was glad she didn't linger with extended expressions of sympathy. That only would have made it worse. She sensed his pain, and his embarrassment at having broken down, and was sensitive enough to leave him alone to put his thoughts in order.

"Will I see you at the same time tomorrow?" Dr. Bloome asked after a bit.

"Of course."

He stood to leave, stuffing his handkerchief back into his jacket.

"You haven't happened to run into Desiree Hohenberg, have you?"

"You asked me that the last time I saw you."

"I was just wondering. I worry when my patients disappear. I'm asking everybody the same question. I apologize if I'm being a pest."

"I have not seen her," the vampire lied. "Is she in some sort of difficulty?"

"She might be."

"Is it serious?"

"It could be. Promise me you'll call immediately if you see Desiree. I don't want to alarm you, but I want you to be careful if she tries to contact you. Desiree might be dangerous to herself as well as others."

"You have my word on it," he said, bowing his head. "I shall be as careful as a vicar's wife."

"What's that supposed to mean?" she asked with a girlish laugh. Abigail Bloome was exceptionally charming when she stepped out from behind her sober physician's persona.

"I do not know," Dante said, returning her smile, "but one would imagine a vicar's wife to be the very soul of cautious deportment."

They were both smiling as the vampire left the office, the lovely Dr. Bloome the subject of his thoughts; progress or no, he could not bear to make himself think about his beloved Lizzie.

33

"EIGHT BALL OKAY with you?"

"Whatever," Dr. Richard Mobius said.

He clamped his jaw shut on the cigar and sat down heavily on a bench that was toenailed into the wall with ten-penny nails and scarred with cigarette burns. The only other customers in Ma's Pool Room were two black men in the far corner who studiously minded their own business. The old woman at the cash register—Ma, Mobius guessed—was watching Ricki Lake on a battered black-and-white portable television. A little daylight managed to filter in through the storefront windows. The bottom half of the windows had been painted green, the tops tinted brown from tobacco smoke. Above the two pool tables, lamps illuminated the green felt tops and brightly colored balls. The air smelled of smoke, talcum powder, sweat, and dust—a strangely powerful aroma.

Mobius had never been interested in games, not even before his wife's death. It was Charlie Miller who insisted they meet in the pool hall.

"You'd never guess a little town like this would have so many freaks," the police chief said, keeping his eyes on the balls as he racked them. "Didn't used to be that way. Times change, I guess."

Chief Miller was a bear of a man, six-four or six-five, with a

211

steel-gray crew cut, big raw fists, and a prominent hawk's beak nose. He must have been the biggest, dumbest kid in elementary school—and, later, a star on the high school football team, Mobius thought.

"I blame newcomers," Miller said, twisting the blue chalk cube around the tip of his cue. "You can't have growth without more people moving to town, but it's brought in an unsavory element. You want the honors?"

"Go ahead."

Miller bent over the table, pressing his belly against the rail. There was a loud crack when the cue ball collided with the other balls, sending them bouncing around the pool table in all directions. Two balls—the one and the five—fell into pockets. Nodding to himself with satisfaction, Miller picked up a Bud tall boy in a paper sack and took a long drink. It was eleven in the morning, too early for Mobius to drink.

"I wanted to tell you something about the Rice kid," Chief Miller said, dropping his voice. "You know, the one we found in the cemetery."

"What about him?"

"We found out he committed suicide. He chopped off his own fucking head."

Miller's face turned a dangerous shade of purple when he laughed. As soon as he recovered from his joke—he didn't seem to notice that Mobius didn't appreciate his sense of humor—he bent over and lined up on the three ball. It was an easy shot. The ball disappeared in the corner pocket. The next shot was trickier, a three-ball combination. Miller made it.

"I was just pulling your leg," the chief said after he missed the next shot.

"Really."

"What I wanted to tell you was it turns out we have two of

these freaks in town. A matched set of vampire wannabes. They were both up at the hospital at the same time. My guess is they met up there. One of them is a local girl named Desiree Hohenberg. Really fucked up. Been in all kinds of trouble."

"Has she ever been to Europe or on any kind of ship or fishing vessel?"

"Shit, no. I don't think Desiree's ever been out of town. I talked to her mama myself." Miller dropped his voice again. "The fucking FBI are looking for her. They think this all might have something to do with a serial murderer."

"Then maybe they aren't completely incompetent. What about the other one?"

"He's some guy with amnesia. He is supposed to be English, but he could just be a good actor. He went into the hospital as a John Doe but later decided his name was Charles Gabriel. Nobody's had any luck tracking him down using that name. My guess is the name is bullshit."

"How did they get out of the hospital?"

"Desiree was discharged. Charles Gabriel signed himself out."

"You can do that?"

"You ought to know that, *Doctor* Mobius."

"My doctorate is in English literature."

The police chief snorted. "Well, professor, I'd still think you'd know it's practically impossible to put somebody away just because they're crazy these days. We wouldn't want to violate anybody's civil rights, you understand."

"Are Desiree Hohenberg and Charles Gabriel together?"

"They could be, though their shrink—they both have the same psychiatrist—doesn't think they are. I'd be willing to bet that whoever killed those people, whether it's Desiree or some

Charles Manson drifter, is long gone. Chances are we'll get Desiree sometime soon. We're working up an arrest warrant on her. She was the last person seen with Danny Rice. We find her, we might find him." The police chief nodded at the table. "It's your shot, professor."

Mobius tried to put the eleven ball into the side pocket. The ball hit the corner of the pocket and caromed off at an angle.

"Nice try," Miller said.

"The Englishman, Charles Gabriel, is the one I'm interested in. What more can you tell me about him?"

"Not a hell of a lot except that, like I said, he and Desiree are both patients of Dr. Abigail Bloome. A Jew." The chief glanced at Mobius out of the corner of his eyes, scouting for signs of Semitic features. "You ain't Jewish, are you? No offense, if you are."

"What has Dr. Bloome had to say about the Englishman?"

"She refused to discuss her patients with the FBI. I'm kind of surprised on that one. She's a pretty little thing, that FBI agent. I expected her and the shrink to hit it off. We did get some scraps of information from somebody else in her office, a foreigner from Hindustan or some damned place who isn't Dr. Bloome's best friend."

"Maybe Dr. Bloome will talk to me. My inquiries are completely unofficial."

"I doubt it, professor. Butter wouldn't melt in that one's mouth. And you won't be able to buy information from her. I hear her parents left her with a fat trust fund. Harold, my banker, says she's worth a cool five million. I wouldn't waste your time."

"She must keep files on her patients."

"Get in there, you little pecker," Miller ordered, but the ball refused to obey him, jumping back out of the pocket. "Your shot."

Mobius lined up again on the eleven ball. "All doctors keep files," he said, talking to himself.

"You wouldn't be thinking about doing what I think you're thinking about doing, would you, professor? Because that would be illegal."

"I'd think of it as 'extra-legal' activity. Don't forget I'm chasing the son of a bitch who killed my wife."

"You're going to have to donate another C-note to my campaign fund if you're going to keep talking like that," Miller said lowly.

"I'll go you one better, Chief. Put me in touch with someone who can help me steal Charles Gabriel's psychiatric file from Dr. Bloome's office and I'll make it an even grand."

Miller gave Mobius a hard look. Mobius knew Miller didn't like Yankees.

"I *might* know somebody, professor," he drawled.

"Stop calling me 'professor,' " Mobius said.

Mobius made the shot, drilling the eleven ball into the back of the pocket.

34

✧

ABBY SWEPT PAST him when he opened the door, giving him no opportunity to refuse her entry.

"I hope you'll excuse my dropping by without an invitation," she said.

She felt his eyes burn into her back, but he did not answer. The interior of number 13 Garden Terrace was a continuation of the exterior's pillared Old South grandeur. There was room beneath the vaulted ceiling of the foyer for a formal receiving line with servants to help guests out of their cloaks—room enough even for dancing. Abby imagined women in hoop skirts and their beaus, waltzing across the terrazzo floor.

The door shut. Abby turned around to discover Charles standing almost on top of her. He meant to keep his face blank, but she could see the emotion in his dark eyes.

"I decided after our session that it was time for me to get to know a little more about you."

"As you wish," he said.

Charles turned to lead the way, keeping ahead with his long strides. He cast a nervous glance up the darkened staircase, no doubt aware that she was noting the absence of furnishings. Abby sensed his anxiety at her penetrating his sanctum. A gentleman like Charles Gabriel would be sensitive about perceived inadequacies in his hospitality. At least Desiree was not in the house. Establishing that one thing was worth the risk of alienating her patient by turning up unannounced. Abby glanced into the immense dining room as they passed, empty but for the built-in china cabinets and the fireplace on the far wall. The house was like its new owner, she thought: an imposing facade that was oddly empty inside.

"I intend to buy furniture, when I find the time," Charles said without looking back at her, almost as if he'd been reading her mind.

"Maybe you don't intend to stay."

He didn't have anything to say to that, but waited at a doorway for her to enter first. Charles Gabriel apparently lived exclusively in the one sitting room, she noted, looking around.

"You must think me foolish to have so much space when my needs are so simple."

Abby turned and looked up into his face. He was awaiting her judgment.

"It is a beautiful house, Charles. I can understand why you decided to move in."

She sat without waiting to be invited in one of the straight-backed chairs at the formal dining room table piled high with books and marvelous sketches. Even the quick studies were good enough to frame, she thought. Abby picked up a book and turned it over to read its title. *The Physics of Immortality.* His taste did not run toward light reading.

"You seem to be fast on the way to acquiring your own private library."

"There is so much that I have missed."

"Missed? Do you mean lost due to your amnesia?"

"There is much about me you do not understand."

"I want to understand," she said.

"Do you really?"

He looked at her a little sharply, as if trying to decide whether her compassion was genuine or part of a synthetic professional manner that she put on and took off like a lab jacket.

"I would never lie to you, Charles."

He looked away from her, as if her words stung him in some way she could not imagine.

"How old do you think I am, Dr. Bloome?"

"Thirty-five."

He smiled and shook his head, his long, curly hair brushing the shoulders of his velvet smoking jacket. "Older."

"Forty?" she guessed.

"I was born May twelfth, 1828."

Abby took in a slow breath to counteract her sinking feeling. Charles Gabriel's delusions were more deeply rooted than she had suspected. "To what do you attribute your eternal youth? Does it have anything to do with *The Physics of Immortality*?"

The frown Charles gave her showed that he understood she was trying to indulge him, but he did not respond with the anger she expected.

"I think not," he said. "I recommend the book to you. I found it most interesting. The author postulates an 'Omega Point,' which represents the future 'completion of finite existence.' The nature of my problem, Dr. Bloome, is that I do not possess a finite existence. I cannot die. Not even eighty years of imprisonment in the sunken wreck of the *Titanic* at the bottom of the Atlantic could end my wretched life. My amnesia and all the rest of it are but complications of the prime aspect of my damnation: My body does not know how to die."

"Do you consider yourself to be a supernatural being, like an angel?"

"Who is to say what is natural and what is supernatural? I only know that science has yet to explain me. Perhaps Stephen Hawking could define me with an equation from quantum mechanics. Or maybe it is much simpler. Perhaps the old explanation is best, and in the end I simply am what I am—a vampire. I see from your expression that this line of conversation is not pleasing to you, Dr. Bloome."

"I had hoped we were beyond that. Forgive my bluntness, but I have never believed there is anything to gain from indulging in patients' fantasies."

"You do not believe in vampires, Dr. Bloome?"

"Not in the sense you mean. Are there people who mistakenly believe they are vampires? Yes, of course. The literature contains a few documented cases of people who felt compelled to drink blood. There is a medical condition that makes people extremely sensitive to light. But vampires who drink blood to sustain an immortal existence are only myths. I do not believe in that sort of vampire."

"What if I prove otherwise, Dr. Bloome?"

"How? By turning into a bat?"

Charles's face darkened. "Of course not. That is physiologically impossible. Bats, crosses, sleeping in coffins—all superstitious Carpathian nonsense."

"I can't allow you to bite me in the neck, if that's what you have in mind."

"There are other ways to demonstrate *Vampiri* power. What if I read your thoughts?"

"It wouldn't convince me you are a vampire, but I'd be impressed," she said with a smile.

His smoldering eyes suddenly seemed to bore into Abby. She felt a strange pressure against her forehead.

"You came here tonight deeply conflicted, Dr. Bloome. You feel trapped between your loyalty to your patients and wanting to prevent possible future murders."

"Not bad," Abby allowed.

"You wonder whether you have a duty to tell an FBI agent where I live. Fortunately, she has not explicitly asked you for information about me, only Desiree."

Abby realized she was staring at Charles Gabriel with her mouth hanging open.

"The special agent's name is Jennifer Avery."

"How do you know that?"

"My *Vampiri* powers. I can read minds, when I want to. Frankly, I find it an ungentlemanly intrusion. I use the power only when I need to."

"Then tell me exactly what I am thinking this exact moment."

Abby felt a slight tingling.

"Let me assure you, Dr. Bloome, whatever else I am, I am not a schizophrenic. I hope it does not offend you that I am flattered you think of me as attractive and intelligent."

"I don't know what to say," Abby responded, for once at a loss for words.

"You still do not believe."

She smiled sheepishly and shook her head.

"I can read a book in less than ten minutes."

"And understand what you've read?"

"Absolutely. The curious thing is that, despite my unreliable long-term memory, I can remember every word of every book I have read since my awakening. Care to test me?"

Abby picked up a book from the table. "What is on page 245?"

"Do you want me to recount the entire page or a specific passage?"

"A sentence or two will do."

"Be careful not to read the passage. I have already proven to you that I can read thoughts. Do not taint the current demonstration."

"I'd already thought of that." She picked a place on the page with her finger. "Start with the second sentence from the end of the paragraph that starts the page."

He closed his eyes and began to quote.

" 'It was useful to remember none of it mattered—not the disagreement, not the frustration, not the disappointment of things going wrong. When things go wrong, sometimes they go wrong completely, not in small ways, not in large ways, but in all ways.' "

"You didn't miss a single word."

"See the glass?"

Charles indicated an empty wineglass at the end of the table. He was enjoying himself now—meaning he was enjoying Abby's reaction. He had managed to amaze and charm her in spite of herself. While she remained firmly convinced that Charles Gabriel was an accomplished magician in addition to his other talents, she found it impossible to maintain her clinically neutral attitude.

"Would you like me to move it to the left or right?"

"Right."

As if pushed by an invisible hand, the glass moved four inches to the right, stopped, then moved back to its original spot.

"Incredible."

"Not for a vampire," he said.

"Jung believed that the human mind has latent powers of

psychokinesis and extrasensory perception. There is a famous story where—"

"I am well acquainted with Carl Jung's ideas. I made it a special point to read him after learning how much you admire him. Undeveloped, unsuspected powers may well exist within every ordinary mortal. I cannot say. All I know is that my transformation from human to vampire gave me the ability to do all of this and more."

Abby looked at Charles Gabriel, no longer sure what to make of him. For the first time she was just a little afraid.

"Jung's ideas about the Shadow are especially interesting to me, Dr. Bloome. Our dark side, our Shadow, is the equivalent of the Devil. It does not seem like an abstract philosophical construct to me. I sometimes feel as if I have *become* the Shadow. I awakened after my long sleep at the bottom of the sea to discover the Hunger had transformed me into the embodiment of my own darkness. I have become my own Shadow, my own Satan."

"Charles, please," she interrupted. "You're running very fast over very difficult ground. Jung's concepts are too complicated to absorb through casual reading."

"I believe my Shadow is what attracted you to me," he went on. "You sensed it in me from the first—the brooding, dangerous aspect of my persona. I have read enough Jung and Freud to understand how transference is supposed to work. You sense in a member of the opposite sex the qualities missing in your own psychological makeup. What missing pieces of your soul do I complement, Dr. Bloome? Is it my darkness? Or is it my passion and creativity? Do my paintings and poems represent the generative forces of your womb that you have refused to heed?"

"Charles," she said, with what was supposed to be a dismissive laugh but came off sounding like nervous laughter. He'd touched a chord deep within her. "You don't know me well enough to have those kinds of insights."

"In some ways I understand you better than you understand yourself, Abigail."

He had called her by her first name. It was amazing how such a simple thing could put him so easily inside her defenses, the professional distance between them breached by a single act of familiarity. The meeting had become intimate in a way Abby wished to avoid. There was an exquisite tension between them, a sense of anticipation in the air as volatile as gasoline vapor.

"Your beautiful mind has enslaved your equally beautiful body. There is no balance. You have turned yourself into a one-dimensional being. You are Logos devoid of Eros. You must not deny your passion any longer, Abigail. You feel it as strongly as I."

"We can't become involved, Charles. Not even if we both wanted to become involved."

His eyes fell to her lips, then her neck. Abby felt herself stiffen, her heart pounding in her ears so loudly that it was almost as if she was hearing *his* pulse, too. She hated herself for becoming aroused, for the secret pleasure she took in his lusty stare. She also hated herself for being afraid. There was a strange hunger in Charles's eyes. She could no longer be certain he wouldn't hurt her. She had been incredibly arrogant to assume she could maintain control over a patient who, in the end, could turn out to be severely disturbed and capable of savage violence.

Charles stood in front of her chair and pulled her gently upward, pressing his lips to hers.

Abby melted into his arms. It was a natural reaction, she told herself, relief to discover that he meant her no harm. For a delicious forbidden moment, she kissed him back with equal passion.

35

✧

"**I**S THIS DRESS on sale?"

"No, ma'am. Only the dresses on the sale rack."

Mrs. McKay made a face. "The ad in the morning newspaper said the sundresses were on sale."

"The sundresses on the sale rack are on sale. The dress you have is from everyday casuals."

"Is this dress going to be on sale anytime soon?"

"Sorry, but they don't let clerks have advance information about sales."

"*They?* And who might *they* be?"

"Management, ma'am."

"That's a stupid policy. You would be much more helpful to your customers if you could inform them about upcoming sales."

"Yes, ma'am."

"I shall write a letter to the store manager and demand a change in policy."

"That would be a good idea, ma'am."

"Are you being cheeky with me, young lady?"

"No, ma'am," the clerk said, her smile intensifying.

"What are those braid things in your hair?"

"They're called corn rows, ma'am."

"Are they." Mrs. McKay smirked.

Ormolu Jackson's eyes flashed, but she kept her mouth shut. She needed to keep her job at Rubin's Department Store for one more semester. After that, she was transferring to Howard University in Washington, D.C.

"Can I box that dress for you?" Ormolu asked sweetly. "It's a lovely print."

"Indeed not. You're absolutely certain it's not on sale?"

"I'm certain. I'll hang it back up for you."

"Not so fast." Mrs. McKay snatched the dress away from the clerk. "I want to try it on."

Mrs. McKay stomped off toward the dressing room. She had no intention of buying the dress. Yellow was *not* her color. She was an Autumn. Maybe if they had the dress in orange, but of course they didn't, the idiots. A Summer could get away with wearing a yellow dress, but never an Autumn. Why, she'd look like a big daisy!

The fitting rooms in Rubin's were all the way in the back of the ladies' department. There were eight small rooms, each with two louvered doors you could latch together from the inside. One of the things Mrs. McKay liked about Rubin's was that you could lock the doors so the clerks couldn't barge in on you while you were in your underthings.

She hung her massive black purse on the metal coat hook on the wall. The walls dividing the fitting rooms only extended down to knee height, and Mrs. McKay was always afraid someone was going to reach under and snatch her purse while she was trying on clothes. She slipped off her shoes and unbuttoned her blouse, draping it carefully over the rattan chair. Getting out of her skirt required considerable wiggling. She'd always been a full-figured woman.

"You doin' all right in there, ma'am?"

"Of course I'm 'doin' all right.' If I require assistance, I shall ask."

"You old bitch."

"I heard that!" Mrs. McKay cried in her most imperious voice.

Hands grabbed her plump ankles. Mrs. McKay was too startled to do anything but look down. The hands were milky white, with bloodred fingernails.

"Help!" Mrs. McKay cried in a strangled little voice.

"Shut the fuck up, you cow," the voice on the other side of the door said.

Mrs. McKay waved her arms above her head and tried to pull her legs free, but she had never been strong. Her assailant gave her ankles a sharp tug. Mrs. McKay felt a sickening floating sensation in the pit of her stomach, like the time years earlier when the late Mr. McKay had talked her into riding on the double Ferris wheel against her better judgment. She grabbed blindly at her purse as she fell, breaking the leather strap an instant before her head crashed into the rattan chair.

Mrs. McKay was unconscious for some minutes. When she opened her eyes, she saw another woman—Mrs. Barrows, whom she knew from church—lying on the floor, staring blankly at her. Mrs. McKay tried to say something, but she couldn't speak. There was a fat strip of duct tape across her mouth.

Mrs. McKay's mind was too foggy at first to understand what was happening. Something was wrong with Mrs. Barrows's eyes: they were slightly crossed and seemed to focus on two different things. The pool of blood streaming out of the gash in Mrs. Barrows's throat—she saw *that* now—touched Mrs. McKay's hands, which were bound with the heavy silver tape. Mrs. McKay frantically tried to turn away, but her back was against the dressing room wall; there was nowhere to escape the warm, sticky liquid.

"Look at piggy squirm!"

Standing over Mrs. McKay were a colored girl—not the clerk, but someone much prettier with straight black hair—and that awful girl she had seen around town. She had heard stories about that one. Her name was Deedee or maybe Deidre. People said she was a witch. She certainly looked like one, dressed all in black.

The colored girl reached down to poor Mrs. Barrows, wetting her hand with blood from the neck wound. She lifted her hand to her mouth and, smiling at Mrs. McKay, began to lick the blood from it.

"Oh, my God, look at her wiggle!" the witch girl cried with delight. "Stop it, fatty! Stop it!"

The white girl began to kick Mrs. McKay with her heavy boots. Her ribs! The pain was so terrible she thought she was going to pass out again. Tears squeezed from her closed eyes. Mrs. McKay heard a sharp crunching—her ribs breaking. If her mouth hadn't been taped, she would have screamed so loudly that they would have heard her all the way at the seashore.

"I get to do this one," the colored girl said. "It'll be easier when we don't have to use these anymore," she said as the witch girl handed her a box cutter.

The colored girl held the razor a few inches in front of Mrs. McKay's face, turning it this way and that, making it sparkle in the fluorescent ceiling lights. Mrs. McKay's eyes pleaded with her not to do it. This couldn't be happening, she thought frantically. It had to be a joke, a prank to pay her back for abusing the clerks at Rubin's. She would tell them how sorry she was, if they'd just take the tape off her mouth!

"Give me the razor if you don't have the nerve to do it."

"Don't rush me, Desiree. I want to enjoy this."

That was the witch girl's name—Desiree.

The colored girl bent down and grabbed a handful of Mrs. McKay's blue-gray hair, jerking her head to the side. The pain was nothing compared to her ribs. Each breath was like a stab from a burning knife. Mrs. McKay's mouth was filling with blood. She was broken up and bleeding from the inside. She couldn't spit because of the duct tape on her lips. She told herself to be careful not to cough or she'd choke.

"Watch and I'll show you the ritual way to bleed out a goat," the colored girl said.

Mrs. McKay's high, muffled scream had a curiously porcine quality. And then, abruptly, the sound stopped.

Ormolu Jackson looked up from her work, listening for something half heard. She'd already dismissed Mrs. McKay from her thoughts. The impossible woman was famous among the clerks. She came into the store regularly to try on clothes and harass the employees but seldom bought anything.

Ormolu returned her attention to the paperwork she did every night when she closed her register. It was after nine and she was anxious to get home. She had an important test in the morning and wanted to study.

36

✧

"YOU SHOULDN'T HAVE kissed me."

The self-possession came back into Abigail's cool green eyes by degrees. He relaxed and let her slip away from him, watching her walk to the window and look out over the garden. The crescent moon was between the trees, a horned moon not yet at the first quarter.

"You cannot deny what is in the heart."

"We have to do what we know is right," she said, hugging herself.

"I used to think that I wanted to be good, Abigail. I am no longer sure it is worth the price."

He went to his easel. He kept it in the corner near the windows, where the light was best in the afternoons. He pulled back the covering sheet. The painting drew Abigail to him, as he knew it would.

"My portrait," she said. Then she saw his image, watching her from the balcony in the painting. "And yours."

"I took the liberty of using you as the model for Proserpine."

"The Queen of the Dead," Abigail said. "I see the pomegranate in her—in my— hand."

"It started as Eve with an apple, but it turned into Proserpine and a pomegranate."

"If I am Proserpine, then you are Pluto?"

The vampire nodded. "I once wrote a poem about Proserpine. Would you like to hear it?"

"Very much."

> "Afar from mine own self I seem, and wing
> Strange ways in thought, and listen for a sign:
> And still some heart unto some soul doth pine,
> (Whose sounds mine inner sense is fain to bring,
> Continually together murmuring,)—
> 'Woe's me for thee, unhappy Proserpine!'

"Would you like to know the truth about me—the complete truth?"

"It's the key to everything."

"Then we must have port. This is a story that cannot be told without drinking a libation to the dead."

He poured two glasses, then led the way outside into the garden. They sat on a stone bench overlooking a bed of tea roses.

"My wife was a beautiful woman," he began, "but she never was very happy. I cannot explain why. Some people seem to be melancholy by nature. However, I must confess that much of her unhappiness was my fault. I was not a very good husband. I had enjoyed many mistresses before we married, and I found this a difficult pleasure to give up after we were wed. Artists are a self-indulgent lot. I think it is because we create our own world through our art. We think that our powers of imagination give us license to create our own rules for living, allowing us to seek our pleasures where and when we choose. I make no excuses for the things I did. I did them, they were wrong, and there is little else that needs to be said about my transgressions.

"Despite my dalliances, I was always devoted to Lizzie. I loved her dearly, and my libertine existence did not alter the fact that she was the queen of my heart. We were overjoyed when we learned she was going to have a child. I suppose she thought having a child would lead me to settle down. As for me, I prayed that a child would give Lizzie the happiness that had always been missing from her life.

"Although Lizzie was frail both in body and nerve, the doctors did not believe there was any reason for concern. I made certain she was well cared for during her pregnancy. I insisted that she lead a quiet life—no parties, no travel, servants to perform even the least demanding of tasks in our household. As for me, I found the discipline to tame my wild Bohemian ways while awaiting our baby's birth."

He broke off and stared for a moment across the darkened garden.

"What might have been? Those are four of the bitterest words in the English language: *what might have been*. And who but God can know? We might have raised a big, laughter-filled family and lived satisfied lives, leaving children and grandchildren to mourn us when we died. But our child, our daughter, was born dead.

"Lizzie sank into the deepest of melancholies after that sad event. I should have redoubled my devotion to her well-being, but I was too consumed by my own grief to recognize my duty. I immersed myself in art, pouring my pain into my paintings and poetry. Lizzie had no such escapes from her black moods. The emotional poison backed up in her heart until it was full to bursting. Her needs were much greater than mine, but I was too blind—too willfully blind—to notice the depth of her despair, and to act to remedy it.

"One night, while I was out reveling, drowning my sorrow in

wine and the laughter of pretty young things, Lizzie poisoned herself with opium. I buried her with a bouquet of her favorite roses in her arms, flowers identical to the ones we had put on our poor baby's grave. In her hands was a notebook filled with my unpublished poetry. My heart died with Elizabeth, and this was the most precious, intimate gift I could give her in death.

"Life is meaningless, even insane. It was only after my beloved died that my career began to blossom, fed by my tears. With my poor, dead wife serving as my muse, I made paintings that sold for ever-increasing amounts of money. Eight years after Lizzie's death, I published *The House of Life*, a book of poetry. It was a success. Nothing I did, it seemed, could fail. My publisher wanted to go to press immediately with a collection of my unpublished work. It was only when I set about gathering my early work that I realized, to my horror, that the only complete collection was buried in Highgate Cemetery in my wife's hands.

"My agent and I had been arguing about what to do over a bottle of absinthe. I was blind drunk when I signed the paper to open Lizzie's grave and retrieve my poems. With that act of self-serving evil, I signed away my soul. The mantel clock began to chime as I scratched my name on the foul document. It was exactly midnight.

"Howell, my agent, looked after the details, including making sure the newspapers knew what we were going to do. He knew it would cause a scandal that would, in turn, ensure brisk sales. I had arranged to be traveling in Scotland during the exhumation, but I disembarked from the train as it started to pull out of Victoria Station. The chance to see my beloved Lizzie one more time, even in death, was more than my heart could resist.

"The exhumation was performed under cover of darkness, as

they always were in those days. The gravediggers built a bonfire to work by. Howell and my publisher were there, hovering in the flickering lights like a pair of devils at the gates of Hell. The ink-stained wretches of the press were there, too. As for me, I waited in the shadows while they got at the coffin.

"Howell arranged for the newspapers to report that Lizzie's body was 'perfectly preserved' and that her glorious hair had grown in death until the book was so intertwined that it had to be cut loose from the tresses. It was a pack of abominable lies. It is impossible for me to think of my beautiful wife without seeing the decayed thing she had become after so many years in the ground.

"I could no longer sleep at night after that. Whenever I closed my eyes, I saw Lizzie as she was in the cemetery the night we disturbed her rest. And when I did manage to fall into an exhausted slumber, I was haunted by unspeakable nightmares. I would wake up screaming, the bedclothes drenched with my sweat. I learned to drink myself to sleep, but as my body grew accustomed to my constant inebriation, I was forced to resort to narcotics. I was killing myself, the same as my poor Lizzie had done, except I lacked the courage to finish the job. If I had, it would have saved me from becoming the monster I am."

He paused a moment, collecting his thoughts, then continued.

"It was a coincidence, one of those odd twists of fate, that led to the transformation responsible for my being here tonight. My mother's maiden name was Polidori. The name may be familiar. My uncle, John William Polidori, a physician, was a friend and traveling companion of Lord Byron's. He was with Byron, Shelley, and his wife, Mary, during that famous summer when they shared a villa and each wrote a ghost story to pass the time."

Abigail frowned but did not ask him to stop, now that his story had crossed over into a territory she did not believe existed.

"Uncle John attended what was the best medical school in the world, the University of Edinburgh, where he was the youngest man ever to take a degree. He was fortunate to have been so precocious, for he did not live a long life, like so many people of his time. The Polidori family had always been involved in literature, and Uncle John did not entirely turn his back on this familial interest after becoming a doctor. In 1819 he published a story that is famous in a small way. *The Vampyre* was the first vampire tale ever published in English. It was the story he started that summer with Byron and the others. Mary Shelley's *Frankenstein* is much more famous, and deservedly so.

"I do not know whether Uncle John had any direct knowledge of the *Vampiri*. My guess would be that he did not, judging from his fanciful creation. Byron, however, knew everything about the race, although not when he was my uncle's friend."

Dante took a sip of port to wet his lips.

"I should not tell you any of this, Abigail, but I have broken so many of my race's taboos that it hardly matters. We—the *Vampiri*—are above all else creatures of culture. Through the ages the *Vampiri* have collected art and artists alike. Keats, for example. He was exactly the kind of person the *Vampiri* like to help, rescuing them from premature death so that their talents might enrich all beings, mortal and immortal alike. But Keats was already dead by the time the *Vampiri* found him in Rome. They were more fortunate with his friend Shelley, who was dying from typhus. They transformed him, saving him. Shelley did not drown in the Bay of Spezia in 1822. That fiction was contrived to cover his withdrawal from mortal society.

"Shelley preserved his friend Byron's talents so that he might complete his cantos. Byron was dying of a fever contracted while helping the Greeks fight for independence against the Turks. It was not a coincidence that the great luminaries of the English Romantic movement died in almost consecutive years in 1821, 1822, and 1824. Except for Keats, they did not die.

"When Byron happened upon me in 1869, a hopeless drug addict on the verge of death, his friendship with my late uncle John caused him to take an interest. Besides, I appealed to his Romantic sensibilities. Byron had read about my obsession with my dead wife; my paintings of her in the guise of Beatrice, the poet Dante's dead beloved; and the poetry I had dedicated to her.

"Byron convinced me to accompany him to Egypt. There, amid the discomforting ruins of the pharaohs' necropolises, he finally persuaded me to join his race. I never would have agreed had it meant hurting people, but that is not the way it has to be for us. A vampire needs but a little blood to keep the Hunger away, though it is not easy to resist the powerful temptation to take more than we require.

"Byron and I traveled to Turkey, thence eastward to India and what is now Thailand, roaming wherever fate led us. The adventures we had, the things we saw—I could fill volumes with the stories of our travels. But that is not why I agreed to join the *Vampiri*. I did not change for adventure or to become immortal. I underwent the transformation because I thought it might make me whole again. I thought the vampire's supernatural strength would enable me to defeat the pain that was slowly poisoning me. Unfortunately, I was sadly mistaken. There was no antidote for the sin of opening Lizzie's grave.

"I parted company with Byron in November of 1910 at the border between the kingdoms of Nepal and Tibet. Byron had heard a rumor about an enclave of ancient vampires living in a monastery on a remote Himalayan plateau, enlightened beings reputed to be the guardians of our race's secrets. I was too miserable by then to care. I had fallen into a state of squalid spiritual wretchedness and wanted only to be alone in my suffering.

"I wandered back to Europe. I spent time in Vienna, attending the opera, finally ending up back in London. There, I hoped to find peace in my old haunts, but that, too, was a mistake. Everyone I knew was dead—my family, my friends, all of them.

"And now you understand, Abigail. I was cast out of human society when I became a vampire. And now my actions have made me an outcast from the *Vampiri*. The members of my race abhor killing, because it is wrong, because it draws attention to our secret race. I am a criminal in two worlds, a monster in two mostly separate realities. Nothing can redeem me, not even loving you, dear Abigail."

She had not taken a drink of the port in her hand, but now she lifted the glass to her lips and took a swallow.

"That's quite a story," she said, speaking slowly. "It is somewhat familiar. I've read about Dante Gabriel Rossetti. I know the story of Elizabeth Rossetti's grave being opened."

"Then you know me. I am sorry I lied to you about my name. I was born Gabriel Charles Dante Rossetti. I have always felt a kinship to Dante, the great Renaissance poet, so when I began to paint I dropped the 'Charles' and inverted 'Dante' and 'Gabriel,' rechristening myself Dante Gabriel Rossetti. There was no point in using my real name at the hospital. So I took parts of my given name, inverted them, and posed as 'Charles Gabriel.' "

He looked at the expression in her green eyes. He was disappointed, but not surprised.

"You do not believe me," he said. "You don't believe I am Dante Gabriel Rossetti."

Her eyes were shimmering, but she shook her head. "No, Charles. I couldn't possibly believe that."

There was a commotion at the door as the girls came out to

the garden to join them. Dante had heard them sneaking into the house, whispering to one another about Dr. Bloome's automobile in the driveway. He could have stopped them easily enough before now, keeping this moment private, but he had to make Abigail understand, even if it meant shocking her the way she had shocked him by forcing him to look at a rose.

"Oh, fun!" Desiree cried. "Do we get to play, too?"

The color left Abigail's face as she saw that the girls were smeared with blood. Dante was furious with them, of course, but he would deal with them later.

"At last you begin to understand, Abigail," he said.

"This fantasy has gone too far."

"You miss the point completely," he said. "This is *not* a fantasy."

"This is my fault," Abigail said, clasping her hands together. "I should have seen where this was heading."

"What more proof do you require to believe that I am what I am? Must you see the footprints of my cloven hooves in the dust to understand the evil I have become?"

"You're not evil, Charles. You're sick."

"I am *evil*!" the vampire roared. "I told you the truth so that you could help me come to terms with the guilt eating my heart alive like an infection of maggots. So tell me, Dr. Abigail Bloome," he said, grabbing her roughly by the arm, "what is the cure when the disease is evil?"

His blood teeth dropped down from their recesses in his upper jaw and snapped into place as he opened his mouth and drew back his lips. Still the maddening disbelief remained in her green eyes. The rationality that opened her mind to so many things kept it tightly locked to this.

"You leave me no choice," Dante Gabriel Rossetti said,

pulling her close and sinking his teeth deep into Dr. Abigail Bloome's throat.

"Save some for us!" Desiree cried.

37

✧

"CAN I HELP you, my brother?" the man called from the altar.

"I'm not sure," Mobius answered. The desk clerk at the Holiday Inn seemed to have written down the wrong street address on the yellow "While U Were Out . . ." message form. Sending him to the African Methodist Church was almost funny, except that he was wasting precious time.

The church's white plaster walls were unadorned, the windows the kind of pebbled glass they used in rest rooms. The only stained glass was in the arched window behind the sanctuary, a raised area at the far end of the room resembling the stage in a school gymnasium. The altar was a rectangle covered in white cloth upon which sat a simple gold cross, with arrangements of flowers on either side. To the left were risers for the choir. On the opposite side was a collection of music gear—a Hammond B3 organ, a set of Rogers drums, and an Ampeg amplifier with a Fender Precision bass leaning against it, as if the bass player had just stepped outside for a smoke.

The man on the altar had a goatee, like the one Mobius had grown, but he was shorter and skinny. He wore what Mobius took to be a Malcolm X getup: a black suit with narrow lapels, a white shirt, and a bow tie. His retro green-tinted glasses evoked

240

the sixties. There was a gold pin in his lapel with a one-carat solitaire diamond. The church must have been having a good year, Mobius thought.

"I'm looking for Willie Williams."

"The Reverend Willie T. Williams, at your service. You must be the Mr. Jones our mutual friend was telling me about."

Mobius nodded.

"I was just cleaning up after the Wednesday night service. The altar guild usually takes care of these chores, but I sent the ladies on home so that we could talk without being disturbed. Take a load off, brother."

They sat next to one another in the front pew. Reverend Williams took out a gold cigarette case and offered Mobius an English Oval cigarette. Mobius declined. The preacher took out a cigarette, tapped it twice on the back of the case, and hung it on his lower lip.

"Mr. Charlie tells me you are on a personal crusade, Mr. Jones," Williams said, holding a gold Dunhill lighter to the cigarette. "He said you have dedicated your life to finding the man who killed your wife."

"Charlie Miller talks a lot."

The preacher leaned back and laughed, blowing smoke toward the slow-turning ceiling fan.

"Mr. Charlie and I help each other from time to time, a little Christian friendliness between the white policeman and the black preacher. It's a Br'er Fox and Br'er Rabbit game, except neither one of us is exactly sure who the fox and who the rabbit."

"And Miller asked you for help with this?" Mobius asked, dubious.

"There ain't nothin' about this town the Reverend Willie T. don't know. If you want something, I know where it is and how to get it, and that includes medical records."

Mobius looked at Williams with new respect.

"I was born and bred in Calhoun, Mr. Jones, but my mama moved us North when I was a child. It's easy for a young man to go astray in the city in these troubled times. I went astray plenty. Once I got out of Attica, I decided to come down home and do something respectable, give something back to the community. And, of course, make a place for myself in the world."

The preacher leaned back, resting his elbows on the back of the pew, and looked around the church.

"Done all right for myself, too. I got this church. I got the Jubal Funeral Home." He picked up a paper fan from the pew and held it so Mobius could see. There was a Bible verse on one side and an advertisement for the funeral home opposite it. "Brother Jubal still runs the place. You might say I am his silent partner."

"Reverend Williams—"

"Call me Willie T., Mr. Jones. Everybody does. So you're here on a crusade. An eye for an eye, a tooth for a tooth. Old Testament justice. I like that. None of this rehabilitation bullshit," the preacher said. "Prison don't rehabilitate nobody, Mr. Jones, take it from me. Jail just teaches you to be a better criminal. It's like college."

"Time is of the essence, Reverend. You have the files?"

"It was a piece of cake," the preacher said, talking with the cigarette dangling from his mouth. "The girl that cleans the office comes in every night at nine. She's a good worker, but she comes in the back door and leaves it unlocked. I cased the place out on Monday to make sure I knew where Dr. Bloome's office was. Last night I waited until the girl got Bloome's office cleaned and went on to the next one. The door to Dr. Bloome's was locked, but I slipped the latch with a credit card. It wasn't a serious lock, you know. I don't think they keep drugs or anything like that at the place, so I guess they don't need no serious locks. The filing cabinet was a little trickier. There's a little el-shaped latch inside the cabinet that the lock turns to hold the cabinet closed. I brought a little strip of metal narrow enough to slip into the crack where the drawer opens and pushed up the latch. It's not hard, if you know what you are doing. That's one of the things I learned at Attica. Yes, sir, I graduated from the University of Attica with honors."

The preacher reached into his jacket and took out two rolls of 35mm film for Mobius to see, but he didn't offer them to him.

"You got the scratch, Mr. Jones?"

"What's on the film?"

"Everything in the files you told Mr. Charlie you wanted."

"Excellent!" Mobius said.

He would have no further need for Medgar Ronson's services now. The former policeman would be more of a hindrance than a help in the end game. Even if Mobius wanted to play by the book—which he didn't—he knew the police would be no match for the vampire.

"Why didn't you just steal the files?"

"Shit, Mr. Jones, then they'd know they was ripped off. You got to be slicker than that if you want to be a criminal. If some-body don't know something was stolen, they don't waste time trying to figure out who stole it. I would've made you photo-copies, but the machine was out in the hall and I didn't want to wait around for the cleaning gal to finish up and leave."

"You're not at all what you seem to be," Mobius said, taking out his wallet.

"We all sinners, Mr. Jones," Williams said, keeping his eyes on the billfold. "That's why I try to do my best to help people like you when I can, earn myself credit in Heaven."

"That's very commendable, Reverend," Mobius said, handing

over a thin sheaf of stiff new hundred-dollar bills and taking the film. "I'd like to make a donation to your church."

"God bless you, brother," the preacher said, grinning. His upper left canine tooth was capped in gold.

38

"DON'T *TOUCH* ME!" Abby almost shouted.

"So now that you finally acknowledge the truth about me—the real truth—the fear comes. As I knew it would."

"How dare you do what you did to me, Charles?" Abby said, shaking with anger. "Or should I call you Gabriel? Or Dante? Or does it matter what I call you? I can't believe anything you have told me!"

The ground seemed to shift beneath Abby's feet. Her knees weakened. She put out her hands to find something to hold, but found only him.

"Call me Dante," he said, holding her from behind and leading her back to the mansion. "I am through pretending with you. But you do me a disservice. When have I lied to you about the material truth of myself? Did I not warn you that I was a monster? I confessed my evil."

Abby twisted out of his arms, steadying herself against the French doors that led back into the solarium.

"You lied about Desiree." She looked into the room nervously, but Desiree and her young friend had disappeared.

"Yes," he said, stung, "but I had my reasons. I thought Desiree was a kindred spirit. I was not thinking clearly, my mind

disordered, my memories lost. But I did lie, and I offer my hum-
blest apology. I now know there is only one person in the world
I can trust, only one person I can turn to for guidance and understanding. That is you, dear Abigail."

Abby didn't know how to respond. The world had become
unhinged, the unreal made real. The idea that she was standing
face-to-face with Dante Gabriel Rossetti, the famous nineteenth-
century artist and poet, was something her rational mind refused
to accept. Yet she could not deny what she had seen with her
own eyes, what she had felt—the curious mingling of terror and
pleasure—when their bodies were locked together in the unnatural embrace.

"I must also beg you, Abigail, to forgive the uninvited liberty
I took with you. There seemed to be no other way to make you
believe. The effects will not last."

Abby looked in the mirror over the fireplace and saw how the
skin on her neck was raised in two circular welts, mounds with
concave depressions in the center. She touched the wounds tentatively. There was an unmistakable anesthetized sensation, as
if a local injection of Novocaine had deadened the feeling. The
punctures healed visibly as she examined them, her skin regen-
erating at an impossible speed, the cells knitting together to
mend the places where the two razor-sharp teeth had momentarily cannulated her jugular.

"No evidence of your wounds will remain in an hour," Dante
said, appearing behind her in the mirror, his face a dark portrait
of the inner turmoil Abby now shared. "Do not ask me how
such a thing is possible. I do not know."

"Does your body repair itself this quickly?"

"You could stick a knife in me—a prospect that might appeal
to you at this moment—and witness the same regeneration. It is

impossible to harm us with weapons or poisons. The *Vampiri* do not grow old. We do not die," he added with a sigh.

"There must be an enzyme in your saliva," Abby said, touching her wounds again. "If such an agent could be isolated and replicated, there is no telling the benefit."

"What you speak of is beyond the range of my knowledge. I come from a time when the medical arts were barely beyond the primitive."

She looked into his dark eyes. "Why did you stop? Why didn't you kill me?"

"I thought I had made my feelings known, Abigail. Though you must loathe me, surely you understand that I am in love with you."

"I do not loathe you, Dante," she said, softening a little. She'd called him *Dante*. She'd taken an important step without realizing it. As incredible as it was, Abby realized she was beginning to believe. But then she thought of something that made her stiffen.

"What about the girls—Desiree and the other one?"

"An unfortunate mistake. I could get rid of them easily enough, but I doubt you would want me to kill them."

"No, you must not do that."

"I would not want to kill them. Killing is wrong. I know that—God, how I know that."

"Yet you have killed."

He shook his head, too overcome to speak.

"But that happened when you were still lacking your faculties," Abby said. "You did things in a sort of amnesiac fugue state, operating with a diminished capacity. You realize you did things that were wrong, and you are now ashamed and sorry."

Abby saw the desperation in his eyes when he looked at her,

as if telling himself not to be so foolish as to hope she might not hate him for what he'd done.

"The Hunger had control of me. I was its mindless beast."

"The other girl—who is she?"

"Her name is Marie. She is involved with the black arts. She was an apprentice to a local necromancer, an odious man calling himself Dr. de la Croix."

"I've heard of him," Abby said.

"She is not as innocent as she looks."

"She didn't look at all innocent when I saw her earlier with blood smeared all over her face," Abby said.

"Unlike Desiree, Marie can control her violent impulses. Desiree, however, has discovered that she enjoys killing."

"Did she murder Danny Rice?"

"The boy in a cemetery? Yes. She cut off his head as a trophy. She thought it would impress me."

"Dear God. Is she like you? Is she a . . ."

"A vampire? Only in her mind. I never should have associated myself with those two depraved children."

"And the woman murdered in the park? Did Desiree kill her, too?"

"Her death was my fault, though Desiree helped. I will never forgive myself."

"Who did they kill tonight—Desiree and Marie?"

"I cannot say. I told them not to leave the house. They defied me."

"They can't be allowed to hurt more people, Dante. And what about you?" She gave him a sharp look. "Do you really have control of yourself again? Are you absolutely certain you can keep yourself from hurting people?"

"I swear it."

She stared at him for nearly a minute. "I believe you," she said finally.

"And now?"

"I'm not sure, Dante. I need time to think. I've never encountered a problem like this before. A lawyer would argue—and rightly, in my professional opinion—that you were not responsible for your actions, that you were temporarily insane. But I honestly can't imagine the court trying you, or making an accommodation for your special need while you were awaiting trial or afterward, if you were sent to prison. That would lead to more tragedy."

"The Hunger will not be denied," the vampire said in a grim voice.

"You have done wrong, Dante. You need to atone."

"My punishment will be an eternity of guilt."

"I said 'atone,' not suffer. There's a difference. Let's deal with the immediate problems and leave the guilt for later. I can help you with that, if we can find a way through the rest of it."

"You are my angel, Abigail. May I have a kiss?"

She shook her head. "I've already lost my objectivity, Dante. Don't make it any more difficult for me."

"Very well, then," he said, and bowed from the waist, a perfect gentleman. A perfect vampire gentleman.

39

DR. VEENA GOVINDAIAH opened the drawer where she kept the little plastic statue of Vishnu. The blue-skinned god looked up from his impromptu shrine, holding in his four plastic hands a lotus, a mace, a discus, and a conch shell.

Like his owner, Vishnu had come down in the world. He formerly resided in the walnut credenza behind the big desk in Veena's original office, which Dr. Bloome had appropriated when she joined the practice. Veena's present work space was cramped, inadequate, insulting. There was barely room for the pathetic clerk's desk, a two-drawer filing cabinet, and pair of plastic chairs. It was shocking to think that a physician so close to completing her residency in psychiatry could be relegated to an inferior, second-rate office no different than the ones assigned to the psychiatric social workers.

Her loss of face would have been unendurable but for the fact that it was temporary. Veena soon would have her license and be gone. Her family had arranged an engagement to a suitable young man, the son of a family of Brahmins. He had an important job working for Microsoft in Washington, where they would live in a house with a cleaning woman and a yard boy after they were married.

Veena whispered a little prayer to Vishnu, asking him to rain misfortune upon her rival's head. She raised her half-empty cup of tea in offering, drinking off the remainder of the tepid Darjeeling.

In the women's rest room, Veena rinsed the bone china teacup with the golden ring around its rim. Although she was not vain, she paused to check her appearance in the mirror behind the sink. Her thick black hair was parted in the middle and drawn severely back. She had a small nose, tiny well-formed ears, full lips, and tasteful golden earrings. Her brown eyes were steady and cool and revealed nothing to the outside world but Brahmin superiority.

When Veena emerged from the rest room, Dr. Bloome was in the hall striding toward her in her typically overconfident American fashion, a smart leather attaché swinging from her right arm, on her way to business outside the office.

"Good morning, Dr. Govindaiah," Dr. Bloome said without slowing. The pleasantness in Dr. Bloome's voice was grating, her friendliness a projection of her self-importance.

"Good day," Veena said crisply and properly as she headed in the opposite direction, careful to avoid eye contact.

Veena found herself stopping unaccountably outside Dr. Bloome's door. She glanced over her shoulder. Dr. Bloome was gone. The hall was deserted. Veena's next client, a smelly old man ordered by the court to get counseling after being arrested for shoplifting, was due in five minutes. James Gold was invariably on time for his sessions. Without pausing to consider what she was about to do, Veena reached for the door handle. It was unlocked. She stepped quickly inside and pulled the door shut, careful not to make any noise.

Dr. Bloome had remodeled the office, expensively furnishing it to resemble a consulting physician's room on London's Harley

Street. The lamps were turned off and the desk clean—evidence of Dr. Bloome's compulsive neatness.

Veena slipped her cup beneath the branches of the leggy fern overflowing the top of the fancy oak-and-brass filing cabinet. She tried the top drawer. It was locked. All the drawers were locked. Dr. Bloome might keep a spare key to the cabinet in her desk, but it was locked, too. Veena looked randomly around the office, disappointment descending on her.

A small flash of red cascaded down the computer screen.

Veena touched the mouse, and the computer came to life. She moved the mouse arrow to the start button in the lower left corner of the screen, then up to the option labeled "Documents" for a list of the documents Dr. Bloome had opened recently. The menu listed only one file, ROSSETTI.DOC. It wasn't anything Veena was interested in reading, but she left the arrow too long on ROSSETTI.DOC, and the document popped open. There, midway through the first paragraph, was the word "vampire."

"Oh, happy surprise!" Veena said. Vishnu had not failed her.

The document contained Dr. Bloome's notes on a slippery character known as John Doe, then Charles Gabriel, and now, it seemed, Dante Gabriel Rossetti. Dr. Bloome had lied. She'd told Dr. Ritenour and the rest of them that the English amnesiac had disappeared. It was obvious from the notes that Dr. Bloome had been counseling this Rossetti. Scrolling through the long document, Veena found references to Desiree Hohenberg. Dr. Bloome had lied about her, too. She'd lied to her colleagues. She'd lied to the FBI agent, Veena thought with glee.

This was the sort of thing that might very well get Dr. Bloome expelled from the practice, when brought to Dr. Ritenour's attention. It might cost Dr. Bloome her medical license. It might even cause Dr. Bloome to be locked in prison for complicity in the heinous murders. Veena had never dared hope for such an amazing reversal of fortune. She was looking at the weapon that would give her the power to destroy her rival.

Special Agent Avery had been in to see Dr. Bloome that morning. Their meeting was brief. Veena had seen the FBI agent from across the parking lot as she left. Jennifer Avery appeared to be quite angry.

Veena glanced up at a movement outside the office window.

"Oh, my gracious!"

It was Dr. Bloome hurrying back toward the office.

There was no time to print a copy of the file. Veena aborted the document and closed the program. It would take time for the screen saver to come back on, but she couldn't do anything about that.

Veena managed to close the door and turn down the hall before Dr. Bloome appeared around the corner from reception.

"Forget something?" Veena asked, a little breathless, though the self-consumed Dr. Bloome did not seem to notice.

"My pager. I swear I don't know where my mind is today."

At that moment Veena did something she had never done before: She smiled at Dr. Bloome. Veena was still smiling when she went into her own office and sat down across the desk from the malodorous shoplifter.

"One moment, if you please," she said, reaching for her notepad.

"You're in a perky mood today, Dr. Govindaiah."

"Perky?" she echoed as she jotted an address from ROSSETTI.DOC across the top of her notepad while it was still fresh in her mind. She glanced up at James Gold. The old fool was grinning like an idiot.

"Yes," she agreed. "I suppose I am."

Veena was almost delirious with joy at her sudden good fortune. Little wonder she forgot the teacup she'd left sitting on the filing cabinet in Dr. Bloome's office.

40

✧

THE DAY WAS dark enough for late morning to pass as twilight. The local TV stations broadcast satellite pictures of the rotating storm, warning that Tropical Storm Patricia would turn into Hurricane Patricia if the tropical depression remained stalled off the Carolina coast.

The front door slammed.

Desiree looked down from the second-floor window. Gabriel was striding down the brick walk in a trench coat, holding a black umbrella against the slanting rain. He was turning the corner by the time Desiree got to the street, splashing through puddles as she hurried to keep from falling too far behind.

Gabriel headed down the hill toward the collection of shops that seemed to materialize out of the gloom. The pocket of gentrified businesses dated from the previous century, brick buildings decorated with ornate ironwork, the copper flashing around the slate roofs green with age. The vampire went into L'Espresso, a coffee bar.

Desiree drew herself up under the green awning in front of Fabrique Interior Design across the street. She watched L'Espresso's proprietress take Gabriel's order and go to the coffee machine. The woman wore her prematurely gray hair in a long braid draped over the shoulder of her Danskin top. She looked like one of those rich middle-aged ladies who take yoga classes.

Gabriel, her only customer, sat turned away from the window, not seeing Desiree standing in the rain, watching. Some people looked lonely sitting by themselves, but not Gabriel. He knew the secret of being completely in and of himself, a solitary creature who did not require the company of others to make himself whole. The vampire was wearing one of the collarless white shirts he bought in Atlantic City. The curls of his long chestnut hair were pushed back over the shoulders of his black velvet jacket as he looked down at the newspaper. His chin came sharply up. He did not look around, but Desiree could tell he sensed her presence.

The woman served Gabriel his espresso and disappeared through a door that led to a storeroom or office. Gabriel had willed the woman to go away, Desiree thought, wishing she had his powers.

Desiree crossed the street and went into the café, sweeping her cloak off with a dramatic flourish, throwing it over a chair by the door.

"What have you done to your lip?"

Desiree extended the tip of her tongue past her lips, which were painted a hue of purple so dark that they were almost black, and touched the silver ring. "Do you like it?"

"It is ghastly."

"You should see what other parts of my body I've pierced."

Gabriel blinked as if to push the suggestion out of his mind. "Where is Marie?"

"Asleep. Last night left her completely exhausted."

"We need to discuss last night."

"Yes, we do. You were selfish not to share Dr. Bloome with us. Not that I blame you. I've always thought she looked delicious."

Gabriel's hand shot across the table so fast that he had grabbed her by the wrist before she even realized he'd moved.

"Listen to me very carefully," he warned. "If any harm comes to Dr. Bloome, being boiled alive in a cauldron of molten lead will seem like pleasure compared to what I will do to you."

"You're hurting my arm."

"You know nothing of pain, Desiree. But if you go near Dr. Bloome, I promise you will learn."

"You've made your point," Desiree said, pulling herself free.

The vampire stabbed the newspaper with his long forefinger. The main story on page one was about Irma McKay, who had been found brutally murdered in Rubin's Department Store, along with a woman named Ann Barrows.

"You have ruined it here for us," the vampire said. "The police are looking for you. Once you attract that kind of attention, a place is over for you."

She stuck out her lower lip in an exaggerated mock pout. "But what else were we to do, Gabriel? We were so thirsty. Drinking those bitches' blood was a rush. Marie and I got so turned on by it that we had to make each other feel good in a special way."

"You have no moral sense at all, do you?" the vampire asked with disgust.

"None whatsoever," she confessed with a smile. "You don't know what you missed. Let your imagination run wild, Gabriel. Think of the possibilities with the three of us, naked, drenched with blood."

"No!" he said, holding up a hand. "I am through with all of that."

"Are you really?"

He looked at her but said nothing.

"You are a rare and precious creature, Gabriel, wild, untamed, and magnificent. Don't let Dr. Bloome turn you into a eunuch. She wants to lock you up in a cage so she can study you. You're nothing more than a medical curiosity to her. I am the one who understands your needs and desires. I would never ask you to turn away from your nature, Gabriel. I give myself to you completely. Kill me, if that is what you want, or use your godlike power to re-create me in your own image as your partner and equal. Only promise that you will never turn away from the miracle of what you are."

The vampire leaned forward, his desperate words almost lost beneath the hush of rain.

"But are we not more than the sum of our desires? Certainly there must be some higher purpose, even for a monster such as I, lost and wandering in the world, my hands dripping with the blood of innocents I have butchered to feed my savage appetites."

"Who is innocent? What is monstrous? You have only done what nature made you to do, Gabriel. You are a vampire, a hunter. Happiness comes from doing what you want to do, not from denying yourself. The blood is our way."

"Perhaps," he said lowly, his head sinking toward the table.

"I know how to make you smile," Desiree said, touching his hand. "The woman in the back room—let's do her together."

The vampire looked up at Desiree through a tangle of hair, his eyes burning with the Hunger. But then he wavered, the lusty fire leaving his stare, uncertainty taking its place.

"I want you to go away."

"What?" she asked, sitting up straight in her chair.

"Things will be much less complicated if you and Marie go away. I want you to go somewhere far, far away—a different country, a different continent. I will give you all the money you need."

"I'm not going anywhere, Gabriel."

"I insist," he said, fixing her with a level stare.

"Don't try to frighten me, Gabriel. The problem is, I believe in you. Dr. Bloome has convinced you that killing is wrong. I bet you've even promised her you won't kill again. Well? Haven't you?"

The vampire's angry look was his only answer.

"So what do I have to fear from you? You can't kill me. You can't turn me over to the police, because I would lead the pigs straight to you. I'm going to continue to do exactly what I want—which is what I have always done. But so you won't think I'm completely unreasonable, I'll offer to make a deal with you. Make me immortal and I will leave town. Otherwise, I'm staying. That's my offer. Take it or leave it."

Desiree stood and picked up the vampire's espresso, drinking it in a single swallow.

"Maybe your little psychiatrist will turn you into a productive member of society. Or maybe you'll come home and find Marie and I naked in one another's arms and succumb to the temptation. Sooner or later, Gabriel, you'll have to acknowledge what you are."

Desiree threw her cloak over her shoulders and walked out of the café, leaving the vampire alone at his table, staring after her, pale with rage.

41

THE HURRICANE RATTLED the windowpanes and made the old house creak and groan. Trees bent backward, pushed close to the breaking point, the wind roaring through the tortured branches to fill the night with the false sound of waves breaking against a rocky shore.

A single candle in a silver candleholder was the only light in the solarium. The storm's invisible hand moved through the room, making the flame dance and flutter, threatening to kill the wan golden light.

Dante sat alone at the table, the chair at a skewed angle, staring into space. The scene might have been a still life of a brooding vampire, in the shadow-painting chiaroscuro style of the Dutch masters. He sat motionless, sensing the intruder's presence, a dim emanation of life force approaching the house. He raised his head a little, sniffing the air, sensing the faint perfume of blood behind the smell of rain and wet earth. The woman's footsteps on the walkway, the anxious tapping of leather against brick. Dante turned his head slowly, eyes narrowing. Her heartbeat filled him—young and strong, its rhythm quick as she came toward the front door through the rain.

The door chimes echoed through the cavernous entryway.

Dante did not move.

The bell rang a second, then a third time. A small fist began to beat insistently on the door. The storm roared suddenly louder as his uninvited guest opened the front door. The draft extinguished the lonely candle on the table. The door slammed shut.

"Charles? I know you're here. I saw the car in the garage."

Despite Dr. Veena Govindaiah's arrogant manner, her accent enchanted Dante. She reminded him of an exotic plant, more hardy than her delicate appearance indicated. How had she found him? Certainly not from Dr. Bloome.

A soft, silvery light appeared in the hallway door. The power had been out in the neighborhood since early evening. Dr. Govindaiah had brought a torch.

"Charles?"

Footsteps came down the hall. The Hunger spoke sharply to Dante, quickening his pulse, flooding him with desire.

The tiny woman's silhouette appeared in the doorway.

Dante got up and went to stand beside the door, moving too quickly for her to see. He focused his mind on the torch. The electric light dimmed and went out, causing Dr. Govindaiah to gasp. She worked the switch several times with her thumb and shook the instrument, all to no avail.

"Charles? Are you there? It is I, Dr. Govindaiah, from the hospital."

Dante felt the warmth radiating off her skin, her aura touching his. The familiar dull ache began in his upper gums as his blood teeth began to descend, but he held them back. He had promised Abigail restraint. The psychiatrist hesitated in the doorway, the useless torch in her right hand, her doctor's bag hanging from her left. Her raincoat was dripping wet. The multicolored scarf she'd worn on her head—now pulled back on her shoulders—was sodden.

An angry gust of wind hurled itself against the house, its

eddy caught up somewhere in the upper eaves, starting a rumble that turned into a long, low moan. Something metal banged through the garden—a garbage can lid blown away from a neighboring house. When Dr. Govindaiah looked out the window after the noise, Dante recrossed the room and sat in his favorite chair.

"I am here," he said.

His voice startled her. Her eyes searched the darkness. She could not see him in the storm's almost absolute darkness. Dante struck a match and touched it to the candle.

The apprehension disappeared from Dr. Govindaiah's face as her mouth reset itself in its usual firm line. She put her doctor's bag and the disabled torch on the table and took off the scarf and raincoat, her eyes never leaving Dante. She had on a sari instead of the cheap American clothes she usually wore at hospital. She snapped open her bag and took out a syringe and vial.

"I am going to give you a sedative, Charles," she said in a tone meant to indicate she would brook no disagreement. "Roll up your sleeve."

Dante did as he was told. Dr. Govindaiah removed the safety cover from the hypodermic and plunged the needle into the vial, holding it upside down in her right hand as she filled the syringe. He noticed her unmistakable sense of triumph as she swabbed the inside of his elbow with an alcohol wipe. She pushed the needle into his arm with a quick, certain movement, and injected the drug. She then covered the wound with another swab, bending Dante's arm to hold it in place.

"I am taking you back to the hospital, Charles," Dr. Govindaiah said. "I have just given you a rather powerful sedative. We need to get moving while you are still able to walk."

A flash of lightning filled the room with blinding brilliance, briefly showing the hardness that had come into Dante's eyes.

The explosion of thunder arrived a beat later, just as a sycamore tree in the back garden burst into flames, the fire arcing forty feet in the air.

"Oh, my goodness!" Dr. Govindaiah exclaimed.

The wind and rain were too hard upon the fire for it to last long. The flames and sparks, whipped madly in the tempest, were smothered in half a minute. Dante straightened his arm and took away the cotton ball. A single bead of blood appeared in the crook of his elbow, a shimmering crimson pearl that made it momentarily impossible to think of anything but his yearning.

"It had not occurred to me until now, but you and I have much in common, Dr. Govindaiah. We are both strangers in a strange land."

"Come along now, Charles."

The vampire did not move. "Dr. Bloome does not know you are here tonight, does she?"

"What Dr. Bloome does not know would fill volumes, Charles. Her preposterous theories have gotten her into a good deal of trouble," Dr. Govindaiah said, unable to disguise her glee.

"You read her notes. That is how you knew where to find me."

"How I found you is of no importance," she replied imperiously, looking down on Dante where he sat. "I am taking charge of your case. I am taking charge of all of Dr. Bloome's cases. Where is Desiree?"

"Who?"

Dr. Govindaiah grabbed his chin and jerked his face upward. "Where is Desiree?" she said slowly, as if speaking to someone retarded. "I know she has been staying with you."

"I have no idea who you are talking about."

"You will tell me, sooner or later," Dr. Govindaiah said with a cold smile.

"I am surprised you scoff at Dr. Bloome's 'theories.' Indeed, your narrow-minded empirical thinking surprises me. You come from a culture that has a rich mythology."

"I assure you we Indians are as capable of thinking scientifically as you Westerners," she said, her tone icy.

"Yet you pray to Krishna."

"My religious practices are none of your business. Now get on your feet, and I will take you to my car. Soon you will be unable to walk unassisted."

The smoldering sycamore split up the middle, half of it falling toward the house. It seemed the tree would crush the solarium. The topmost branches scraped loudly against the outside wall, breaking several panes in the French doors lining the garden, smashing a large, ornate trellis and the corner of the back porch.

"Do not be afraid, Doctor."

Dante was standing now, towering over Dr. Govindaiah, their nearness exaggerating the difference in their heights.

"Charles," Dr. Govindaiah said, trying to sound as if she were still in command of the situation.

"You intend to destroy Dr. Bloome."

"She has violated . . ."

Her voice trailed off as she eased herself backward a step. He advanced a step, maintaining the intimate distance between them. His ears were full of the wind and rain coming into the room through the broken windowpanes. Her big brown eyes grew even bigger as his hand flashed out and cradled the back of her head in his palm. Her braided hair felt coarse beneath his hand, like a mare's mane. She began to tremble, but she did not try to pull away from him. He smiled a little, allowing the blood teeth to drop down and lock into place with a dull click. His voice was barely audible over the storm.

"Dr. Bloome is competent and dedicated to her patients'

well-being—qualities you would have done well to emulate, Dr. Govindaiah. Abigail's only failing was having the misfortune to become caught up in something almost impossible for her to understand. In this, and this alone, you and she are similar."

The words barely registered. Veena Govindaiah's terrified eyes were locked on Dante's mouth, which he slowly brought close to hers.

"I could never allow you to destroy Abigail," he whispered.

She did not resist when Dante kissed her full on the lips, his mind conquering hers with hardly any effort at all. He moved his lips down her neck, yawning at the last to give the fullest extension to the gently curving blood teeth. Dr. Veena Govindaiah gasped harshly as he stabbed the razor-sharp incisors into her soft golden flesh, arching her back, her hands clutching empty air.

Outside, the storm howled.

42

✧

THE BLACK LEXUS splashed to a stop in front of the saltbox house. There were no lights on in the house or on the street. The storm had knocked out the power in that part of town.

Dante Gabriel Rossetti opened the door and uncoiled his lanky frame from the automobile. He wore a long black raincoat that reached to his ankles. The coat and his long hair seemed to float about him as he moved quickly and gracefully around the car, coming toward the house. A welcoming golden light appeared through the window, growing brighter as he reached the porch.

The door opened as Dante reached for the handle, and he found himself face-to-face with Dr. de la Croix. The root doctor was dressed the same as before, in white shoes, white trousers, a white short-sleeved dress shirt with red suspenders. He still wore a panama hat and sunglasses, despite the night. He carried a kerosene hurricane lamp in his right hand, the gold-headed cane in his left. He had been carrying the cane like a cudgel, but now he set it down and used it to relieve his feet of some of his weight.

"Come in, monsieur."

"Were you expecting someone?" Dante asked.

"Only you. Who else would be out on a night such as this? The cards told me you would come."

Dante went past him into the house, down the hall in the darkness, not needing a light to see. Dr. de la Croix followed, the floorboards crying out against his heavy footsteps. The room where the root doctor held court was ablaze with the light of dozens of red, white, and black candles burning on the makeshift altar. The red candles were for love, the white for good magic, the black candles—these by far the most numerous—for curses.

"You are in better health, sir."

"Thanks to you, monsieur. I'd be on the other side by now if you hadn't freed me from Mama Coretta's curse."

"Is there really another side?"

"Oh, yes indeed," Dr. de la Croix said with a lugubrious nod. "Would you like me to put you into contact? Is there someone you would like to talk to?"

"No," Dante said emphatically.

"Just as well, monsieur. There are many angry souls awaiting you there."

"That is not what I came here to discuss," Dante said, suppressing a shudder.

"I know," Dr. de la Croix said, pulling down his dark glasses so he could peer at Dante with his weird blue eyes. "Where are your minions?"

"You are referring to Desiree and Marie?"

"You are no longer enchanted with those two."

"A mistake," Dante admitted. "In truth, I have made a series of disastrous mistakes, including my involvement with those girls."

"You come here looking for a way out of your dilemmas."

The vampire started to say something but stopped himself. There was no point in denying it.

"I would like to have my apprentice back, monsieur."

"You are welcome to her."

"Very well, then. That is the price I will charge you for my assistance."

"How could you assist me?"

"If you didn't think I could, you wouldn't be here, monsieur."

De la Croix lowered himself into his easy chair, filling it, spilling out of it, leaning forward on the cane he held between his two hands. Dante threw himself into a plain wooden chair covered in chipped white enamel paint.

"Monsieur Rossetti," the witch doctor said, rolling the name around in his cavernous mouth with great pleasure, as if it were some especially delicious morsel. It took Dante a moment to determine the source of the man's amusement, but then it came to him: he had never told de la Croix his name.

"You are lost, monsieur," de la Croix said. "You are desperate. You fear that your every move will result in another tragic misjudgment." He leaned his head back as if looking at the ceiling. "Your nerves are so brittle that they would crack at the slightest touch. Now the storm has blown you like a lost leaf to my doorstep. The cards tell me everything."

"Can your cards tell me anything useful about the future?"

"But of course!" Dr. de la Croix exclaimed with a wheezing laugh. He slid a rickety card table in front of him and began to shuffle a well-thumbed deck of tarot cards. "Only remember your promise, monsieur. You will return Marie L'Enfant to me."

The vampire nodded.

De la Croix shuffled the cards, held out the deck for Dante to cut, and put them facedown on the table in two stacks. The witch doctor tapped the stack on his right three times with his middle finger before turning over the first card.

"I see the dead queen and her eternal rest disturbed."

Dante jerked in his chair.

"You need not fear her," Dr. de la Croix said. "She bears you no malice. Indeed, she will love you forever."

Dante's upper lip trembled.

"But you disturbed her rest, and that made the spirits angry. They have not been uninvolved in your life since then. Fortunately, time has made them mostly forget you. Spirits are by nature inconstant beings with fleeting interests."

Dr. de la Croix turned over the next card. "Ah, here it is."

"What?" Dante demanded.

"This card signifies a great transformation. I see you dropping your mortal form to adopt a disguise that appears mortal yet is different." He turned over the next card. "Death by water. Your death. And yet . . ." He gave Dante a curious look, then turned over the next card. "How strange. Death and yet not death. You were trapped in a sunken ship."

Dante did not answer, but he didn't have to.

"Just so," de la Croix said, turning his attention to the other stack of cards. He tapped the cards three times, then turned over the first card.

"You are pursued by enemies."

Dr. de la Croix picked up the next card and one eyebrow shot up over the frame of his sunglasses.

"What is it?" Dante asked.

"The woman you killed tonight is not the hidden enemy you need fear most."

"Damn you!"

"You don't frighten me," Dr. de la Croix said, grinning broadly. "I will not die at your hand, monsieur." The root doctor nodded at his cards. "I know very well when my time will come. You will play no role in my death."

De la Croix turned over the next card.

"You are being hunted by someone of great intelligence and cunning. He also has great resources, which makes him even more of a threat." He consulted the next card. "His weakness is at his center. He has lost his way in life. He no longer knows the difference between good and evil. This makes him dangerous. You have done him some harm in the past. Ah, here it is," de la Croix said, consulting the next card. "You killed his wife."

"Who is he?"

"I cannot see his name," Dr. de la Croix said. "He is very near and a threat not just to you."

"What is that supposed to mean?"

"He represents a danger to someone you care about. The next card is the queen of cups, you see. Love." He picked up the last card and frowned. "There is love in your life after a very long time, and yet you continue to go from one extreme to the other, driven by inner forces you do not understand.

"There is someone else you have to fear," de la Croix said. "A woman—a lovely young woman with beautiful red hair. She has something to do with the authorities. I believe she is an FBI agent. I do not get the sense that she is near at the moment. She has been called away to another state to deal with some aspect of her business. To testify in a trial, it seems. But she will return soon, and when she does, she will come after you with a vengeance. Do not underestimate her tenacity and resourcefulness."

"So how will it all turn out?"

De la Croix shrugged.

"The reading is somewhat ambiguous, monsieur. The tarot signifies an indeterminate course. The future remains ill-defined. Stars are crossed, meanings uncertain, outcomes hidden in a fog of possibility."

"Do not play the artful dodger with me, de la Croix."

"On my honor, monsieur, I am telling the truth. There are times we simply must work out our own destiny. Your tomorrow is unborn, like a child within the mother's womb. Make the most of it."

"This is exactly the ambiguous claptrap I expected from a fortune-teller."

"If I wanted to bullshit you, Monsieur Rossetti, I would bullshit you," de la Croix said, looking at Dante over the top of his sunglasses with his blind-dog eyes. "Love and death walk with you, one on either side. My best advice to you is to proceed carefully or you will upset an extremely delicate balance."

De la Croix gestured with his gold-headed cane toward the voodoo altar, a surreal junk heap of candles, bones, rum bottles, and jars of graveyard dirt. "If you wish, I could light a candle for you."

"There will be no need for that," Dante said, getting to his feet, his raincoat sweeping around him as the wind screamed louder around de la Croix's modest little home.

The root doctor held up a thick index finger. "Don't forget Marie," he reminded.

"And Desiree? I would be happy to send them both to you."

"Desiree is your problem, monsieur. She is possessed by a particularly stupid sort of evil. It has no application in the arts I practice. Perhaps Dr. Bloome will know how to deal with Desiree."

"How do you know . . ." Dante let his voice trail off, subsumed beneath de la Croix's wheezing laughter.

"The cards, monsieur," de la Croix said breathlessly, tapping the tarot deck.

"Good night, sir," the vampire said, turning away.

"Be careful, Monsieur Rossetti," Dr. de la Croix called after him. "It is not a natural state of affairs when the hunter becomes the hunted."

43

RICHARD MOBIUS DROVE his rented Ford Taurus through the storm, a hard scowl pressing down the corners of his mouth. The hotel manager had warned him not to go out; maybe the supercilious ass had been right. Slanting sheets of rain made it difficult to see more than a few dozen yards beyond the windshield. The wind shook stop signs and toppled trees. Mobius was forced to take an indirect route, detouring around blocked or flooded streets and downed power lines. Electricity was out in most of the town.

A section of twisted metal—once a store awning—drunkenly rolled out of the darkness into his lane. Mobius whipped the Taurus onto the wrong side of the road, but there was no oncoming traffic to worry about. He seemed to be the only person out this night.

The white frame church appeared in the headlights. A big blue tarp was draped over a corner of the roof, lashed down with a tangle of nylon rope, a loose corner snapping angrily in the wind. It reminded the former English professor of Gulliver tied down by Lilliputians. Near the eaves, part of the building's skeleton was exposed, the ribbing of the trusses naked where the storm had torn away the shingles and plywood.

Mobius pulled into the parking lot and turned off the motor.

The rain drummed noisily on the car roof. There was no point waiting for the deluge to ease. He kicked open the door and got out. The wind almost pushed him off his feet. He moved stiffly toward the church, his body angled forward, as if he were climbing a steep hill. As he reached the vestibule, he heard a gas generator running somewhere.

The Reverend Willie T. Williams was alone in the church, staring up at the roof, assessing the damage to his investment. About a quarter of the roof was gone to the beams, the artificial blue sky of the tarp visible, the ceiling illuminated by work lights tethered to a Honda generator by orange power cords. All was havoc within the church: rows of pews were knocked over, the walls plastered with pieces of wet paper and leaves. The drums had been flung about the sanctuary, thrown in all different directions by the storm. The Hammond organ was shiny with water.

"Williams!" Mobius called, shouting to be heard above the generator and the storm.

The preacher turned around. He looked older than Mobius remembered, his thin, tired face and goatee making him resemble a tortured priest in an El Greco. Williams had traded his Malcolm X costume for a work shirt, bib overalls, and a Day-Glo yellow rain slicker.

"Mr. Jones!"

There was irony in Williams's voice. The message he'd left at the Holiday Inn had been for Mr. *Mobius*, not Mr. *Jones*. The police chief must have told Williams his name. Charlie Miller wasn't any more trustworthy than Willie T. Williams.

"I didn't expect to see you tonight, brother. I called this afternoon, before the storm turned ugly." Williams smiled for the first time, giving Mobius a glimpse of his golden tooth. "You find the cat you were looking for?"

"The files you photographed in Dr. Bloome's office conveniently fail to mention Charles Gabriel's address."

"That's a bitch."

"It's a delay, but no great matter. I'm sure the psychiatrist will lead me to Gabriel when the storm lets up."

"You looking for one scary motherfucker. You think the dude actually kills people to drink their blood?"

"You read the file?"

Williams nodded. "I got kind of stuck while the cleaning gal waxed the hall floor. Figured I might as well."

"I haven't the slightest doubt he drinks his victims' blood. He's a vampire."

"You believe in vampires?"

"Charles Gabriel is a vampire. I intend to find him, and when I do, I will destroy him."

"You have more balls than I do, Mr. Jones," Williams said with a slight shudder.

"He killed my wife."

"And that's a damn fine reason. You'd be doing us all a favor. I'm scared shitless just to be here with somebody like that wandering around in the night. But of course, I don't exactly have a choice," he added, glancing up at the damaged roof.

"Reverend Williams," Mobius said, shutting his eyes as he tried to control his impatience. "Why did you drag me all the way out here?"

"This might help. It was written on one of them little yellow sticky notes on the outside of Charles Gabriel's folder. I copied it."

The preacher dug in the pocket of his overalls and came out with a piece of paper. Mobius unfolded it—expensive watermarked stationery with DR. ABIGAIL BLOOME engraved at the top. Scrawled on it in Williams's hand was an address: No. 13 Garden Terrace.

"Why didn't you give this to me before?"

"I was saving it for a rainy day." Williams gave Mobius another flash of gold tooth. "And brother, is it ever raining."

"You cheated me."

"I gave you exactly what you paid me to get: the contents of Charles Gabriel's and Desiree Hohenberg's patient folders. The address wasn't *in* the folder."

"What else are you holding back?"

"Not a thing, my man. I swear. You got it all now."

"I suppose you think I'm going to make another contribution to your church for this."

"It's going to cost a whole lot to repair the roof. My congregation is too poor to afford insurance on this building. They're humble people, Mr. Jones. Honest, working folk."

"Maybe they should pay you less, Reverend."

"Could be," he agreed with a golden flash. "Small churches like ours have few wealthy benefactors. That's why I know it was the hand of divine providence that led us into our business relationship. I know you're a rich man, Mr. Jones. Mr. Charlie says you've got millions."

"Why do I have the feeling you're going to be tempted to pester me for future donations?"

"I would never think of such a thing, Mr. Jones. I'm asking just this once."

"You'd blackmail your own mother."

"Chill, Mr. Jones. We're partners, helping one another."

"I have eight thousand dollars in cash in the car. I don't know if it's enough to repair your roof, and I don't particularly care. It's the last anonymous contribution I'm going to make to your church. If you ever try to shake me down again, Willie, I will make you regret it."

"I'm sure the congregation will be most grateful for the help."

"Come outside and get the money. I'm not going to be out in this weather any more than I have to be."

They trudged together through the wind and rain, every step a fight in the fierce wind. Mobius put the key in the trunk lock and turned it. The wind held the lid down.

"Help yourself," Mobius yelled into the preacher's ear. "It's in the Samsonite briefcase. Just take the whole fucking thing so the money doesn't blow away."

Grinning, Williams forced open the trunk lid with both hands. There was no briefcase in the trunk. The space was empty and lined with clear plastic held to the sides with silver duct tape. "Shit," Williams said, mouthing the word, the wind carrying away the sound.

Mobius put the gun barrel on the yellow slicker until it pressed the base of Williams's skull. The .22 made a small, snapping report that was almost lost beneath the storm's freight-train roar. His big gun hung heavily in the shoulder holster; using it would have been overkill, exploding Williams's head into a messy shower of bone and brain fragments, blowing a hole in the trunk lid, too.

The preacher toppled into the trunk, his legs hanging out the back when the wind pushed the lid down.

Mobius held the trunk open. There was a small hole in the slicker, brown around the edges, looking like a cigarette burn. The reverend's sightless eyes stared ahead, the white of his left one clouding an ugly purple. Amazingly, there seemed to be no blood. No wonder assassins preferred .22s, Mobius thought, flipping Williams's legs in and standing back to let the wind slam the trunk closed.

The generator was running low on fuel, making the lights

sputter as Mobius started the car. He was turning onto the road when an apparition appeared in the sky in front of him, a gigantic amorphous mass. Mobius threw up his hands, realizing a split second before impact that the blue phantom was the tarp that Willie T. Williams had used to keep the rain out of the church. Torn loose from its lashings, the tarp hit the car with a wet scraping noise and was gone the next instant, disappearing into the darkness.

Mobius stomped on the accelerator, making the Ford spit gravel and fishtail. As the car accelerated down the debris-strewn road, Mobius dug in the glove box for the city map that would show him how to get to number 13 Garden Terrace.

44

✦

TREES DANCED MADLY in the headlights, some now naked of leaves, twitching skeletons bent low by the hurricane. The unlighted residences hunkered in the darkness, the yards and gardens littered with branches and debris that crawled and twitched, animated with the storm's spirit.

Mobius parked across the drive to number 13 Garden Terrace, blocking it.

A faint light appeared in one of the second-floor windows—a candle. The flickering light disappeared after a moment, a hint of the evil the house harbored.

Mobius hauled out his gun—the big one—and checked it.

Would killing the vampire make him feel happy? Would it make him feel anything at all? Mobius no longer felt things the way he once had. Bitterness had gradually settled into a chill numbness. Like Melville's Ahab, the obsession for vengeance was the only thing that kept his heart beating and the air moving in and out of his lungs.

Mobius slid the gun back into the shoulder holster.

It didn't matter what happened when the vampire was dead. Time could end, the future limited by a single defining act of revenge. When the vampire was dead, Mobius might well turn the gun on himself.

He fought his way through the wind and rain toward the house. The porch flooring creaked under his boots, but the storm masked the sound. He took out the gun, flicked off the safety, and reached for the door latch. The house was unlocked.

Mobius had already decided long before that boldness was his best strategy.

He flung open the door.

"Hello?"

Mobius stared fiercely at the darkness at the top of the stairs, watching for the candle or the slightest sign of a presence. There was a vague gathering of the shadows on the landing, more of a suggestion than something that could be seen. Mobius took a Maglite out of his pocket and turned it on, shooting a beam of light through the gloom.

The girl at the top of the stairs hid her eyes behind her hand. She was dressed in black, her skin white as milk. When she slowly lowered her hand, he saw her lips were bloodred, her blinking eyes heavily outlined in black. She'd dyed a widow's peak into her purplish hair. Her nose and bottom lip were pierced.

Desiree Hohenberg, Mobius thought. He recognized her from the description in her hospital file. He knew all about her, and Charles Gabriel, thanks to the Reverend Willie T. Williams.

"Get that fucking light out of my eyes." Her little girl voice made the profanity seem even more inappropriate.

Mobius lowered the light, putting the pistol behind his back.

"My car died in front of your house. I was hoping I could take refuge here until the storm let up."

Desiree started down the stairs toward him, an enigmatic smile forming on her lips.

"I thought you were someone else. Frankly, I'd welcome your company. The hurricane has me freaked out."

"You're alone?"

She nodded, pouting with her lower lip. "It's scary in this big old mausoleum with the power out." She glanced at his crotch. "And boring."

Mobius raised the pistol and pressed it against the girl's forehead. "Where is he?"

"Who?"

"Don't play fucking games with me, Desiree, or somebody will be scraping your brains off the walls. Where is Charles Gabriel?"

"I don't know."

"Liar," Mobius said matter-of-factly, pressing the gun barrel harder against the girl's forehead.

"I swear I don't know! If he comes back and finds me in his house, I'm dead—and the same goes for you. The only reason I'm still here is because of the storm. Help me get away. He'll kill us both if he catches us here."

"Give me the razor."

Desiree lifted her hand from the folds of her skirt. Mobius put the flashlight down on the square newel post and took the box cutter from her. He retracted the blade, seeing the dark brown material encrusted in the mechanism. Dried blood. If she had to rely on such a crude tool, she was still human—if someone who had done the things she had done with the vampire could be considered human.

"It won't be easy to kill Gabriel," Desiree said.

Mobius raised the gun. The girl spun away, but he was not aiming at her. The roar was deafening, and the recoil so strong that Mobius thought his arm was being torn from the shoulder socket. Mobius picked up the flashlight and pointed it through the gun-smoke haze. The hole in the wall was nearly a yard across. The explosive shell had penetrated the plaster and wood lath and had made another hole in the far wall of the next room.

"This weapon ought to compensate for any special powers the vampire possesses," Mobius told the girl. "You'll be able to scrape up the pieces once I'm finished and fit them into a shoe box."

Desiree tipped her head to one side and looked up at Mobius, the tip of her tongue pressed against her upper lip. Mobius found himself staring at the silver stud implanted in the middle of her tongue.

"I'll help you kill him," she said, making up her mind.

"Why would you help kill your boyfriend?"

"Gabriel is not my boyfriend. I hate the fucking bastard."

"Then tell me where he is."

"I honestly don't know, but I can get him to come to us. I can fix it so that he walks into a trap. You can blow the ass-licker straight to hell."

"Okay," Mobius said a little doubtfully. "How are you going to make it happen?"

"What do I get for helping?"

"The satisfaction of ridding the world of a vicious killer."

"That's not enough."

"I won't turn you over to the police."

"Oh, that's a given. I'm not going to help you unless you promise to let me skate afterward."

"Fine. What else do you want? Money? I have plenty of money. I'll give you enough to buy a new life wherever you want to go."

"I want something else. Something special."

"Name it."

"I want some of Gabriel's blood after you kill him."

Mobius gave the girl a hard look. Could she use the blood to turn herself into a vampire? Why else would she want such a macabre souvenir in payment for her treachery? Of course, the first order of business was to destroy the vampire. Mobius could agree to anything now and decide later whether to honor the commitment. He didn't have any special animus for Desiree, but it would probably be best to kill her, too.

"You can have whatever you want, Desiree, if you help me destroy the monster."

"It will be a pleasure," she replied sweetly.

45

"DR. BLOOME? THIS is Desiree."

"I can't tell you how glad I am to hear from you, Desiree. Where are you?"

"I hope I didn't wake you up."

"I doubt anybody is sleeping tonight. I'm amazed the telephone still works."

"They buried the lines after the last hurricane."

"Where are you?" the psychiatrist asked again.

"I'm with a friend, Dr. Bloome. Don't worry, I'm not with *him*."

"We need to talk."

"I'm so afraid, Doctor."

"Try not to become upset, Desiree. It only makes things harder."

"I've done terrible things."

"Taking responsibility is an important step."

"He made me help him kill those people. I never would have gone that far if it wasn't for Gabriel."

A crackle punctuated the uneasy pause. The underground telephone lines were not entirely immune from the storm.

"I'm going to turn myself in to the police. I'll make them

understand I didn't have anything to do with what happened, Dr. Bloome. It was all Gabriel."

"We need to think this through together before you talk to the police."

"I'll testify against him, if they want me to," she said, her voice breaking.

"You need a good lawyer, Desiree. And you need me. I don't want you to do anything until we can get together. Do you understand?"

"If you think that's best."

"I know it's best. The radio says the eye of the hurricane will be here in two hours. Tell me where you are. I'll pick you up when the wind dies down."

"You know where the African Methodist Church is on Waterhouse Road? Meet me at the church."

"I'll be there. Don't give up hope, Desiree. There's always hope."

Desiree hung up.

"That was a credible performance," Mobius said. "Are you sure the vampire will give a damn about Dr. Bloome?"

"Oh, he gives a damn. Gabriel is in love with Dr. Bloome, although I don't have any idea what he sees in her." Desiree fell back on the bed in Mobius's hotel room, pulling her skirt up, exposing the creamy flesh of her thighs.

"So," she said in a teasing voice, "what do you want to do for the next two hours?"

46

DANTE GABRIEL ROSSETTI could sense the violation the moment he touched the door.

The hurricane's eye had enveloped the town with deathlike stillness. The vampire stood with his hand on the latch, listening to the water drip from the trees, his raincoat thrown over his shoulders like a cape. Even from outside, the house reeked of treachery.

Sighing, he went in.

There could be no mistaking the meaning behind the dramatic hole in the foyer wall. There were footprints in the plaster dust on the terrazzo floor. One set belonged to Desiree; the other, a man in boots. There was no smell of blood in the air.

The telephone began to ring.

Dr. de la Croix had been right. The immortal hunter had become the hunted.

Dante strode down the hall toward the ringing telephone, snatching the receiver from its cradle. How quickly he had learned to despise the intrusive modern device!

"Hello, Desiree."

"How did you know it would be me, Gabriel?"

"A guess."

"He has Dr. Bloome."

Dante's hand tightened around the telephone until the plastic started to crack.

"Are you still there?"

"Yes," he said.

"He'll kill Dr. Bloome unless you do exactly what he says."

"Who is 'he'?"

"Dr. Mobius. You killed his wife."

"Yes," Dante replied wretchedly. "I believe I did."

"Come to the African Methodist Church on Waterhouse Road. Look at the map in the phone book if you don't know where it is."

"Why are you helping him, Desiree?"

"He made me."

"You lie, but it hardly matters. I understand why you hate me, Desiree, but what has Dr. Bloome ever done but try to help you?"

"She doesn't *really* care about me."

"How do I know Mobius has abducted Dr. Bloome? How do I know she is still alive?"

There was a thump in the background, followed by a pained cry.

"Make sure that no further harm comes to Abigail, Desiree. I will kill Mobius for this, but if you protect her, I will be merciful with you."

"Fuck you," Desiree said.

The line went dead.

47

✧

"I KNOW WHO he is."

Abby sat on the edge of the wet pew. The handcuffs behind her back made it uncomfortable to lean back, so she sat straight up.

"You must be very clever, Mr. Mobius," she said.

"Your compliment is suspect, given the circumstances, Dr. Bloome, but I'll accept it anyway. And it's *Doctor* Mobius."

"Why don't you unfasten these cuffs, Dr. Mobius? My wrists hurt."

"I'm afraid I can't do that. What about you? Do you know who he is, Dr. Bloome? Has he told you?

Abby tried to give him her blank look, but the smirk on his face told her she'd given the truth away.

"So you do know," Mobius said.

He used the gun to gesture toward Desiree, who watched the conversation warily but made no effort to join in, like a child observing adults having a veiled disagreement.

"She calls him Gabriel, short for Charles Gabriel. An angel's name for a devil: how ironic. His real name—the name he was born with—is Gabriel Charles Dante Rossetti. That wasn't euphonious or pretentious enough, so he mixed things up a bit and reinvented himself as Dante Gabriel Rossetti. Do you want to know how I figured out his identity?"

Abby drew in a slow breath and told herself to stay calm, silently repeating her private mantra: *Stay calm, stay calm, stay calm.* She'd called Jennifer Avery, as promised, after Desiree's phone call, not knowing exactly how much she was going to tell the FBI special agent. Abby had only gotten the answering machine, with a recorded message from Avery saying she was traveling. Abby left a general message, asking that Avery call her when she was back from her trip.

"I'm sure you know the derivation of the word 'amateur,' Dr. Bloome."

"It's from the Latin *amator*."

"Very good! I'm an amateur in the art world—a lover of art. I have a small but respectable collection of nineteenth-century art. Nothing too noteworthy, but still an exquisite collection in its modest way. Which is not modest at all, considering the fortune I spent acquiring it."

Mobius sat down and crossed his legs, resting the big silver pistol against his thigh.

"I realized there was something strangely familiar about the photograph in Rossetti's psychiatric file the moment I saw it."

"How did you manage to look at my files?"

"Don't look so surprised, Doctor. I paid someone to break into your office and copy them. I didn't think much about the photo at first, but it started to eat at me after a while. I was sure I had seen his face somewhere, but I couldn't put my finger on it. The mind is a slippery thing, but then you know that far better than I. I haven't spent a minute thinking about art since my wife was killed, but I found myself in the public library yesterday, perusing its collection of art books. I suppose my subconscious mind must have played a role in my taking down a book about Rossetti. And there he was. Actually, I am not a fan of Rossetti's work. I have never cared for the Pre-Raphaelites. They are too sentimental for my taste."

Mobius shook his head.

"It's difficult to accept, isn't it? Rossetti didn't die in 1882. If I didn't know better I'd think I'd lost my mind."

"I'm not sure we haven't all gone mad," Abby replied.

"Come now, Doctor. Dante Gabriel Rossetti is a vampire, and we both know it."

"What is it you want, Dr. Mobius?"

"Justice."

"You want to kill him."

"Say his fucking name!"

"Dante. You want to kill Dante."

Mobius's face was red in the lamplight from his outburst, a blood vessel on his forehead throbbing visibly. "I am going to kill the monster that murdered my wife."

"And you would consider that justice?"

"It is the closest thing to it I will know on this earth. When he is dead, the world will have nothing more to fear from him."

"Killing Dante won't make you whole again."

"I know that. Nothing will."

"Perhaps I'd feel the same, if I were in your shoes."

"He must be stopped, Dr. Bloome. You know that as well as I. You should want to help me."

"I can't."

"Why? Are you afraid of him? Do you want evil to triumph?"

"It's more complicated than that, Dr. Mobius. Dante Rossetti is not the killer you think he is."

"The trail of corpses I have been following is a figment of my imagination?"

"He has done bad things, Dr. Mobius, but I question whether he was responsible for his actions."

"Don't make me laugh, Doctor."

"I don't expect you to be sympathetic to my point of view."

"Take your shot, Dr. Bloome. Convince me that Rossetti was temporarily insane when he killed my wife. That is, unless you have something better to do while we wait for him to show up."

"Dante was trapped in the *Titanic* when it sank eighty-five years ago. He should have drowned with the others, but he didn't. By some mechanism I do not pretend to understand— the explanation must be medical, not supernatural—he went into a state of deep hibernation. He remained in that state until he was awakened by the salvage crew trying to lift a section of the ship off the bottom of the ocean."

"I always thought it amounted to grave robbery," Mobius said in a grim voice.

"Except that one of the passengers was not entirely dead. At that point, Dante didn't know who or even what he was. He had been reduced to what he refers to as 'the Hunger.' No sense of self remained, no self-control, no conscious understanding of his actions. Only later, after being hospitalized here, did he regain enough of his personality to understand the things the Hunger had driven him to do."

"If you're going to feel sorry for somebody, Dr. Bloome, I suggest you feel sorry for the people he's murdered. Feel sorry for their families."

"I do," Abby said.

"No, you don't." Mobius was on his feet, pointing the gun at Abby to emphasize his words. "The balance of your pity goes out to the monster that killed my wife. You probably think of him as some sort of doomed romantic figure. He's not. Rossetti is evil incarnate."

"I don't believe that, Dr. Mobius, and waving your gun at me won't change my mind."

"Are you really naive enough to think he will do anything but continue to kill unless I destroy him?"

"I'd like to think so."

"You'd '*like to think*,'" Mobius said, mocking her. "We're too far down this bloody road to indulge in we'd 'like to think.' Are you prepared to guarantee Rossetti will never hurt another human being?"

"There are never any guarantees," Abby said after a pause.

"Force yourself to think clearly about this, Dr. Bloome. There is no margin for error. No matter how charming the vampire is, no matter how fascinating you find his story, you've got to focus on the fact that he needs to drink the blood of living human beings to survive. The things that make him attractive to you as a woman and a scientist are the things that make him dangerous."

Abby caught herself beginning to nod in agreement.

"Classical literature is rich with tales of bloodthirsty monsters—the Minotaur, Lamia, Circe. When I was a college professor, I thought these stories were born of man's need to explain the incomprehensible forces in nature. Now I know these creatures—some of them, anyway—walk the earth. These beings are more than curiosities, Dr. Bloome. They are the enemies of mankind. They prey upon us. They hunt us for their meat, while we smugly refuse to acknowledge their existence. We are like peasants who refuse to believe in the tiger that is dragging our loved ones off into the jungle each night to be devoured."

The wind was beginning to blow again, a harbinger of the returning storm.

"All right, Dr. Mobius." She turned sideways on the pew and

extended her cuffed wrists. "Unlock these handcuffs. I'll help you."

"Don't believe the lying bitch," Desiree hissed from the shadows.

"You're going to need all the help you can get to keep him from turning the tables on you, Dr. Mobius."

"Don't trust her," Desiree said. "Gabriel has her twisted around his little finger."

A car splashed up outside the church, the tires skidding on the wet loose gravel.

"He's here!" Desiree cried.

"What are you doing to do?" Abby asked.

Mobius did not answer. She wasn't sure he even heard her. His eyes were on the door, watching for the vampire.

48

THE CHURCH'S DOUBLE doors swung wide on Dante
Gabriel Rossetti, who stood there motionless, as if a spirit
materialized out of the swirling air. The automobile's headlights illuminated the vampire from behind, casting him in silhouette. He stood with legs planted apart, his hands on his hips.
The wind lifted his long coat and hair, making it float about him.
As he turned his head a little to one side, his eyes caught the
lantern light, a brief golden glitter within the dark outline of his
form, as if he were a cat in the doorway.

Rossetti opened his mouth, not saying the things Mobius
expected him to say, but quoting Coleridge:

> ". . . Beware! Beware!
> His flashing eyes, his floating hair!
> Weave a circle round him thrice,
> And close your eyes with holy dread,
> For he on honey-dew hath fed,
> And drunk the milk of Paradise."

The weight of the weapon hanging heavily at the end of Mobius's right arm was reassuringly real to him at that surreal moment. He could have raised it in an instant and pulled the trigger,

yet he was in no hurry now that this moment had finally arrived. He wanted to savor his revenge so he could look back on this night for the rest of his life—however long that might be—and remember it in perfect detail.

The shingles on the torn roof fluttered overhead like a flight of angels. The wind was beginning to rumble again, like the approach of a distant freight train. Fast-running clouds scraped their bellies so low in the sky that they seemed to touch the roof. The air was becoming clammy with moisture. When the rain came back, it would be another deluge.

"Are you afraid to come in," Mobius asked, "or is there truth to the folk wisdom that a vampire must be invited to enter?"

The Lexus's headlights turned themselves off. Mobius jerked the gun into position but there was nothing there for him to shoot. The vampire had vanished. The church doors began to swing back and forth in the wind, banging loudly several times before closing themselves with a tremendous slam.

Dr. Bloome let out a little frightened cry, looking past Mobius. He knew why even before the vampire—close behind him now—spoke.

"You have gone to an extraordinary amount of trouble to meet me, Professor Mobius," he said. "I trust my acquaintance will not prove a disappointment."

A wind blew through the church, riffling pages of hymnals, picking up small scraps of paper and sending them skittering around the walls like the spirits of minor demons fleeing an exorcism. Mobius turned and raised the weapon in one fluid motion. The vampire did not try to jump out of the way or grab the weapon, apparently realizing that either move would have been instantly fatal.

"I'm going to blow you into a thousand bloody little pieces," Mobius said without emotion.

"I am quite aware of what your weapon can do," the vampire said, equally cool. "You left rather a mess at my house."

"Rather," Mobius said. "Your photographs don't do you justice, Rossetti. You more closely resemble your charcoal self-portrait of 1847, although I think Holman Hunt captured you best in his 1853 study."

"You know your subject, sir."

"I have been interested in art far longer than I have been interested in you. But to be completely honest, Rossetti, I never was much of a fan of your paintings—or your poetry, for that matter."

"I share your disappointment. I failed to live up to the standards I set for myself," the vampire said. "But perhaps we can discuss my professional failings another time. I came here tonight to convey my regrets to you, Professor Mobius."

"Really?" Mobius arched one eyebrow. "And I thought you came because I had taken Dr. Bloome hostage."

"I wish to offer my most sincere condolences," the monster said. "I also wish to apologize for the death of your wife, Patricia."

"Apologies won't bring her back," Mobius said, his hand tensing on the weapon.

"No, they will not."

"Do you know what it is like to have your wife taken from you?" Mobius asked, his voice beginning to quaver. "Can you conceive the hollowness it leaves behind—and the rage?"

"Aye," the vampire said with a heavy voice. "Most regretfully, I do."

"If you know that, you must also know I am going to send you straight to Hell, where you should have gone more than a hundred years ago."

"You would be doing me a favor by stopping the pain of my wretched existence. I am my own living hell, Professor Mobius. Like Milton's Satan, wherever I go, my hell goes with me. Death would be a welcome escape from the guilt."

"Do not think you can trick me into believing that I would hurt you most by letting you live."

"Do not treat the matter of guilt lightly, Professor Mobius. You carry your own burden, though it has not yet begun to weigh on you. How many felonies have you committed in your quest to destroy me? There is blood on your hands. You have killed."

"I did what I had to," Mobius said, defiant.

"But that is *my* excuse, Professor Mobius. Perhaps Dr. Bloome can help you, as I once hoped she could help me."

"It's too late for you, Rossetti."

"It is very much too late for me. I cannot escape the evil I have done to others, and the evil that has been done to me. In the end none of us can. The wounds and grief become as much a part of us as our flesh and bones. Life is a carriage that cannot be gilded. It is a rude and battered conveyance, ill-made and damaged by innumerable collisions, a rough ride to a destination no one wants to reach. But perhaps it is not too late for you, Professor Mobius."

"Spare me your compassion," Mobius said.

"I wish only for you to understand that killing is as abhorrent to me as it is to any moral being. I was trapped at the bottom of the ocean for the better part of a century. When I was at long last awakened, the angel of my better self—that precious spark of divinity that exists within our souls unless we snuff it out—remained asleep for a time. My immortal Hunger possessed me, making me its mindless slave. I tell you this only so that you will know I bore your wife no special animus. It was not me that killed Patricia, but the beast that lives within me, a beast that lives within us all, I fear."

"You bastard!" Mobius exploded. "Do you actually expect me to forgive you?"

The vampire lowered his head.

"I will never forgive you!" Mobius roared. "Never!"

The vampire had a stricken expression on his face, his eyes shimmering with moisture as he looked to Dr. Bloome.

"Is there any real forgiving in this life, Abigail?" he asked, speaking to the psychiatrist in an intimate way, as if they were alone. "How can we learn to forgive one another when we do not know how to forgive ourselves?"

"Enough," Mobius said, leveling the gun at the monster's head.

"No!" Dr. Bloome cried, jumping to her feet. Had she had another change of heart, or had she only pretended to side with him against the vampire earlier? It hardly mattered.

"Now, die, you son of a bitch."

There was a sharp metallic click, but no explosion. The gun did not fire. Mobius pulled the trigger a second time. The same impotent click. The vampire smiled sadly, confirmation that he had somehow prevented the weapon from going off.

"Unfortunately, Professor Mobius, I could not permit you to destroy me. Even though I want to die, my mind will not allow it. I did not stop the gun consciously, you see. Something in here did it," he said, touching his temple. "Dr. Bloome would call it a defense mechanism."

"I told him you were too powerful to let him kill you, Gabriel," Desiree said, emerging from the shadows. "I played along just to get him here so that you could kill him." She grinned at Dr. Bloome. "And her. I hope you let me do her myself."

"You have never known how to lie, Desiree. Kindly move away."

The girl moved sideways, wary eyes on the vampire, until she was out of Mobius's line of sight.

"Dr. Bloome, your restraints," the vampire said. The handcuffs seemed to open of their own accord, clattering to the floor.

"Don't hurt him, Dante," Dr. Bloome said, chaffing her sore wrists.

Mobius met the vampire's stare. He let the gun fall to his side, but he did not back away. Fear was one thing he would never show his nemesis. Even if Rossetti killed him, he would never give the vampire the satisfaction of seeing him show fear.

"I am finished with hurting," Rossetti said, turning away. "Indeed, I am finished with everything." He wandered toward the altar, bending to pick up a wedge of splintered oak broken from one of the pews. Even with his back toward them, Mobius could see that the vampire was positioning the wooden point over his heart.

"There is perhaps one bit of truth in the nonsensical tales people tell about the *Vampiri*," Rossetti said, looking over his shoulder toward Mobius. "There is one perfect way to kill a vampire."

Dr. Bloome tried to get to him, but the vampire was rushing forward before she could move. He hit the wall at a dead run. There was the sound of a collision and tearing cloth followed by a sharp, guttural gasp. The oak wedge was driven completely through the vampire's body, the point sticking out the back of his coat, the wood shimmering red with blood.

The vampire turned slowly toward them. His face was an ashen mask as he looked longingly at Dr. Bloome. He loved her, Mobius saw, and the look in her eyes made it seem that she returned the dying vampire's affection. The fiend's eyes moved slowly, as if even this small thing required all of his strength, until they settled on Mobius.

"Try to forgive me," Rossetti said. "And try to forgive yourself."

The vampire sank to one knee, grabbing for the edge of the altar to steady himself. Dr. Bloome helped lower him to the floor, laying him on his side.

"One last kiss, my love?" he said weakly, closing his eyes.

Dr. Bloome pressed her lips against his. His fingers brushed her cheek and then fell to the floor.

The vampire was dead.

49

✧

THE TENSION WAS gone from Dante Gabriel Rossetti's face, and with it the haunted, hunted look Abby had come to know too well. He was finally at peace. The returning storm was nearly upon them, the wind a vast prolonged roar that threatened to batter down the insubstantial shelter the broken frame church could provide.

"He's dead!" Desiree clapped her hands, her eyes sparkling with madness. "Remember your promise, Dr. Mobius."

"I remember," he replied dully. He looked at Abby, sitting with Dante's lifeless head cradled in her lap. There was nothing of the exultant victor in the strangely quiet Dr. Mobius. Dante's death had not suited him nearly so well as he'd expected, Abby realized.

"You said I could have his blood," Desiree said, unscrewing the cap from an old mason jar.

"Don't let her," Abby warned.

Mobius was already turning away, no longer interested. Perhaps he did not understand that Dante's blood contained a retro-virus that would give the psychotic girl Dante's preternatural powers.

"Mobius, listen to me!"

A screech rent the air as one of the beams that held up the

church roof abruptly dropped several feet, stopping with the shrill complaint of nails being wrenched from wood. Desiree looked up, her silver-studded mouth open in an expression of mute amazement. The girl was too startled to move when the beam gave way and plunged toward her.

The beam lay across Desiree laterally, her ribs crushed. The compound fracture in her left arm indicated that she'd raised her hand at the last moment to try to deflect the blow. The corner of the beam had caught her in the upper right part of her head, leaving a wicked right-angle indentation in her skull. Brain matter seeped through the fracture. There was nothing Abby could do.

"Is this what you wanted?" Abby demanded of Mobius, feeling the tears starting to come.

"Yes, I suppose it is," he said in a flat voice. His face betrayed no hint of emotion, a blank slate. Now that the denouement was past, Mobius saw only what was left behind in its wake—broken bodies, broken lives.

Mobius turned and moved toward the entrance, preoccupied, isolated, alone—more like Dante than he knew, Abby thought. The silver weapon hung loosely from his hand as if he'd forgotten it. He went heavily up the stairs and outside. The doors banged in the wind after him.

Abby gently rested her hand on Dante's, ignoring the storm's returning fury. She had already decided to resign her position and go away, assuming FBI Special Agent Jennifer Avery didn't arrest her for complicity as soon as she returned to Calhoun to resume her investigation. Abby needed to sort out everything that had happened and decide what it all meant. She had stepped far over the professional line trying to help Dante Gabriel Rossetti. A psychiatrist should never allow herself to become emotionally involved with a patient. She was more than involved. Looking at

Dante, beautiful even in death, she realized she had fallen in love.

Would it have made a difference if she'd adhered to the rules, like the martinet Dr. Govindaiah? If she had, Dante and Desiree might still be alive. Or maybe the result would have been even worse. It was impossible to know.

"I'm sorry I couldn't help more," she whispered to Dante's silent form.

The splintered triangle of oak had worked its way an inch out of the dead vampire's chest, which was curious. Typically, muscles spasm around a projectile, holding it in the wound.

A splash of rain fell through the torn ceiling. Abby had to leave the church before the full force of the hurricane returned.

"I have to go," she whispered. "Forgive me for leaving you."

The oak wedge pushed itself another two inches from the wound in Dante's chest. Transfixed, Abby watched the lethal splinter rise, shuddering at the viscous scraping of rough wood against flesh. Wet with blood, the wood balanced precariously on Dante's chest, then fell and rolled onto the floor.

With trembling hands, Abby pushed back the edges of the tear in Dante's shirt. Through the ragged gash in his chest, she saw the interior halves of the wound drawing together.

Dante drew in a sudden ragged breath. His hand shot out and clamped onto Abby's forearm, his grip viselike, painful.

"Do not be afraid," he said hoarsely, relaxing his grip. "It is only Lazarus, returned from the dead." He opened his eyes and smiled. "Where is Mobius?"

"Gone away."

"Hallelujah for that."

"I can't believe you're alive. It's a miracle."

"Or a curse, depending upon your perspective." The vampire

laughed a little, wincing with pain. "I cannot say this was an experience I am anxious to repeat."

"Did you know it wouldn't kill you?"

"I suspected as much. I thought it was worth a try. It seemed like the only way to get rid of Mobius without killing him. I knew you would not like it if I hurt him. I meant what I said earlier. I am through with all of that. Please help me sit up, my darling."

"You've lost a lot of blood."

"I am afraid I will have to do something about that."

"Take some of mine, Dante. I offer it to you. I want us to be together."

"We shall see," he said, putting his hand around her shoulder. His eyes hardened when they settled on Desiree.

"She won't be coming back to life, will she?"

"No, Abigail, and I must confess I am glad of it. She was as close to pure evil as anyone I have ever known, mortal or *Vampiri*."

"I failed her."

"You did your best. That is all any of us can do. She was determined to join the damned, and now she has her wish. Help me to my feet, my lady. This poor church cannot stand much longer against the tempest."

"I'm not afraid."

"I know you are not," he said, letting her help him toward the door. "And neither am I. As long as we have one another, we have nothing to fear."

50

"I WOULD NOT be too harsh in my assessment of Professor Mobius, Abigail. His wife's death drove him beyond reason."

Dante moved his hand over the candle absently, perhaps reflecting on his own experiences at the edge of madness. They were seated at an outside table in a restaurant in a small fishing village on the western end of Jamaica. Their sailboat was anchored in a natural harbor inset into a rocky crescent, the crew and captain awaiting their pleasure. The beacon in the lighthouse at the far end of the bay turned slowly, casting its silvery beam across the water. The moon, almost full, climbed high in the eastern sky as they sat talking after dinner.

"What do you think will become of him?"

"I would not be surprised if Mobius went back to university. Not soon, but in a few years' time. I sensed that without realizing it, he missed his old life—his books, his scotch, his paintings, and his crackling summer fires. He drank deep from the cup of revenge and found it a far less satisfying experience than expected. But how satisfying can revenge be? Acts of destruction leave only emptiness in the heart. Acts of creation are where joy is to be found."

Dante took her hand and kissed it gently.

"I love it when you do that," Abby said. "Of course, you've had a lot of practice."

"Honesty compels me to confess to you, my lady, that I was one of London's most scandalous rakes in my day. But that has all changed."

"Has it?"

"Entirely," he said with a great show of sincerity. "If I err in the future, it will be in the direction of virtue."

"That's a good answer."

"Rakes are no longer much in fashion. I am now a resident of the twentieth century. Fidelity is a virtue today, unless you are a politician."

"It will be the twenty-first century before you know it," Abby said, picking up her wineglass.

"Do not remind me! Things change so fast that I can hardly keep up. So many things still perplex me."

"Such as?"

"The lack of social classes."

"What's wrong with that?"

"Everything!"

"Sometimes you amaze me, Dante. Equality and freedom are a higher level of social evolution. People have the freedom to rise to their own level."

"Or not to rise, but to sink."

"True."

"This amorphous social arrangement contributes more to the general unhappiness than you realize. In my time, a beekeeper was a beekeeper. His father before him was a beekeeper; his son after him would be a beekeeper. There was a stability, predictability, balance, and order."

"It sounds horribly stifling," Abby said.

"It *was* stifling, in a sense, but in another sense it was completely liberating. People were not responsible for inventing themselves, the way they are today. In Queen Victoria's time, we knew who we were, and in most cases we were content. Today, a beekeeper must not only care for his bees, but he must also worry whether he has achieved his potential. Perhaps he would do better to become a businessman, an agent to other bee-keepers, a distributor of honey. His wife may think he should give up his apiaries altogether and become a shopkeeper, like her sister's successful husband. In the back of his mind, the bee-keeper wonders whether he is making a mistake by continuing to live his entirely pleasant life. Where's the contentment in that? Nothing is certain today, nothing is assured. In a nation where any boy can grow up to become president, those who do not have reason to think themselves failures."

"I think you're rather overstating the case," Abby said with a smile.

"Only for rhetorical effect. Take Dr. Govindaiah. One hundred years ago she never would have dreamed of putting herself forward the way she did."

"One hundred years ago, Veena Govindaiah would not even have been able to get into medical school. Only men could go to college."

"A point for you," Dante conceded.

"I only wish I'd found her teacup in my office sooner," Abby said, looking away from Dante.

"It would not have made any difference in the end."

"Probably not," Abby agreed, "but it would have put me on my guard. I might have seen what was coming and thought of a way to stop it."

"I could not allow her to destroy you, Abigail. Dr. Govindaiah would have been content with nothing short of your ruination."

"I know," she said, touching his hand. "But still . . ."

"No more regrets, Abigail. We must put them behind us."

"I will never forget."

"Of course not, Abigail. Nor shall I. Forgetting is one of the things a vampire cannot do. It is part blessing, part curse. Yet we must remember the good along with the bad."

Their eyes met, hers shimmering.

"A few lines my namesake penned come to mind, Abigail." The vampire closed his eyes and quoted Dante Alighieri:

> "The day was now departing; the dark air
> releasing the living beings of the earth
> from work and weariness; and I myself
>
> alone prepared to undergo the battle
> both of the journeying and of the pity,
> which memory, mistaking not, shall slow.

"There is one important distinction between Dante Alighieri and Dante Gabriel Rossetti," the vampire said, smiling at Abby across the candlelit table. "I am no longer alone. I will not forget, but my salvation is that I am no longer alone."

There were tears in Abby's eyes—tears of love, regret, and memory. Pain and joy were both part of it, contrasting strands woven together to make the greater tapestry. Good and bad, light and dark, pain and pleasure, life and death—they all came together to create a seamless whole. Someday in the future—in a year, in a decade, in a century, perhaps—she would look back on it and smile a little sadly at Dante, remembering the terror and wonder of how it all began.

I, VAMPIRE

Living forever, he dwells among the mortals. Connoisseur of the finest in life—beautiful women, well-aged wine, and classical composers—he has no need of guilt. For he is neither good nor bad, neither angel nor devil. This is his story.

THE VAMPIRE PAPERS

An invitation to study the life of the *Vampiri*, those creatures who are joined by blood and cursed to live out their days in lonely immortality.

THE VAMPIRE PRINCESS

Come aboard the ultraluxurious *Atlantic Princess*'s maiden voyage and cavort with a glittering array of millionaires, movie stars, and royalty, all with their own dark secrets. But not one of them has a past as evil as the ravishing Princess Nicoletta Vittorini di Medusa's. And not even you will be able to resist the siren call of the deadly ecstasy she offers. . . .

THE VAMPIRE VIRUS

A mysterious death will lure you deep
into the jungles of Costa Rica. There, in
the hot zone, an unknown and potentially
devastating new virus has made its first
lethal appearance. Yet an even more hor-
rifying evil is waiting in a lavish estate.
carved from the savage wilderness, where
an extraordinary man rules, the master of
a forbidding world. And he himself is
slave to a centuries-old hunger. . . .